CW01067190

Tattoo of a Naked Lady

by
Randy Everhard
as told to
B. D. Kwiatek

"There," says he, "if that line don't fetch them, I don't know Arkansaw!"

-Mark Twain

The Invisible College Press, LLC
Arlington VA

Publisher's Note:
This is a work of fiction. Names, characters, places, and incidents
are either the product of the author's imagination or are used ficti-
tiously, and any resemblance to actual persons living or dead,
events, organizations, carnivals, or locales is entirely coincidental.

ISBN: 1-931486-01-X

Cover Art ©2001 Juliana Peloso
Cover Design ©2001 Michael Yang
First Printing

The Invisible College Press, LLC
P.O. Box 209
Woodbridge VA 22193-0209
http://www.invispress.com

Please send questions and comments to:
editor@invispress.com

PART ONE: THE BIG BUILD-UP

Fate, chance, karma, whatever you wanna call it -- when Miss Fortune spreads her legs for you, you're already in over your head. Believe me, I know.

Bunny LaFever looked like a dame with more curves and venom than Reggie Peeler's Land O' Snakes.

But she wasn't a real dame. She was a she-devil. That golden bush of hers was nothing but a welcome mat to hell.

But now I'm getting way ahead of myself. Bunny had a way of doing that to jerks like me. She twisted us inside out and turned our heads around so we couldn't think straight anymore.

So lemme begin at the beginning...

* * *

Carnies got a word for a crooked game operator like me. They call me "flattie" cuz I'll flat-out rob you and make you like it.

My name's Randy Everhard and I've got a million ways to take your money. One of my personal favorites is the "hopper shot." It's tossing softballs into toilet seats, which you've seen on every midway in your life.

I could gaff the joint to make it impossible to win. But where's the fun in that? I work it so any chucklehead can win all night long.

Cuz once I've hooked a live one into thinking he can take *me* for a ride, that's when I nail him with the "build-up."

Caught up in the excitement of winning game after game, the rube's built up to play twenty games at two bucks a pop. And the only prize he's going home with is a teddy-bear that cost me three shekels per, wholesale. You do the math, Einstein.

The problem with selling three-dollar plush for forty scoots is that the build-up only pays off if you've got a steady string of suckers. And that night was turning out to be a real larry.

The Laff Riot carnival was a flattie's wet dream. The grab joints and flashy rides were a front for the real action: flat stores, alibi and percentage joints, crap tables, slot machines, fortune wheels.

The show was running wide open. Everybody crooked and every joint gaffed and nobody doing a damn thing to stop it. I figured the cops were greased slicker'n Liberace's asshole.

It should've been like shooting trout in a barrel. Too bad nobody was taking my bait. I was up shit creek without a paddle to piss on.

My first goddamn night with the show, and already I was itchy for a new angle.

I can't remember which one of them I saw first: the blonde come-on dressed like she had an exhibitionist streak a mile wide or the square in the coke bottle glasses who was eyeballing her like she was nothing but something to look at.

Of course, that Coppertone beauty really was something to look at. She was turning heads and raising dicks all over the place. But I didn't like him getting his eyes all over this piece of 100% corn-fed cocktease.

She was stacked like a double-decker Ferris wheel with nipples that could cut glass.

The red double-0's stenciled on her football jersey were stretched over humongous hooters. She looked like a shooting gallery, bursting at the seams. You couldn't miss those twin titty targets.

I'm talking knockers so big you could still see them when she turned around. And believe you me, she was one woman who looked as good going as she did coming.

She wore a pair of daring Daisy Dukes that were so short and tight her crotch sucked them in. The denim over her ass was thread-bare, blown out like a retread.

And if that wasn't enough, she was doing a number on a grape Popsicle to make your peter wish it was frozen on a stick. That girl was one carnival ride I wanted to jump on quick, and I didn't care how many tickets it cost.

In my racket, though, business comes before pleasure. And this looked like a golden opportunity to work the key scam. It's the oldest con in the carny book.

I jumped the counter and made my way over to the chump with the steamed-up glasses. I was like, "Hot enough for ya? And I ain't talking about the weather, fella."

At first he didn't buy it when I told him I was the "manager" of this fine talent. He just stood there mopping his brow with a hanky.

"I don't fuck chickens and I don't shit feathers," I said, "and I wouldn't lie about a piece of ass like that, neither."

I gave myself a hard-on feeding him the fast talk: screwing her would make a man think he died and gone to heaven, where the streets are paved with solid gold snatch.

"She's a sight for sore eyes, ain't she? And if you think *I'm* giving you lip, you oughta see *her* go to town on a dick. Life-transforming, friend. *Life-transforming.*"

I pulled out an old key I kept for just such an occasion. Dangling it before his bug eyes, I spieled how it was the key to her room at some motel outside of town.

"I'm talking once-in-a-lifetime opportunity, pal. She's the reason hard-ons were *made.*"

He swallowed it all -- hook, line and sinker.

* * *

Chuckling over what he was going to tell his wife when he came home minus his paycheck, I made my way over to the sultry sex kitten.

She was throwing heat like a furnace. Melting chocolate bars at twenty paces. It was too hot to fuck, but next to her, that scorcher felt like a cool, seaside breeze.

"I just made you twenty bucks, and all you had to do was stand here looking gorgeous, Gorgeous."

She didn't say anything, just looked me up and down and blinked those big baby blues.

The sheen of sweat on her face glowed under the neon lights. She'd sucked all the flavor out of the end of the Popsicle, so the tip was white.

I fished out a crisp, new bill and passed it over. She let it rest in the palm of her hand as she stared at it, confused. She tried giving it back to me, but I stopped her.

8

"See that guy over there?" I asked, stepping aside to give her a glimpse. "He just paid me a lot of money to sleep with you."

"He *what*?" she goes, insulted. She threw down what was left of her Popsicle and took a step closer. Her eyes burned like a butane flame.

Like most women, she looked better when she was steamed. But I didn't want her making a scene. She was liable to blow the act.

"Don't get yer panties in a bunch," I said, shutting her cakehole with my hand.

I told her about the con and then nervously took my hand away. I was sure she was gonna blow up again. But she kept quiet.

I told her we had to scram and didn't give her a chance to say no. I just put my arm around her waist and steered her toward the exit gates. I gave Pops a back-handed wave as we booked outta there double-time.

My dick is long and my cons are short. *Cop and blow*, that's my motto -- take the money and run. Otherwise things got a way of getting ugly.

* * *

Two minutes later, we were hauling ass down the highway in my supercharged Chevy Menace. It was an acid green two-door with cheetah seat covers, four on the floor and dual exhaust. Twin cams and 440 horses under the hood.

"Say," I said, "what's your name, anyway?"

I was hoping to get to know every inch of her better. She smelled like coconut oil. Her tanned skin gave off heat like asphalt that'd been baking in the sun all day.

"Bunny," she goes. "Bunny LaFever." She was a real piece, too. I couldn't wait to do all sorts of dirty things to her. "How much you take him for?" she asked.

"Two-fifty." In actuality I scored three-fifty. But if there's one thing I know about women, it's never tell them exactly how much money you've got.

* * *

Back at my room at the God Bless America Truckstop Motel, she showed me that that sweet and innocent show was just a put-on. I was glad, though. I prefer a girl with some experience under her belt.

Before I knew it, she was all over me like stink on shit. Purple from the Popsicle, her tongue sprung to the back of my throat and then snaked all over the inside of my mouth like she was mining the gold fillings out of my teeth. Despite all the tongue wrasslin', her hands were nowhere near where I wanted them to be.

My dick had been so hard for so long I thought it would blast off like a rocket, but she kept her distance. The teasing was cute at first but enough was enough. I grabbed her hands and planted them on the tent pole in my pants.

She pulled away and took a few steps back.

"You trying to insult me? You think you can have this body for free?" Bunny squeezed her 'lopes together, serving them up for my hungry eyes: "These tits alone cost five bucks to look at."

I chuckled nervously. "C'mon," I go, "quit screwing around."

"I'm totally serious. Five bucks or I'm gone."

I started laughing for real, digging the little swindler. What else could I do but pay up? She had me right where she wanted me.

This was one of those times in a man's life when he knows his dick's doing the brainwork but he doesn't care. Whatever the dick wants, the dick gets. That right there's the whole story of my life.

I plucked a five-spot from my wallet and waved it like a flag of surrender. She just looked at it. "I don't want your money now," she goes. "Pay me later."

"Whatever you say." And I just eased back on the bed to enjoy the show.

She peeled off her T-shirt and out bounced those giant, all-natural juggs. She had razor sharp tan lines from the sling of a skimpy bikini top. You could tell from her nips that the air-conditioning was on full-blast.

Bunny danced around the room, wiggling and shaking everything her momma gave her. I looked her up and down until I could've guessed her weight. She had all the right parts in all the right places and then some.

She neared the bed and leaned over me to let those massive, all-American melons swing inches above my face. "Wanna taste them?" she goes. As if she had to ask.

I lifted my head to suck the tantalizing titties into my mouth, but she snatched them away.

"Five bucks," she goes.

"All right, five bucks."

"Five bucks *each*, big spender."

"You got it."

"Pay me later," she cooed, and moved closer to bury me beneath her treasure chest. "Mmm," she purred, "you suck real good."

"Damn straight," I mumbled. "You're getting my money's worth."

She only laughed as her fingers spider-walked down to my crotch and unzipped my fly. "You'd like a tit-fuck, wouldn't you?"

It wasn't a question. It was a statement of fact. Some girls are mind readers, but Bunny LaFever was the first dick reader I ever had the pleasure to meet.

"Twenty bucks," she barked.

I was like, "A bargain at twice the price. Pay you later?"

"That's right, bright boy."

We switched places on the bed so that she was on her back. I kicked off my shoes and pulled down my pants and underwear. This dick of mine's got its own zip code and time zone.

When she gripped the shaft, her fingers didn't reach all the way around. She was like, "Lucky for you I'm still in my size-is-everything phase."

"Me, too," I said, dropping to my knees to straddle her. My hard-on slipped between her cleavage like a hot dog in its steamed bun. She pressed them together to make the sandwich good and tight as I began my strokes.

I humped her hooters harder to push my dick closer to her succulent mouth. She stuck out her pink tongue and tick-led the tip. Back and forth it fluttered over the head.

"There's a freebie," she giggled. "But I won't take one in the mouth for less than twenty."

"How much to swallow?"

She had to think that one over. "Thirty," she answered. "And that's only cuz I like you."

I dismounted and stood beside the bed. She sat on the edge of the mattress to let her mouth get better acquainted

12

with my cock. Her tongue twirled over my shaft until it looked like a monument of polished marble.

She blew me good and slow, repeatedly bringing me to the edge of orgasm and then stopping until the urge melted away.

The build-up felt so good it hurt. I never begged anyone for anything before. But tortured by her talented tongue, I was actually begging for mercy.

After some more tongue lashing, she finally let me fill her mouth. She swallowed, too, and it felt like my whole body was sliding down with it.

* * *

My hard-on was history, but the rest of me wasn't ready to say good-bye. Me and Bunny were just getting acquainted. My hands pored over that porno-perfect body, feeling the taut muscles and smooth skin of her legs and stomach.

My fingers tried to squeeze down the waist of her tight shorts, but only got a touch of underwear elastic. I was like, "How much to lose the shorts?"

"Twenty."

"*Twenty*? It only cost ten to see your tits!"

She got out of bed and made with the hand-on-the-hip. "Inflation, baby. Twenty bucks or I get dressed right now and take *these* with me," she threatened, grabbing her grandiose glandular globes.

"Okay, whatever you say. Take 'em off, take 'em off."

"Hold your horses, cowboy -- I'm worth the wait."

The hootchie-kootch she put on burned holes in the back of my eyeballs. She began her bump-and-grind real slow and

13

steamy, undoing her fly one button at a time. Sashaying that fine ass back and forth, she peeled off her shorts.

"Lose the panties," I go. My throat was as dry as yesterday's toast.

"Twenty bucks," she said.

I nodded. My dick was in no state to dicker.

She whipped them off. I could see she was a real blonde, if you know what I mean.

Next to the bed now, she lifted her leg over my head and planted her foot beside my cheek. She smelled sweeter'n a crisp fifty dollar bill.

"Eat it," she goes. She meant business, too. "Eat me for ten dollars more."

It didn't take much to get her there, squealing and trembling as orgasm bloomed in her belly.

After that climax, her legs were a little wobbly. She joined me on the bed. I saluted her with my stick.

"Ram that in me." Her voice was a smoky whisper as she seized my steely shaft and pulled me toward her.

I was like, "How much?"

"We'll settle it later."

She got down on her hands and knees and impatiently wiggled her assets at me. I've been all around the world and seen many things, but nothing beats the business end of a woman.

I entered her dead-center on the first stab. Inside she was like grainy satin. Bunny screwed selfishly, using my cock to get herself off.

But I didn't care. I was getting the best of it, too. One hand washes the other.

She was making animal noises I'd never heard before or since. We were waking up the neighbors. Somebody pounded on the paper-thin walls.

Digging the pucker of her asshole, I got a big idea. Without missing a stroke, I grabbed her handbag and dumped its contents on the bed. I found what I was looking for: a squeeze-bottle of suntan oil.

I slopped oil over my hands and her backside, and slid my fingers up and down her crack. "How much?" I asked, poking half of my index finger inside and rotating it in slippery circles.

"All of it," she grunted. "I want all of it."

I didn't know if she was talking about my money or my dick. But I didn't give a damn either way. She could have 'em both.

* * *

Something like six hours later, we fell into an exhausted heap, panting and listening to the early morning rumble of idling eighteen wheelers. I watched her tits rise and fall with every breath. They jiggled when she started to giggle.

"Ante up, bright boy," she laughed.

I groped for my wallet and slapped two hundred-fifty from that afternoon's score into her open palm. "Easy come, easy go," I sighed.

"Spoken like a true carny."

"How would you know?"

"Cuz I'm *with it*," Bunny explained. She meant she was with the show. "My folks were carnies. I learned every scam years ago."

15

That explained how Bunny knew about the build-up. She played that con like a pro. Just goes to show that sometimes you *can* shit a shitter.

I rolled over and reached for the remote. My head was still buzzing. We crashed with the help of a handful of goofballs.

* * *

The both of us talked over the early bird special at the truck stop restaurant. I had a hot meatloaf sandwich served open-faced with a side of crinkle-cut fries and brown gravy slopped over everything. She picked at a plate of mac and cheese.

"So you're with it," I said.

"With it and for it," she goes in that unbelievable smoky voice that made even the clean words sound dirty.

With it and for it, the carnies say. If you're with it, you're never alone. If you're for it, you've always got something to live for.

But those words never meant a damn thing to me. They were just something to say until I met Bunny LaFever. And then suddenly I knew what life was all about.

Twenty-four hours with one woman was a new record for me. I'm normally the love 'em and leave 'em type. Don't get attached and all involved. That's when your troubles begin.

But sitting there in that diner, I was *with* Bunny. I was *for* Bunny. It was just us against the world.

Like every other joe in the joint, I couldn't keep my eyes off those generously giant juggs. They were like moneybags. I saw two big dollar signs.

"Baby," I said, signaling to the waitress for the check, "it's time you and me went to work."

* * *

That same night at the Laff Riot, I worked the inside of the bottle joint. I was behind the counter, selling baseballs to knock over a pyramid of three milk bottles. But my real job was to look way too stupid to take these chuckleheads for a ride.

Bunny was the sucker bait, working the outside. She hung around the joint letting it all hang out. That milk maid had more rubberneckers than a ten-car pile-up.

A one-woman breast-fest, she was enough to rope in every rube on the lot. Those big tits had their own gravitational pull. They sucked suckers straight into our trap like turds down a toilet.

Our first mark of the night was your typical geezer.

Seeing Bunny, he bellied up to the counter and gave it a shot. He was old enough to be her daddy. Married, too, I bet -- the wife off looking at quilts and blackberry preserves.

Gramps wasn't really in the market for a piece of ass. He was just looking at what might have been if he'd taken the trouble to make something of himself.

Bunny squealed with delight when he killed those bottles. "I've been standing here for half an hour," she lied, "and nobody's made that shot yet! You ain't someone famous I should know about, are you?"

"W-w-why, no, ma'am. I-I-I'm nobody a-tall."

Ha! She really had him going. He was trying his damnedest to impress her. That made him an easy mark for the build-up. Bunny kept talking and I kept taking his money.

Fifty or a hundred bucks later, he had his prize -- a big pink dog. And then he gave it to her before walking off like he was God's gift to easy women.

17

He probably went home and banged his broken-down wife for the first time in who knows how long. Hell, when you look at it that way, we were doing a good deed -- performing a necessary service.

Bunny gave him a hard-on and he felt like a young man again. The attention of one hot bitch is better than gallons of any medicine. You just can't buy that kind of dick-n-ego boost.

A short time later, one of those jarhead ex-marine latent homo types stumbled our way. He was drunk off his ass. I whistled through my teeth to signal to Bunny.

As he got nearer, Bunny started to make some noise about me ripping her off.

"Shay, whash the problem here?" he slurred, stepping in and puffing out his pecs.

"This mean man's ripping me off!" she said, this close to tears. What an actress! A real Academy Award winner. "This game is rigged!"

He reached across the counter and grabbed me by the front of my shirt. "Ain'cha got shomething better to do'n cheat women?" He was a real square-jawed fuck. All boozed up, Captain Courageous.

I pleaded with him: "B-but I k-k-keep telling her, m-m-m-mister -- this game's on the up-and-up. Anybody can w-w-win." The stuttering made it sound even more pathetic.

The peckerhead looked me over like I was a lying sack of civilian shit. "I betcha got them bottles glued down or shomethin'." Lemme tell ya, you had to wake up pretty early to put one over on G.I. Jerk.

"T-try it for yourself, s-s-sir. Take a shot f-for f-free. It's on t-t-t-the house."

Of course, he blew them bottles away, easy. Bunny giggled, turned red. "Gosh, you're good," she gushed, measuring his bulging biceps with her fingers. "Do it for me?"

Who could resist that blonde come-on? Those blue eyes, those big tits that sold themselves. There ain't a man alive who wouldn't sell his soul just to come near her pussy -- much less cum on it.

He dropped a bundle to win her that goddamn pink dog. But now the horny sonofabitch wanted to take her home. Cash in on his investment.

"Lessgo," he said, pulling her away. That's the bitch about playing to drunks -- they're easy to outsmart but also unpredictable as hell. Some can be violent, too.

We had to give him the blow-off but quick. Bunny thought fast to save her butt. "Okay," she said as she fumbled around in her purse, "but I gotta take my medications first."

"I'm all the medicine you need," he said with a big, goofy gap-toothed grin.

"Hold up, baby," she said, standing her ground.

"What, you got a headache or shomethin'?"

"I got the clap and gonorrhea and damn if I can't rid of these crabs once and for all. That ain't a problem, is it?"

"Aw, that don't matter, li'l darlin'! I caught all them friggin' diseases in Bangkok!"

Suddenly he swept her off her feet and carried her in his arms like some kinda goddamn Neanderthal. Her legs dangled helplessly. Her eyes went wide in alarm.

'R-A-N-D-Y!' she mouthed in mortal terror. I cursed under my breath as I watched her wavy blonde hair bobbing away under the neon lights.

I grabbed a blackjack I kept under the counter for just such an emergency and started after them, whapping the duct-taped weapon against my palm. But I didn't get five hundred feet when, totally outta nowhere, I got grabbed.

* * *

The meaty, hairy arm belonged to Peanut Gaines. I knew him all too well. What was coming wouldn't be pretty.

Suddenly I forgot about Bunny's perniciously perilous predicament and started worrying about my own ass.

Peanut Gaines ain't the man you wanna piss off. His muscle was going to pot, but he still had enough to throw me face-first against the backside of the Flying Bobs.

"Hey, boss," I said, my lips squashed flat.

My teeth scraped metal. I tasted iron. The thud-thud-thudding bassline of three year old pop music vibrated to the back of my skull.

"What's the big idea, fuckface?"

He spun me around and pinned my back against the truck. I didn't know what he was talking about. It could've been anything. I'd been scamming all night long.

He dangled a key in front of my eyes ferociously. It was the one I gave to the square in the coke bottle glasses the night before.

"I oughta shove this up your asshole sideways!" he blustered as he crammed the key into my mouth. And then shook me till it rattled against my teeth. "That rube you burnt was some big-shot in town!"

The rest of the story fell into place. When the mooch tumbled his hot date with Bunny was a rip-off, he squealed to Peanut.

20

Peanut was the show's patch. He squared up the law and fixed beefs between carnies and outsiders. Made sure everybody went home happy -- or, in most cases, just went home.

He hoisted me by the seat of my pants like I weighed nothing at all. This was one bout I was gonna lose. Before becoming patch, Peanut's first job with the carny was wrasslin' orangutans.

It was a good act, I hear. What's not to love about monkeys? Except when the big ape is tossing you ten feet.

I did the only thing I could do under the circumstances. I went limp.

It wasn't the flying part that was so bad -- it was the unhappy landing. Hitting that hard dirt knocked the wind right out of me. I was stunned, gasping for breath.

Peanut's white loafers got in my face. The black socks were stretched over calves like two grapefruits. He picked me up and crammed me head-first into this rusty garbage can.

Don't get me wrong. It's not that the big bruiser had something against hustling. He was on the take, same as anybody with half a brain. Twenty percent off the top bought me protection from losers who raised a stink.

But it seemed I never got around to paying Peanut his percentage. He thought I was going south on him -- pocketing his fair share, that is. And so this tear-a-new-asshole bit was just to make an example outta me.

He drum-rolled me out the back gate, past an audience of carnies. It was a big show so everyone could see what happens to hold-out artists. I was surprised. Normally Peanut is kinda short on ceremony. Long on punishment, though.

I got up, a little wobbly and weak in the knees. My head was still spinning. I could barely hear the words coming out of my mouth: "Peanut, man, I'm sorry. I'll give you your percentage. Whatever you want."

"Listen, you fuck," he said, grabbing me by the front of my shirt.

Those icy blue eyes burned the fog off my brain. A blood vessel had popped in one, turning the white all red. His dimpled chin and salt-and-pepper flattop snapped into focus.

"You're new here," he growled, "so maybe you don't know no better..."

Suddenly he slugged me in the gut. The blow doubled me over. He got a handful of hair to straighten me up. I thought I tasted blood in the back of my throat.

He kept on talking like nothing had happened: "But that tight-ass you been carrying on with is the boss's wife."

I was like, "*Bunny*? She's married to *O.B.*?"

O.B. Krass, that is. He owned the Laff Riot. But what did Bunny want with an old fart like O.B.?

He was a cripple and a relic, hobbling along on a crutch and popping pills every other minute to keep himself alive. Why bother? One look at the sorry bastard and you wanted to take him out back and shoot him just to put him outta his misery.

But don't get me wrong. It's not like I had something against the old goat. It's just that I had something for his wife -- every damn night I had something for her.

And she had something for me. No wonder, too. I was the only one who could keep up with her.

"That's right," Peanut said, "so I'm gonna cut you some slack." He kneed me in the balls and I dropped to my hands and knees. My eyes watered and I wanted to puke but it never came.

22

Kee-riiiiist, why was this jerk-off taking it so personal? I mean, you would've thought *he* was the one married to her. But I guess Peanut thought it was his duty to look out for the old man's interest in everything.

"Get up," he goes, offering his hand. "Stand up, boy. C'mon now."

I grabbed hold and he yanked me to my feet like a puppet on a string.

He was like, "Now gimme yer goddamn money."

He wiped his brow. Sweat rings stained the underarms of his canary yellow sport shirt. Erect nipples were visible under the sheen of polyester.

"How much?"

"All of it. And I'll let it slide just this once. But from now on, stay the hell away from the boss's old lady. We're the jealous type..."

"*We*, huh?" I asked as I handed over my hard-earned tens and twenties.

"That's right, bright boy. So do us all a favor and stay the fuck away."

* * *

When somebody tells me not to do something, I go right out and do it. I can't help it. It's this little problem I got that gets me into bigger problems.

So instead of forgetting all about Bunny, I snuck back on the lot to get her out of that jam with the jarhead. They could be anywhere.

I started searching off the midway, keeping my eyes peeled for Peanut and sticking to the sinister shadows. I'd dropped the blackjack during my run-in with the patch. So I

23

improvised, lifting a monkey wrench from a ride truck and wrapping an oily rag around the business end.

I darted in between empty trucks and rattling diesel generators. I was winded. My lungs were searing. My pounding heart was ready to burst inside my chest.

At last I heard the unmistakable sounds of fucking and defilement. With a renewed energy, I followed the grunts and groans. Each one a knife in my heart.

At long last I reached the source. He had her on the ground and was banging down the front door.

His back was to me. His pale butt hung out below his T-shirt. The muscles in his cheeks dimpled with every violent thrust. He was still in his shoes and socks, the no-class bastard.

Bunny's long legs were in the air, bent at the knees. They bounced up and down as he piledrived her over and over. White panties waved from one ankle like a flag of surrender. I saw red.

I ran up and swung the wrench at the back of his skull. It hit with a dull thud. He was out like that, falling against her while dropping to his knees.

"Oh, shit," I said.

Bunny wasn't Bunny.

She was somebunny else.

She wasn't even a blonde.

She was a brunette.

And she was pissed: *"Who the hell're you?!"* she goes.

She didn't know me, but I knew who she was. She was the show's gypsy fortuneteller. Her mitt camp supported something like two dozen of her closest relatives.

24

And that jarhead I knocked out wasn't her husband. Gyps don't truck with outsiders for nothing. So she must've been taking the sap for a ride he didn't know about.

And here I was, blowing her hustle. My face flushed with embarrassment. "Uh, sorry?"

"I'm the one who's sorry!" Sparks flashed from her black eyes like a toy ray gun. "You coulda let me finish first!"

She grunted, cursing me in Romany as she pushed the dead weight out of her lap. His dick was shrinking away like a burnt match stick.

Her nose was too big but I wasn't looking at her face. Not when she made such a wicked spread. She could've been headless for all I cared.

But my conscience pulled me away.

"Just where do you think you're going?" she hollered at my back.

I turned around, protesting. "I got something to do."

"Damn right you do. Get back here -- or I swear I'll call the cops!"

I didn't believe her, but her red bra was pushed up over her tits. They weren't big but you couldn't call 'em small, neither. You could palm one pretty easy.

How could I say no to an argument like that? She had a need, and I was there to fill it. But that's just me -- always aiming to please.

* * *

Her tongue was in my mouth. My cock was in her cunt. We fit together like two pieces in a jigsaw puzzle.

It was a tight squeeze in the possum-belly of that ride truck. Wall-to-wall sex. We were a crowd of two, packed in like sardines.

She lay on her back. Her breasts were squashed against my chest. Hard nipples scraped my skin. Her right leg was wrapped around my waist. Her left knee was pressed against her face.

It was pretzel sex. We were all twisted up together. And the tangled knot of flesh got tighter with every hump.

My hand kept falling asleep. Every few minutes I had to shake the feeling back into it. The ceiling was so low my ass bumped it on every pull-out. I got a charlie horse and screwed her harder to keep from howling.

I'll be the first to admit, that possum-belly wasn't the choicest spot on the lot. But it was safe from Peanut. Any port in a storm.

That gypsy thief was a force of nature, too.

She had more ebb and flow than the Atlantic Ocean. We were a tumultuous tempest of seething sex. Her jet black bush was like the Bermuda Triangle and I was the doomed sailor.

But I didn't give a damn. I was glad to go down with the ship. I was screwing the eye of the hurricane. She was a whirling vortex around my dick.

The air was thick with the smell of old grease and sweaty sex. You couldn't see shit in that storage space, either. The only light was from a flashlight. It rolled wildly when we kicked it. The beam danced about, catching flashes of detail.

Her face was made up like a circus wagon: blue eye shadow with glitter in it. Black eyeliner and thick mascara.

Eyebrows that looked like she painted them on with a stencil.

She looked like a real slut. All part of her come-on. But who cares? I love an honest whore. I'm a real sucker for it. You can trust a girl who fucks for something.

Long strands of black hair were plastered to her face. Glowing green eyes stared me down. The fortune teller gritted her teeth. She huffed and puffed, her cheeks ballooning and deflating. She was gonna hyperventilate if I didn't pop her cork soon.

My powerful thrusts had us wedged into a corner. Her head was bent at an awkward angle. Our bodies pitched and crashed together.

I tongued her ear and took the lobe between my lips. That was the final straw. After that it was over. She was done for. She let out a cry as her pussy began to spazz up and down my shaft. My ears were still ringing as her whole body began to shake.

"Uh-huh-uh-huh-uh-huh-uh-huh-uh-huh!" she grunted in time to my quick piston. She started speaking in her native tongue, rolling her R's through a string of growling gobbledygook.

"I hear ya, baby! I hear ya!" I cried.

The Romany race has its strange and ancient ways. But boy can they ever fuck. Those gypsy girls can screw themselves inside out. I was having some visions and hallucinations of my own.

The whole world stopped as pent-up seed came bubbling up and out. I was a shook-up pop bottle, exploding warm fizz all over the place.

"Aaiii-aaiiii-aiiiiyyyeeee!" she sighed as I doused her flaming snatch.

27

She squeezed me dry. Her pussy was like a warm bed on a cold morning -- I hated to leave it. But my cock was shrinking away.

She gazed deeply into my eyes, reading my fortune in them. "You will be betrayed by a woman."

"*Ha*! Tell me something I don't know."

"Someone has put a curse on you," she said. "Very bad, very evil. It follows you like a black cloud."

"I'll take my chances."

"I can remove it. My magic is powerful."

"I'll say."

"No charge," she said seductively.

Her black eyes narrowed and a smirk played in the corner of her mouth. That spell wouldn't work on me, though. When a broad like that says *No money*, she really means *More money*.

"You talk a good line," I said. "Feed it to some other mooch."

"Suit yourself," she said, suddenly sounding bored. The charm was turned off like a TV. Her mind was already somewhere else, planning her next scam.

We tumbled outta the possum-belly, stretching sore arms and legs and pulling on ruined clothes. Greasy black fingerprints were all over her face, legs and arms. I had a crick in my neck that I'd be feeling for a week.

I watched her go. Her ass in its sheathe-shaped skirt disappeared in the dark. My dick was barely dry when everything went black for me.

It was like a light bulb burning out. There was a pop of white lightning and then total darkness. I took a swim in a deep pool of black ink.

A bucket of cold water brought me out of it. Coughing and sputtering, I sat up too fast.

My head was swimming in pain that radiated from the back of my head. Weird green and purple blobs flotated before my eyes. I tried to shoo them away like flies.

The veil of fog slowly lifted. It hurt to look up. Standing over me was the curvaceous silhouette of a gal who could decorate mudflaps. Details slowly emerged.

It was Bunny all right. Her hands were planted on her hips. Her eyes narrowed ferociously. "Well?" she wanted to know.

"Well, what?"

"You ditched me, you jerk! Ain't you gonna say you're sorry?"

"Yeah, I beg your pardon, *Mrs. Krass.*"

She looked at me and didn't say anything.

"Oh, yeah," I said. "Peanut told me all about it. *Somebody* had to, I guess."

"You didn't ask!" she yelled, all defensive.

"I gotta ask?!" Un-fucking-believable! I grabbed hold of her bare hand: "You don't even wear a ring! How's a guy supposed to know any better?"

"So we're married," she said, blowing it off. "It's not like it means anything. It's just a carny marriage."

Carnies don't need a church or a preacher or any of that bullshit to get married. All they need is a merry-go-round. They get on holding hands and, one turn later, they get off as man and wife. No courthouses, no blood tests, no paperwork.

Hell, the only thing neater than a carny marriage is a carny divorce. You get on and they run the carousel backwards. When you get off, you're divorced. That's it -- clean and simple. No damn lawyers making a buck off your misery.

"So divorce the sonofabitch," I said, "if you hate him so much."

"Randy," she goes, "you just don't understand women."

"The hell I don't. You're a gold digger. I understand that."

"Just admit it," she said.

"Admit what?"

"You're jealous."

"Jealous of what? I'm the one who gets your body."

"That's right -- you get my body and O.B. gets nothing. I've got that dirty old man wrapped around my finger."

"Listen," I said, "whatever you got going, leave me out of it. It ain't my hustle."

She grabbed my arm and held fast. "Let's run off somewhere. Anywhere, I don't care. You and me -- what a team we'd make!" she squealed.

I sniffed around her neck.

"What?" she asked nervously, letting me go.

"That perfume you're wearing, what is it? No, wait, I know what it is -- smells like trouble."

"Shut up."

"I've known you less than twenty-four hours, and already I'm in a world of shit. I lost all my money cuz of you."

She sighed and thought for a moment. Then her face brightened. She cocked her hip. "Like, aren't you gonna ask me if I'm okay? It's the least you could do after letting me get carried off like that."

"You okay?"

A sly smile appeared on her face. She had teeth so smooth and white, I wanted to run my tongue across them.

Being with Bunny LaFever was like being locked in a padded room. No matter which way you turned, you ran head-first into a wall of sex.

"Of course I'm okay," she giggled. "We got to his car. He yakked and passed out. I got his wallet."

She waved a fan of bills at me. Raised by carnies, Bunny had picked up a thing or two about the grift. The apple don't fall too far from the tree. I began to wonder if her momma could screw half as good as her.

But I should've tumbled to it right then and there. Bunny LaFever took care of herself first. She had an angle same as everybody else.

"So I guess we're through," she said, slipping me the entire score. "That's for your trouble. Now we're even."

Blame it on the knock-out, but I still wasn't thinking straight. Those tits and ass went together like guns and booze. The girl was bad and bad for you.

I was like, "C'mon. We'll figure something out."

"What about Peanut?"

"No muscle-bound gorilla's gonna tell *me* what to do. What about Krass?"

"O.B. will be mad, same as always. But what can he do?" she goes. "Besides, we don't even share trailers. He might not even notice I'm gone."

Krass never should've married her. He was too old and she was too full of fire. He could only give her money. But she was mad for kicks, and it'd take more than dough to tame that animal inside her.

We took off in the Menace. The entire drive back to the truck stop motel I kept feeling the knot on the back of my head. It was as big around as an egg.

"God*damn*," I grumbled. "You didn't have to hit me so hard, did you?"

"I'm not the one who sapped you. You were knocked out when I got there."

Like I said, it just wasn't my night. But Bunny more than made up for it later on. We had a helluva time -- so good that I forget the details.

But I can tell you that there's no screw like an evil screw, and screwing another man's wife is the evilest of all.

* * *

Give a man a rope and he'll hang himself with it. That's why Bunny and I started carrying on pretty regular after that.

When we were feeling bold, we'd fuck right there on the lot, in her trailer. Once we did it in the drive-thru car wash with the soap suds and hot wax flowing around us. But mostly she'd sneak off the lot at night and I'd pick her up and drive her back to my motel room.

Those crazy weeks are all a blur now but I remember this one time coming to with a solid boner that I knew wouldn't be going down anytime soon. The ceiling was scorched and my eyebrows were singed. Must've been spitting fireballs with grain again.

Rubbing my aching head, I heard the shower going full-blast. Clouds of steam curled around the open door. Bunny came into view, naked.

I wondered if her pussy was worth the trouble of all this sneaking around behind O.B.'s back. Hell, if you think about it, no pussy's *ever* worth the trouble. But if you let that stop you, you'll never get laid.

And right now, there was nothing between me and her but twelve rock-solid inches. She slowly opened her eyes. Her dreamy stare drifted to my cock that jumped at her like a dowsing rod.

"I couldn't wait," she murmured, sounding a little bit guilty.

"You wanna get clean or get dirty?" I asked.

"Both," she goes, looking back at me as she grabbed my dick and led me into the shower like a dog on a leash. The water was piping hot. It felt incredible as it pounded our backs.

I embraced her from behind, cupping her slippery breasts, weighing them in my hands. My mouth slurped the water off her flesh. Hair streamed down her back like blonde ink.

My eager cockhead nudged her firm backside, and I carefully guided my hard-on between her cheeks.

"We gotta stop meeting like this," I said as I reached between her legs and played with what I found. "We'll catch hell."

She bent over. "Don't get soft on me," she goes.

"Does this feel like I'm getting soft on you, baby?"

Dicks just don't come any harder than mine. Especially when it was sealed in her snatch. She fit me like a sheathe. I was snug as a bug.

But a cunt is a cunt is a cunt, no matter how tight. She's got to have the technique to back it up. And the right attitude.

She's got to meet me half-way. Give me something to work with. Put a little life into it. Not just stand there taking it.

I like my whiskey on ice but I want my women on fire.

Which is why I was so crazy for Bunny. Here I was, pounding her pussy, but she wasn't above giving some back. Hell, no. She was pushing herself backward to meet my thrusts and drive my shaft deeper.

"Fuck me!" she cried as I slammed away.

I picked up speed when I saw that she couldn't get enough. My thighs slapped against her cheeks and my balls knocked her pussy. Bath water sizzled as it hit our burning parts, cooling the intense friction.

Suddenly her cunt seized up on me. It was like sticking my cock in a light socket. My hair stood on end. The electric charge shot through my body. Sparks flew off my fingertips.

She blew me away. I poured everything I had left into her. "Oh, Randy," she gushed.

"I wish there was two of you," I said. "I'd love one and then I'd love the other."

"I wish there was two of me, too," she said as she turned around.

Her lips were wet and open as they locked onto mine. It was like a turbojet taking off. The shower pounded us as her mouth sought my neck, then my ear.

"Randy," she goes, whispering close, "what do you want outta life?"

"A million bucks and a blonde to blow it on. I got the blonde, and now I just need the million bucks. How 'bout you?"

"I want everything," she said.

34

"Nobody's got everything. But at least we're together."

"No. Not as long as O.B. is alive."

That kind of talk spooked me. *Not as long as O.B. is alive.* I knew what she meant.

But I wasn't a goon working the strong-arm. I was a flattie. When you got smarts you don't stoop to violence, and it annoyed me how easily the words poured out of her lips.

Once you bring up murder, you can't put it back in the bottle. It's out there. It hangs over you like a storm cloud, turning your happy little picnic all to shit.

I tried to make light of it. "Shaddap," I go, kissing her on the forehead. "Yer crazy." I reached for the faucet and abruptly turned off the shower.

"Crazy about you."

"Then don't fuck everything up," I said as I wrapped a towel around her shoulders and smacked her on the ass. "We got a good thing going here."

"But I hate him," she goes.

"Who?"

"Who do you think?" she snapped. We both damn well knew who she was talking about. "He's *old* and *ugly* and *horrible* to me."

"You stuck with him this long."

"You don't understand," she bitched as she towel-dried her hair so vigorously her tits were a blur. "You don't know anything."

She was wrong. I knew one thing -- she loved his money as much as she hated the man. That's for damn sure.

35

At least we both agreed that we couldn't keep it up like that for long. We were just begging to get busted by Peanut Gaines. So we decided to cool it for a few days.

* * *

I tried to carry on like there was nothing between us but it hurt like hell knowing she was right there and not having her.

Wanting Bunny was like a hunger that's never satisfied. It's always there, gnawing at your insides. Reminding you that you still haven't got it.

It gets so bad you don't give a damn once you've fallen in love with the pain.

Maybe it was lucky for me, then, that Peanut started giving me heavy shit. At least dealing with him kept my mind off Bunny. Like stubbing your toe and pounding your thumb with a hammer to forget about it.

Deep down I bet we're all a little sick and twisted and wouldn't mind giving some poor sap static. But Peanut brought all that sick and twisted-ness to the surface. Day in and day out, he rode my ass and busted my balls and even asked for more money up front.

"What the hell for?" I asked him this one time when he was really getting to me. "Your cut's enough. I bring in more money than all the agents here put together."

"And you get more complaints than all the agents put together," he goes. "I spend half my time cleaning up your shit."

"That's your *job*, boss. That's what they pay you for. That's what *I* pay you for."

"Fuck that. I get paid to keep things running smooth. And you are fucking things up royally."

"What is this -- a Sunday school show, or what? Nobody ever bitched at me for scoring before."

"You're a risk around here, flattie."

"What the hell's that mean?"

"It means from now on you're on the Banana Boat."

"The *Banana* Boat! Fuckin-A!"

Talk about adding insult to injury! The Banana Boat was in the back ass of the midway, next to the line of port-o-sans and away from all the action. Nowheresville.

"If you don't like the way I run things," he goes, "you go talk to the boss. We'll tell O.B. about everything that's been going on around here."

Peanut finally had me where he wanted me. He knew damn well that I wouldn't beef to Krass. When you make your hell, you gotta burn in it.

I put up with the Banana Boat for a few hours but the longer I stood there doing nothing but thinking, the madder I got. Randy Everhard does not bend over and thank you for fucking him up the ass. I cut outta there before 10, but I knew I'd be back.

* * *

The very next night I was single-o and on the sneak, hiding out behind the merry-go-round. I was grinding the old Razzle Dazzle routine.

The game looked like an ordinary briefcase from the outside. Popped open, it was an instant count store.

The bottom made a place on which to throw eight dice. Pasted on the inside of the lid was a chart to convert the toss into point values.

The gist was to accumulate a hundred points or more, with a ten to one pay-out. Of course, the pay-outs were strictly one way -- straight to my wad.

The Razzle was a sure thing, but I was sweating bullets. If Peanut caught me, my ass was grass and he was the lawn-mower. But if I ain't running from trouble, I'm looking for it.

A flattie spends half his life waiting. I spent half the night in the shadows waiting for the perfect mark. He was some old yahoo you wouldn't look twice at. But you could stand around all damn day staring at that delicious redhead on his arm.

She must've been half his age. A real banner broad -- a good looker that made him look good. It actually hurt to tear your eyes off her.

That pop tart's topography was enough to stuff three or four cropped T-shirts. Somehow she packed her up-tilted tits into one. There they hung, defying gravity like a couple helium balloons.

Her legs were the color of honey. When she toyed with her leather miniskirt, I saw she had a thing against under-wear. She knew damn well what she was doing, too.

Anyway you looked at her, she was a hard-on magnet. Dicks pointed at her like a compass needle pointing straight-up north. My flag was flying like Old Glory.

To afford an expensive habit like that, I made him for a rich cat from the get-go. Sugardaddy here was the perfect mark. The blood was in the water.

"Speedway, Speedway," I spieled, "the fastest game on the midway. Score one hundred miles and go home a win-ner. And tonight the boss is paying off at ten to one. A buck'll get you ten."

To help make up his mind, I shoved the cup of dice into his hand. "First roll's on the house. Go on -- it's free. You can't lose."

That beleaguered basset hound hadn't shaved or slept in a week. Dark circles ringed his sunken, bloodshot eyes. His bags had bags. In a daze, he shrugged and let those bones fly.

I fairbanked him as I scooped up the dice, miscounting to let him win and lure him in.

"Four and two plus five, carry the one, plus three, plus seven and ten makes thirty-three, now add the fifteen, makes a grand total of forty-eight. Check the chart, chum, and see what forty-eight gets you."

The robust tomato saw it first. "Oooh, looky!" she goes, bending over to point at the chart. She had this lazy Confederate drawl that was all heat and humidity. "Fifty miles!"

Her bountiful bosom swung low like overblown bunches of grapes. I couldn't resist copping a feel of that firm flesh. She didn't mind, either. She nearly swooned when I pinched a nipple.

"Today's your lucky day," I said to sugardaddy. "You're halfway to a hundred. Try it again -- one dollar will get you ten."

He peeled off a one-spot and put it in my money box. She pouted her full lips and blew on his dice for good luck. With a piece of ass like her, he was already a lucky stiff. But his streak was about to turn bad.

I fast-counted him a total of twenty-one. It gave him fifteen miles. "Look, mister," I go, "now you're only thirty-five points away. A dollar again will get you ten."

He put down another ace and rolled. "Twenty-six," I said, announcing the total.

"Twenty-six says *Add*," he goes, reading off the chart.

"Right you are, sir. That means you've got to add another dollar to your next bet if you wanna keep playing. You'll win plenty when two bucks gets you twenty."

Moochie chanced it. I added up forty-one. "That's another fifteen miles. Now you're only twenty away from the jackpot. Why not bet ten? When you score those twenty points, I'll give you a hundred dollars of the boss's money."

I flashed him the garden of green in my wallet. Eyeballing that fat bankroll, he got the look of a sucker about to get in over his head.

I almost forgot his wife in all the build-up, but suddenly she let out a big yawn. "Honeykins," she whined, "I wanna ride a ride. Y'all *promised*."

For a sec I feared she was gonna pull him out of it. But she said, "Y'all keep on playing and win me something BIG."

He'd already given her something big. On her finger was a rock the size of New Jersey. But a wedding ring didn't stop the little missus from returning my wink as she smooched hubby on the cheek.

"You heard your wife," I said as she walked away with a wicked ass-wiggle. "Grab it and growl!"

He ponied up a tenner. It was like taking candy from a baby -- except I never gyp kids, pregnant women or cripples.

"Eleven gets you nineteen points," I said, counting his roll. "You're at ninety-nine miles. One more mile and you win the whole enchilada!"

He may as well have been a million miles away. No way in hell was he gonna get that last point. I'd string him along till he was busted flat.

Another ten-spot got him twenty-six: *Add* again. He was up to twenty dollar bets.

He slapped it down without a second thought.

He rolled and I gave him another twenty-six.

He put down forty and rolled a big fat zero.

Suddenly, his wife's squeal of delight broke the tension. "*Wheeeee!*" she cried, waving as she whirled by on a painted pony. She quickly lifted her skirt to flash me before spinning out of view.

I looked at hubby, dumbstruck. He didn't say a word. I figured he didn't catch the tease. Another forty dollars was in his trembling hand. He was like a junkie.

"Lookit me!" she cried as she spun our way again.

She rode like a jockey, standing up in the stirrups, knees bent, and crouching forward. Hubby missed seeing her flip up her skirt to show off an ass that was illegal in fourteen states.

After that shameless sexhibition, I had trouble minding my business. Luckily the rube was willing to do all the work. He tossed the dice and came up with nothing and instead of walking away he threw down another forty.

I've played enough losers to know how they think. When a mark's in the hole, he's afraid to cut his losses. Instead of pulling out, he only digs deeper.

"Whee! Giddyup!" she cried again and again, owning my eyes at each go-round.

She rode side-saddle, spreading and raising her legs. She stood up, lustily grinding her pelvis against the brass pole. I carved out a woody for her to trick-ride like that.

The mark finally ran out of moo. He was like, "Take a check?"

41

It wasn't the first time a mark begged to take him some more. I shook my head. "Nothing personal, buddy."

Just then his much better half turned past on the slowing machine. She gave me one last flash of her ass on the dismount.

Was she half-dressed or half-naked? It all depends on how you see the world. The pessimist sees her as half-dressed. But I'm an optimist in a big way. She was half-naked to me. The way I figured it, I was halfway there.

I was like, "Okay, I'll give you one more roll."

"For what?"

His wife skipped back and slid her arms around her old man's neck. "Win me a big prize?" she asked, sweet as sugar.

"Make me an offer I can't refuse," I said, looking hard at his wife.

He didn't get me at first. But then it hit him. His eyes brightened.

The low-down dirty bastard actually smiled as his fingers curled around the dice. Some guys would sell their mother for one more chance.

But as far as I was concerned, that deal was like a sore dick -- you couldn't beat it.

* * *

We were barely inside the motel room before my prize came on strong. Her lusty embrace knocked me back against the door, slamming it shut behind us. She wrapped her body around me like a Buick around a telephone pole.

Her leg snaked around my waist and squeezed. Our tongues wrassl'd as I groped for the light switch. I wanted to see what I'm getting myself into.

42

"My name's Brandi Lustre," she said in between some frenetic frenching.

"I don't give a shit," I said, looking into her amazing green eyes as I hiked up her skirt.

My hand roamed over her shapely ass and dipped between the slippery folds. She was juicier'n a supermarket tabloid. After turning herself on all night, her snatch was practically steaming in the cold AC.

She was like, "Is it true what they say about carnies?"

"Yes."

"You didn't wait for the question."

"Don't have to. Whatever it is, I got your answer right here --"

I undid my pants to free my thickening tool. She reached in to weigh my balls in her hand, rolling them like a pair of loaded dice.

"Y'all are absolutely right," she goes. "A hard man is good to find."

She planted one leg on an armless plastic chair for easy access. Suddenly she thrust herself closer, plunging me into the carnal clutches. It was slicker than a Slip-N-Slide in July. I was in to the balls.

"Fuck me!" Brandi cried as I began banging away. "Fuck me hard!"

We were a slick sex machine, grunting and grinding to get each other off.

Cradling her ass in my hands, I swung her over to the dresser. It was the perfect angle of attack. She was at just the right height.

Her hands gripped the edge of the cheap furniture. The fake wood was scarred with knife cuts. She whispered impatiently: "C'mon, c'mon, c'mon!"

Her legs spread as I went deep. They closed around my waist like a trap, locking at the knees. Her green eyes looked up at me.

She pulled me against her. When I pulled out, she jerked me towards her again. She was driving the rhythm. She wanted control.

Fuck that. She was mine. I stole her fair and square. I pummeled her faster than her legs could keep up.

Brandi's bikini tan lines were as clear as night and day. It was like a pencil outline for her blazing bush. She was trimmed as neat as a golf course.

Inside her cropped top, those big breasts were positively alive. They jiggled and knocked around like puppies in a bag trying to get out. I pushed up her shirt and out they bounced. I got my hand on one.

The back of her head bumped against the mirror. Knocking time with my thrusts. I was driving her to Cum City and when we got there the mayor would hand over the key.

"Wheeee!" she cried giddily as her universe suddenly expanded. "Whooo-hoooo!"

I didn't even have to touch her clit. She went through life on the verge of cumming. I didn't let up but dug in deeper as she rode out her orgasm.

I drilled until I didn't hear her. For a second I blacked out, spinning in the outer space of her body. Back on Earth, I came so hard and long that I could've signed my name across her back.

She got off the dresser and moved to the unmade bed, on her back. I kicked off the rest of my clothes.

Writhing eagerly, she spread her legs to show me the goods. I got down and rubbed my face in her scent.

"Quit beating around the bush," she gasped. She lay back and lifted her knees to either side of her face.

I plunged face-first. She was a puddle of arousal. Gushing like a faucet.

"Eat my pussy," she groaned. She crossed her powerful legs over me, crushing me deeper into her lunch box. She would've crammed my whole head and body inside if she could. "Make me cum all over y'all's face --"

I sucked her clit into my mouth and circled the hardened knot of nerves with my tongue until she shivered head to toe. She had a pussy you could pour over pancakes. I slipped three fingers inside.

She was pressing her tits together and pinching nipples. Her back arched as she came. Tidal waves of butt-bouncing ecstasy washed over her.

My face dripped with her juices as I came up for air. My tongue was shot. Lips numb. Cock reloaded. She was really asking for it now.

"Gimme, gimme!" she goes. "I want more!"

Before I knew it, she was on top, straddling my waist. My erection twitched between her thighs. She grabbed the head and rubbed it back and forth over her swollen clit as she shook out her long red hair. That was one girl who knew how to take the bull by the horns.

She shoved the knob inside. She leaned forward and planted her hands on my shoulders. Her tits swung into my face. I stretched a nipple between my lips and sucked hard as she impaled herself on me.

She began wrenching my prick at an agonizingly slow pace. She raised her rump until the head was just inside.

Then bore down inch after inch until I was embedded to the hilt.

That supercharged, sex-cylindered slut rode me hard. She had the strongest pussy I'd ever felt. I swore she'd rip it off she jerked me around so hard.

After several build-ups, she stopped and pivoted on my pole. Moving into a reverse cowgirl, she re-plugged her sopping quiff. I hung on to her ass, spreading the cheeks wide to scope the scene.

"Y'all feel so good," she drawled as she bounced around. "So good. So, so-o-o-o good." Her words became as short as her breaths. "So, good, so, good, so, good!" she huffed and puffed, rhythmically stoking the fire between us.

I was cooked to the boiling point. I couldn't hold back any longer and exploded inside her. She kept pumping my dick until it went Mister Softee inside her.

I should've known right then and there that I was in over my head. But pulling out didn't even cross my mind. I was too hopped up to think. Over the years I'd won a fucking lot, but never a lot of fucking.

I was red and raw, but she was still hot and bothered. If sex was electricity, she had enough drive to light up the midway. Lucky for me she kept a plastic arsenal in her purse.

We had a ribbed Dildosaurus in her pussy, a smaller dick-shaped vibrator in her mouth, and one end of a double-dong in her rear. It took the both of us to keep them all sliding in and out. She gave those schlongs a serious shellacking.

Just then I heard the key scratching at the lock. Bunny suddenly stepped into our shamelessly sordid scenario. My mind reeled with excuses and explanations.

* * *

"Bunny! How --? " I said, standing up quick. I tried to tuck my hard-on between my legs but it kept popping out at her. "This ain't what it looks like!"

"It ain't?"

"It ain't a private orgy," Brandi piped up, "if that's what y'all think."

"It ain't. But now that *y'all* mention it..."

"I'm Brandi," she said, taking Bunny by the hand and leading her to the bed.

As usual, you couldn't wrap a stick of gum with what little Bunny had on.

Whatever scrap of clothing was hiding her privates, Brandi took care of. Bra and panties flew across the room. Soon the bodacious blonde was wearing nothing but her tan lines.

Lucky for me Bunny had an open mind. She was a real swinger. Like the flying trapeze. She went both ways. The feeling was mutual.

Brandi Lustre would screw anything that moved. Girl or boy, it didn't matter. So long as her cunt was covered, she was one happy harlot.

They lay head to head and bush to bush. Naked bodies writhed like a lesbian knot. Taut bellies undulated. They slowly humped, flesh grinding against flesh.

They frenched good and slow. Pink tongues intertwined. Bunny nibbled and licked Brandi's lower lip.

Brandi reached down between their legs and felt up Bunny.

"Y'all're so wet," she sighed. "I'm so wet, too. Touch me." She guided Bunny's fingers to her soaking snatch.

47

They looked deep into each other eyes and, without exchanging a word, moved into a scorching 69. Brandi took the topside, burying her head between Bunny's thighs. She studied her snatch like she was gonna find the meaning of life in there. Bunny lifted her head into Brandi's tawny muff.

Fads and fashions are here today and gone tomorrow, but two hot babes gettin' it on is forever. I circled the bed, feeling like a kid in a candy store. Everything looked so good I didn't know which to fuck first.

So many holes, so little time. I'd of given my left nut for a second dick right about now.

Their tongues were flashes of pink, lapping at girlholes. Brandi moaned. Sucks and slurps filled the air.

Fully inflated, I horned in on the girl-girl act. I planted my hands on Brandi's ass and pushed the cheeks apart as Bunny tongued her button.

I piled in. She gasped at the solid invasion. Bunny frenched her clit while I fucked her slow.

I pulled out as they moved into a new position. They sat facing each other. They leaned back and spread their legs.

Brandi scootched closer till their pussies were only inches apart. She grabbed the flexible double-dong and fitted one end into her pussy. Bunny inserted the other end into her own open cunt.

They were both plugged in. Bunny held it in place. Her fingers barely fit around the thick shaft. They worked their pelvises back and forth to fuck themselves. Their hips were hypnotic as they thrust themselves onto the dong.

Rivulets of sweat ran between their breasts. Their hard stomachs glistened. Bushes were damp and matted.

I stood next to Brandi. She was eye to eye with my growing hard-on.

Her mouth sprung toward me, gulping the head into her mouth. She gobbled me like a geek taking the head off a chicken. Her head jerked back and forth to get me rock hard.

Bunny stopped servicing herself and began to tongue my sac. She held my balls in her mouth as she slid the dong in and out of Brandi.

"I want the real thing," Brandi said as she jumped out of bed, leaving Bunny holding the dick.

"Where?" I asked.

"Here," she said.

Turning around, she bent over and grabbed her ankles. High and tight, her butt pulled apart in a deep cleft. I slipped a saliva-coated finger inside and wound her up.

My cock pulsated eagerly as I greased it with spit. Pushing her cheeks apart, I went in the hard way.

She moaned uncontrollably, swaying her head from side to side with my thrusts. Her long hair swept across her back. I pulled it like the reins of a horse and drove the hussy hard.

I pulled all the way out. You could've driven a truck through her. I plunged back inside, then pulled out again like it was a second pussy.

Strumming her own clit, she'd never stopped cumming. One orgasm melted into another till she was a rippling fuck puddle.

I don't know how many orgasms she'd had that night. I'd stopped counting. It didn't matter. She only wanted more. Some women're never satisfied. Try all you want. There's just no pleasing 'em.

* * *

I was twelve inches in the hole, but I'd already invested a gallon of goo in Brandi. It was like adding fuel to the fire.

She was turned on even more. And there was no turning her off. No satisfying that impossible appetite. She was like a convenience store -- open 24-7.

We went at it in twosomes and threesomes, girl-girl, boy-girl, girl-boy-girl, full frontal, ass backward, every which way in the little book they sell in its own slot in the rubber vending machines at every truck stop in the world.

Now we were writing a new book. One for sex fiends. Get the creative juices flowing. We were desperate. We made crazy shit up.

Brandi sat in a chair with her legs bent over the arms. I screwed her in the cunt. Her upturned face was in Bunny's crotch, eating away. Bunny sat on the chair's back with her feet pinned under Brandi's knees.

Bunny shook her head in dismay. She was like, "I don't get it. There's two of us and one of her."

"Even if we had a roomful of dicks, we'd still be out-fucked."

She was so horny it wasn't funny. You always hear about nymphomania but until you're on the wrong end of it you don't know it from squat. It's murder.

I had to face facts. Brandi was a vampire, sucking the life and soul out of me through my dilapidated dick. Her cunt was a black hole no mortal man could escape from.

"Stop the ride, I wanna get off!" I begged, praying for the impotence that didn't come.

"No way, buster!" she shot back though clenched teeth. "Y'all won me fair and square!"

Suddenly I got wise to their set-up. Lustre had let me take his money and wife. My erection was a stand-in. Bunny and I were being sacrificed to Brandi's endless appetite.

Tortuous hours went by. Clamped in the clutches of her bottomless cunt, I passed in and out of stupors. I had visions and hallucinations. Her pussy flashed an evil grin. It was full of teeth. It was actually cackling at me.

I came to, breaking out of this waking nightmare of hairy hellholes. I thought I saw the grim reaper in the corner. But it was just Bunny. Cowering, shell-shocked. A fat lotta good she was. It was all up to me.

In a jockey's crouch over me, the noxious nympho bounced up and down on my shaft. Brandi's hair was wild, her look crazed. Her pussy, once silky smooth, was like stinging sandpaper against my tenderized meat.

It was all up to me. I had to act fast or I was a dead man. "Hold up, baby, I gotta take a leak."

"Oooh, golden showers!" she gushed. "Pee all over me!"

"Sorry, dollface, that ain't my bag," I said as I pushed her away. I limped into the john to think. The salaciously sinister sex fiend needed to be tranquilized, and fast!

I reached into the toilet tank. Bobbing inside were a few orange prescription bottles -- my secret stash. I selected one, cracked it open and shook a few pills into my hand. Seconal, Nembutal, Valium, Quaalude.

The bitch had a built-in fix, but I could cheat, too. There's nothing that can't be done without the creative use of modern pharmaceuticals. That dizzying dosage was enough to dope a baby elephant.

"Come to bed, baby," she purred as I limped back into the bedroom.

I offered her the barbies in my hand and told her they were bennies. "The quicker picker-upper. Keep you going for hours."

I went to the fridge for something to wash them down with.

"Three beers?" she asked when I came back with three cans dangling from my finger on the plastic rings.

"One for you, one for me, and one for peter."

I hadn't been so raw since the first time I met Rosy Palm and her five sisters as a punk and made an all-nighter getting to know that gripping girl gang. I held my beat-up schlong in my hand and started to pour. My glowing red poker hissed and steamed when that cold beer hit.

"Aaahhhh," I sighed in relief.

"Bottoms up," she goes, popping the pills and taking a long drink. Her throat jugged as she drained the can. When she was done, she burped and covered her mouth and blushed.

I hoped the shit was fast-acting as she made a move for me. My fingers were still in her pussy when that knock-out cocktail hit her. The drugs didn't let me down. Her eyes went out of focus and she smiled dreamily.

"I shouldn't drink on an empty stomach," she giggled. She couldn't stop yawning. "I'm so sleepy all of a sudden."

I slipped my hands from between her legs. "Baby, don't stop," she said quietly. "Don't...ever...stop...." Her eyes closed and she was on her way to slumberland.

I nuzzled a dildo against her lips. She sucked it like a pacifier, clutching it in her sleep. How something so dangerous one minute could look so damn cute and innocent the next was beyond me.

I got dressed and pulled Bunny, still naked, out the door with me.

* * *

We barreled down the highway, running for our lives, dazed and confused. Not knowing the time of day -- not knowing what day it was, even.

The rushing wind revived us like smelling salts. Freedom burned our senses -- it hurt like hell but at least we knew we were alive.

Bunny found some clothes in the glove compartment. Most of her wardrobe was shoved in there. Lucky for her she didn't wear much.

We were excited, talking like a couple of drunken crazies. Yammering just to hear yourself cuz you narrowly escaped death and couldn't shut up about it. I gave her the whole scary story, beginning to end.

"Anyway," I said, "you shouldn't have come back here but I'm glad you did. But now you gotta go back to the Riot."

"Don't ditch me!" she cried. I could see in her eyes that she was scared. "You can't ditch me!"

"You can't ditch her!" somebody said out of nowhere. Frank Lustre's head suddenly reared up from the back seat.

Bunny and I both screamed. My heart skipped a beat. I clutched my chest.

I'd forgotten all about Brandi's husband in the back seat. He'd been taking a snooze during the entire ordeal.

"You can't ditch her," he said again.

"Promise me you won't," Bunny begged. Her fingernails dug into my arm.

"Not in a million years, darlin'."

"Swear!"

"Cross my heart and all that."

"You better!"

She didn't have to worry about me blowing anytime soon. After all, this was one sweet set-up. Between the grift and the boss's wife, I had all the bases covered. Money takes my mind off pussy and pussy takes my mind off money.

"Wait a minute --" said Frank, scratching his head. "I thought we were talking about my wife."

"I don't wanna even *think* about your wife, pal."

"So you're bailing?" he asked with a yawn. He sounded more sad than angry. "But you can't. You can't let her down."

I was like, "Mister, you can't disappoint a nymphomaniac. No matter how bad the performance, you always leave 'em wanting more!"

He nodded sadly, running his hand through his thinning hair. "Ain't that the truth," he moaned.

We got to talking. He said he was her fourth hubby in as many years. Brandi went through men like other women go through shampoo.

He was always on the lookout for a fresh supply of cocks. It was life or death. He was only thirty years old. But stress and exhaustion had made him an old fart with one foot in the grave.

I've heard more sob stories than I care to think about, but his got to me.

Sympathy's a price I can't afford in my line of work. But I knew where he was coming from. That's the only explanation for it.

So I felt sorry for the poor bastard -- so fucking sue me.

Call me a boy scout, but the gears started turning as I U-turned the Menace and made for the Laff Riot.

* * *

I dropped Bunny off a few blocks away from the lot so I could drive in alone.

Peanut Gaines was easy to find. Just look for the nightmare of powder blue polyester. In his sport shirt and matching coach's shorts, he looked like a retired robin's egg wearing black socks and pale yellow loafers.

I cut myself a fat slice of humble pie. "Lemme make it up to you," I begged. "I saved a piece for you this time -- if you know what I mean, and I think you do."

* * *

Brandi Lustre was just coming out of it by the time we got back to the motel. "Oooh, my head!" she said, stirring naked in the bedsheets.

For me? he asked silently. The hopeful grin of an idiot was frozen on his lips.

"She's all yours, Tiger," I answered. I slapped his back and pushed the poor sap into the room. "See you in the funny papers!"

"There's only one cure for a hangover," she growled. Her sultry r's rolled in her throat. I shut the door behind him as she finished her thought: "A big, long orgasm."

Payback with interest, I thought to myself as I roared away, leaving those freaks in my dust. *That's the Randy Everhard way!*

* * *

I kinda figured that after that stunt my days were numbered as an agent. So I started hanging around the G-top.

55

That's the private gambling and drinking club for showmen and lawmen -- Grifters and Grafters.

Carnies can't make a wad without blowing it on cards and booze. Easy come, easy go. I simply followed the smell of dirty money into the tent.

Inside of ten minutes I picked my mark: Fat Jew Baby.

I figured the slob for a D.G. -- a degenerate, an addict, easy pickin's. Fat Jew Baby was a lousy gambler to boot. The worst D.G.'s always are. They never learn.

"I got a system," he kept insisting through his losing streak.

"Systems're like assholes," I cracked. "Everybody's got one and they're all full of shit."

But you can't tell a D.G. anything. All you can do is take their money. I took that sorry bastard for a grand at draw poker.

"Pay up," I told him at last. It was four a.m. and I wanted some sleep. My eyeballs were cracking like old paint. "I'm outta here."

"Not yet!" Fat Jew Baby whined. "Gimme a chance to win my money back!"

Like every other loser, he didn't know when to call it quits. Just goes to show that a mark's got no business with money -- even if he's carny.

"No dice. I'm cutting you off. Win your money back tomorrow night."

"But I ain't got a thousand to give you," he sighed. "I guess I gotta owe you. You got my word."

"Hot air's good for nuthin' but balloons. What else you got?"

He pulled out a blue velvet-flocked ring case. I was about to tell him to keep his damn jewelry cuz I ain't no pawn shop, but then he opened the box. Inside, instead of a ring, a yellow, raggedy sliver of toenail rose from the white satin cushion.

I was like, "What the hell's that?"

"Know what this is?"

"Disgusting?"

"Elvis's toenail."

"No shit. Where'd you get it?"

"Graceland. Ever been?"

"Who hasn't?"

"So you've seen the jungle room."

"With the furniture made outta tree stumps and green shag carpeting everywhere."

"Right," he sighed.

"So how'd you get it?"

"Okay, so there I am, standing there in the jungle room, and I happen to look down, right? And lo and behold, stuck in the carpet is this toenail. Right there in front of me, practically. But I saw it right away, snagged in the carpet. It was shining like a diamond or a star. I had to sort of reach through these wrought iron bars they've got to get it, but other than that I could reach it pretty easy. It was stuck in there pretty good, too. I had to pull and pull but I finally got it loose."

"How d' you know it's his?" I asked.

"Whaddaya mean?"

"I mean, how do you know it's his?"

"Sometimes a person just knows something, ya know?"

"Yeah."

"Fate, call it. All those years and nobody else had ever seen it before. But I saw it right away."

"Okay."

"I mean, whose else would it be? Who else would've been walking around barefoot in Elvis's favorite room in Graceland? You don't think he would've let just *anybody* walk around barefoot, do you?"

"I guess not."

"Okay, maybe his momma, but she was dead by then," he said. "So..."

"So," I said, "what else you got?"

"Aw, hell, Randy. This is the chance of a lifetime. Elvis's *toenail*, fer crissakes!"

"I know, Baby, I regret it already. But what else you got?"

"Nuthin'," he sighed. "I got nuthin'. I'm tapped."

"What about your joint?"

Fat Jew Baby owned and operated the Bobo joint. It was the dunk tank concession named after the clown who perched on the precarious plank, razzing passersby. Three softballs for a buck gave them a chance to drown the clown in revenge.

The joint was a grind but it made some decent coin. Better yet, Peanut wouldn't be able to take it away from me. He didn't have much truck with honest joints. He made his nut off the flatties.

"You wouldn't take a man's joint, would you?" Fat Jew Baby goes.

"Only if he bet like he was good for a grand when he wasn't," I said. "That's a goddamn lie in my book."

* * *

And that's how I found myself standing around with my thumb up my ass the next day, finding out first-hand what a hemorrhoid owning your own joint was. Especially one that ain't crooked as the devil's dick.

It was high noon. The midway was lousy with marks. And my goddamn clown was a no-show.

"Where's he at, Pappy?" I asked the nearly-toothless geezer who'd sold the softballs since the beginning of time. "Where's Bobo?"

"Jimmy, you mean?" he croaked. On his head, leaning a little to the right, was one of those big fuzzy hats like a drum major wears. The white fur was mangy and dirty. The vinyl strap bit into his grizzled chin. "Jimmy gets here when he gets here."

I was already pissed-off and frustrated and annoyed, and here's why:

First the garbage man wanted ten bucks to clean up my shit. Then the juice man wanted twenty bucks for the electricity. Then the lot manager wanted a hundred scoots for taking up space on his midway.

Operating expenses, they call 'em. Carnies call 'em *dings*. Those rat bastards were dinging me to death and I had nothing to show for it.

This was the first and the last time I ever play it on the level. There's no percentage in it. By the time everybody gets their cut, you couldn't wipe your ass with what's left over.

59

I was about to climb in the damn tank myself when Bobo finally shuffled in at one. Jimmy Flair was his name. He was hung over from the night before.

White greasepaint was slathered over stubble. A limp cigarette dangled from the corner of his red mouth. A shapeless blue cap flopped off-kilter on his head. His Dickey coveralls were so baggy in the ass he looked like he'd just shit his pants.

He didn't say a word as he climbed up the side of the tank and onto his red-carpeted perch like a king ascending his throne. He tapped the mike and cleared his throat and hocked a big lugie off the side.

"High and dry," Jimmy drawled, warming up the vocal cords. He stretched his lips, exercised his jaw, rolled his head to crack his neck. What came out of that painted mouth was pure magic.

The nasal buzz of his voice cut through the tin roar of the carnival. "Hey, lookit skinny! C'mere, you pencilneck geek! Get a load of ole spaghetti arms! He can hardly lift the softballs."

You can tell the quality of a heckler by the size of the crowd he draws. In all my years on the carny circuit, I never saw a Bobo build a tip so fast. Inside of ten minutes Jimmy had an audience ten bodies deep.

Jimmy was all mouth. He raised the art of the insult to new lows. It actually sent shivers up and down my spine to hear him work the crowd.

"Hey, tub-o-lard! Looks like you never met a meal you didn't like! Ladies and gentlemen, fer yer own safety keep yer hands away from his mouth."

Up in his cage, he was the rajah of retort, the barbarian of barbs, the poet laureate of piss-and-vinegar perturbation. Jimmy didn't take a break the entire day. He just sat up there

60

chaining cigarettes and ripping off insults like farts at a chili cook-off.

He was a natural born Bobo. It wasn't just his work -- it was his life. His whole reason for being.

Around about seven, Sissy Flair came by with a thick ham sandwich for her husband. That strawberry blonde was easy on the eyes but hard on the dick.

I love a girl who's up-front, and that's where this dazzling dairy queen put it. Those torpedoes were stuffed into a red and white striped spandex top. No bra on those babies, either.

Believe me -- you could fry an egg on those hooters they were so hot. There was plenty more where those tits came from. Her hourglass figure was more like an hour and a half.

She was barely in some denim shorts. Button-fly half undone, peeled back to make them hip-huggers. I thought I glimpsed brown bush. Or maybe I was just dreaming.

I wanted her so bad I could taste it. That sweet mystery spot between her legs was a-calling. When she walked away, her asscheeks rolled, grinding against her salaciously swiveling hips.

"Wait up," I said. My dick was a big dog on a leash, pulling me after her and licking its chops. "What about me?"

She turned around. Arched an eyebrow. "You wanna sandwich or something?"

"Or something. You look good enough to eat."

"You talk sweeter'n a glazed donut."

"I got that gift of gab."

"A silver tongue is what you got."

"Silver? This tongue is pure gold. This tongue works miracles."

"I'm in the mood for a good miracle right about now." She came close to whisper in my ear. "I mean, I love Jimmy. But drinkin' and clownin's all he cares about. He don't know the first thing about lovin' a woman."

That was all I needed to hear. My conscience won't let me pass up a damsel in distress. I live for unsatisfied wives.

We made for the Flairs' aluminum Dynaflo RV parked outside the lot.

* * *

She crossed her legs around my neck. Her denim shorts and panties dangled from one ankle. She was still in her white tennis sneakers.

My tongue tickled the dripping pink folds of her tawdry twat. Her sauce was as tangy as South Carolina Bar-B-Q. She grabbed handfuls of my hair as I honed in on her clit.

My tongue stroked that electric lovebud. My nose was buried in strawberry blonde bush. I sniffed her musk and swooned at the pungent perfume.

In the distance I could hear Jimmy razzing some pip-squeak. "Hey, shorty, howzabout standing up? The only thing you can look down on is yer self-esteem! Watch yer step, people -- you might step in this little turd!"

One of those funny old car horns was hooked up to the target. When Napoleon finally hit the bullseye, the horn hacked one out of its throat: *Owooo-ga!* I could just see Jimmy going down.

"Hey, mister!" Sissy barked angrily. "Who the hell told you you could eat pussy?"

I looked up at her, positively perplexed. Her face looked down at me from between those mountains of mammary magic. They rolled to either side.

"Is that a tongue or a sponge?" Sissy bitched. "I'm dry like the Sahara down there!"

I reached up and tweaked a nipple.

"Oooh, baby," she goes, rolling her eyes impatiently. "What're you, tuning a radio? This your first time with a woman, Don Wannabe?"

She grabbed the back of my head and shoved my mouth back onto her belligerent beaver. I made some trouble with the tongue twister. It was personal now. I had something to prove.

"C'mon, Junior!" she yelled, keeping up with her terrible tirade as I lapped ferociously. "You couldn't turn on a faucet! What's a girl gotta do to get an orgasm around here?"

I tried to ignore her as I did my best to get her off. But my best wasn't good enough for that snarling shrew.

"What're you, a queer? Don't you like girls?"

For the first time in my life, I almost walked out on an open cunt. No wonder Jimmy Flair stuck to drinking and clowning. Who the hell could stand the verbal abuse?

Normally, I would've left. But there was one thing keeping me around. Revenge. Nobody talks to me like that and gets away with it.

That miserable bitch was just asking for it now. My world-famous, patented "shocker hold," that is. With my right hand, I slipped an index finger in her cunt and a pinkie straight up her ornery ass.

Sissy got a charge out of that two-pronged penetration. Especially when I started sliding them in and out. That double-digit joy buzzer shut her up. For a minute, anyway. Once the shock wore off, her trash-talking mouth was back.

63

"That's a cute gimmick, buster. Cheap gimmicks like that are for guys who ain't got the balls for an honest fuck."

"One honest fuck, coming right up." I yanked my pants down. The bitch actually pointed and laughed.

"Hurry up already, schoolboy -- I ain't got all night!"

She got my goat alright. She got me hard as hell. I pushed her down on her back and slid into her trap. My big boner opened her up like a can of clam chowder.

"If yer hung like a jackass," she goes, "you must be dumb as one, too! All the blood's flowing down there instead of to yer brain!"

That vituperatin' verbiage was just an act to get me going. But it worked. I had to give her that. I gave her something else, too. Twelve angry inches. I really laid into her, steamrolling her across the floor.

"You wimp! I've seen more muscle in a wet dishrag!" she complained. "Yer leaving me high and dry here! High and dry! High and dry!"

Her knees were next to her ears. I plunged into her over and over as her shrill voice echoed inside my head. I pounded hard, trying to bottom out. I lobbed my balls for an hour.

It was useless. She took every inch. It was bottomless. I kept at it.

"You couldn't screw a cork, you pathetic bastard!" Her voice was hoarse and raw. Hair lay plastered to her face. Perspiration pooled between her tits and in her bellybutton. A trickle of sweat ran down my asscrack. A hot lather fizzled in her bush.

She huffed and puffed, sounding off a loud raspberry, Bronx cheer. Spittle hit me in the eye. "Who taught you to fuck -- yer mother?!" she panted through gritting teeth.

"No, yours!" I shot back. "And this is what she taught me!"

Sissy was finally gonna get what she deserved. I pulled out and flipped her over on her hands and knees. I was seeing red and white. It looked like a bullseye painted around her bunghole. It was open season on ass. This bitter bitch was going down big time.

I aimed my arsenal up her arse. Inch by aching inch I screwed my angry joint inside that anal clamp. She grunted and groaned with every push until I was balls-deep. And then I fucked her big bad ass.

"You know what they say about guys who dig anal, don't you!" she screeched.

Now she was getting nasty. Fight fire with fire, I always say -- so I grabbed her by the hips to pull her onto my thrusting dick, then pushed her forward as I pulled out.

She wasn't talking trash anymore! She didn't say a damn thing. Twelve solid, slippery inches of the randy rod knocked the wind right out of her sails. She didn't know what hit her.

I slapped her cheeks as I rammed her rectum. Stinging pink handprints spread across the milky white skin. I upped the pace til I smelled smoke.

I went hell-for-leather. My back ached. The RV was spinning around me. My balls were a pressure cooker about to explode. I pushed it into the red.

It was a beautiful thing, finally nailing that target. Forgiving's for rubes -- vengeance was all mine! It never felt better to unload my balls. She'd think twice before opening her big mouth again.

* * *

The next day, Pappy and Jimmy were AWOL. It was after two in the p.m. when I finally tracked down the toothless
Pappy at a grab joint, gumming a hamburger.

I was like, "What the hell's wrong with you? Where's
Jimmy?"

"I ain't talking to you."

"Sure you are."

"No, I ain't." He made like he was zipping his lip, locking it and throwing away the key.

"Aw, fer crissakes." I passed him a fiver. He started
singing.

"Jimmy got it all figured out about you and his old
lady," he said.

I guess that stretched-out asshole of hers was impossible
to alibi. She could've passed a grapefruit after I got through
with her. That ain't the kind of thing you can hide from a
husband.

"So?" I said.

"So he ain't gonna work for you no more. Nobody's
gonna heckle for you, neither."

"Why the hell not?"

"It's the Code."

"What code?"

"The Bobo Code. You do dirt to one Bobo, you do dirt
to 'em all. You won't find anyone to replace Jimmy."

Pappy might've been a geezer, but he was right on the
money. I was clownless. High and dry. A Bobo joint is
worthless without a Bobo.

I thought so long and hard my head hurt. I was just
about to give up when the answer brained me like a bolt of

lightning. I raised a tent around the tank and threw up a banner:

DOUBLE-D DUNK TANK!

WET-N-WILD T-SHIRTS!

MEN ONLY!

* * *

No Bobos were necessary for this joint -- just boobs. It was a cinch finding the talent, too. The lot was loaded with lovely ladies who were more than willing to get wet.

Some of them were co-eds who needed denero for college. The others were townies eager for easy money. And nothing could be easier than the dunk tank. It was like falling off a log.

Tits are what I call instant money. Just add water. By suppertime a line of horny bastards wound from my tent to the cotton candy shack three hundred feet away.

It was the first honest enterprise of my life. Real American know-how! This was why we fought the Big One. To save the world for tits and ass. My chest swelled. I choked back tears of patriotic pride. Let freedom ring!

Around eight o'clock Cutie Beaucoup was in the tank. Talent like that was hard to come by. It was hard not to cum just by looking at her.

When heaven was passing out tits, Cutie got seconds. She had heaping helpings of hooters. When she threw her shoulders back and thrust out her chest, those magnificent mams separated and lifted.

"High and dry," she drawled into the microphone as pitch after pitch missed the target. "You bozos couldn't hit the broad side of a barn, much less the side of a broad! Let's get a real man up here!"

This little skinny guy finally nailed her, dead-on. *Owoooo-ga*! squealed the horn as the hinged bench swung away, dropping poor Cutie ass-first into the Plexiglas tank.

The crowd exploded into hooting cheers of eyeballing ecstasy. They finally got what they'd paid for. She really knew how to deliver, too.

She went under in slo-mo. The impact drove her T-shirt up, baring her bounty of boobs. They were milky white orbs that floated up like big balloons.

You could almost feel them in your hands. The soft flesh against your fingers, the rosy nipples between your lips. There was more wood than a lumberyard inside the joint.

A million white bubbles swirled around her kicking limbs. As her ass hit the bottom of the tank, her legs spread apart in a shameless spectacle of sex. The fluorescent pink crotch of her string bikini was no bigger than a postage stamp.

Waves of long blonde hair drifted off her head. Her eyes were wide open. You could almost hear her shocked squeal. She jumped back up and resurfaced, gasping for breath.

"That water's ice-*cold*!" she squeaked.

Her T-shirt was still pushed up over her tits. Those pink nipples went in soft but came out hard as 24-carats. Goose-pimples rose on the naked flesh.

She scooped them up in her hands, displaying them to the crowd like loving cups on a trophy shelf. And then, just as quickly, she tugged her shirt back down. If they wanted to see them again, they'd have to pay.

Cutie was no dummy. She knew she was working on percentage. Half of the take from the balls went into her pocket. She worked that crowd for all she was worth.

68

Wet T-shirt clung to a canyon of cleavage. Grinning ear to ear, she lifted her arms high and wiggled her chest. Her twin talents swung back and forth.

Half an hour later, her shift was up. She had two frozen tits and a snatch that could use thawing out. But that was nothing that a little friction couldn't fix. If you know what I mean, and I think you do.

Parked just behind the tent was a trailer belonging to Junior Gutbucket. He let me borrow it, and I let him hang around the show for free. This side of a morgue, it was the closest that in-bred would ever get to so much naked flesh.

Inside, I was packing her pussy with my prick. Her teeth were chattering like castanets. Her goosepimples had goosepimples. Her nipples were blue. It was like sucking ice cubes.

The first stab was like jumping into a cold shower -- I nearly screamed from the shock of sticking my dick into her. But she warmed up pretty quick.

Her knees were on either side of her face. I plunged into her again and again. Stroke after stroke, my heater put the color back in those cheeks.

* * *

My tool was barely inside my pants when the door banged open and in barged a bloated, backwater blow-hard.

"Fornicators!" he bellowed with double chins jiggling and one helluva dick-do. You know what that is, don'cha? That's when your belly hangs lower than your dick do.

"Godless perverts!" he cried, more full of himself than a pregnant lady. Blood rose to his face like red on a thermometer. His wavy white hair was swept up and shellacked into a pompadour of evangelistic proportions.

Cutie made a noble effort of trying to wrap a towel around her naked self. It was useless. She was too much woman. As soon as she had one part hid, another'd pop out.

"You tramp! You hussy! You Whore of Babylon!" he spat as he gave her the once-over, over and over. "You ought to be ashamed!"

"Nothing to be ashamed of on that body," I said.

"And *you*," he said, turning on me like a pit bull. "They told me that disgusting display of filth and perversion belongs to you!" He gesticulated at the double-D dunk tank.

"Everybody else seems to like it."

"Sinners! Shameless fornicators!" he sputtered. "Every last one of them!"

"It's a free country, friend."

"Over my dead body, boy. We don't like your kind of filth in West Tarwater."

"If you don't like it," I said, "there's plenty to see at the other end of the midway."

"Ah've seen enough."

"Who the hell're you?"

"Ah'm Roy Rayford Quimby! Ah'm a member of the Legion of Decency."

"You're a member, all right."

"Ah've got powerful friends in this county! Judges, lawyers, preachers..."

"Yeah, and they're all at the dunk tank!"

"Don't sass me, boy," he growled, stabbing his finger into my chest, "or Ah'll run you outta town on a rail."

"What is it you really want, Quimby?" I asked. "Money?"

"*Bribery*," he pronounced smugly. "Ah'll add that to the charges when the sheriff gets here."

"What sheriff?"

"Sheriff Billy Grimes is gonna shut you down, sinner. We got morality laws 'round these parts."

Cutie slipped out the door, and I couldn't blame her. This was my fight. I didn't need her tits anyhow cuz seconds later in walked my best girl, Pepper Sinclair.

She was fresh out of the tank. The generous curves of her tits were shrink-wrapped in wet T-shirt. Pepper was stacked like the pyramids of Egypt with an ass you could take to the bank.

"Scuse me," she said to Quimby, "But I gotta get outta these wet clothes."

"Ah'm not going anywhere, you tramp," he said, folding his arm across his chest. He couldn't stop eyeballing the brown nipples that poked through the transparent cotton.

"Suit yourself," she said as she shot me a wink on the sly. I got the hint.

I was like, "I reckon I'll wait outside."

I went to the other side of the trailer and peeked in the open window. She peeled off the shirt. As her buoyant boobs settled into place, they bounced and bumped together like twin pontoons.

She had so much talent up top, Quimby had to take a step back to take it all in. He was dumbstruck and slack-jawed. His mouth was wide open but nothing came out.

She wore a pair of denim cut-offs. The wetness made their tight fit even tighter. It clung to her skin like a coat of blue paint.

She wormed her fingers under the waist. Her hips shot back and forth to help tug the material down over her wicked ass curves. She had two deep dimples where her back ended and her ass began.

She showed off some beauteous butt cleavage as she stripped down. Smooshed together, her cheeks looked like two titanic tits tied up in a denim corset.

She swiveled her hips and, grunting with the effort, pushed the waistband down. It finally crested her bulging rump. It was all downhill from here. Seconds later she was naked.

She stepped out of the pile of soggy jeans and turned around in her full naked glory. She ran her fingers through her bush, fluffing the tawny curls. Quimby was staring shamelessly, mopping his brow with a hanky.

"Take a picture, fat man," she drawled. "It lasts longer."

"If God wanted us to walk around naked, young hussy, He wouldn't have invented clothes."

"If God wanted us to wear clothes, He wouldn't have invented *these*," she said as she palmed a tit in each hand and lifted them proudly. You'd have to look far and wide to find two better arguments for public indecency. Her nipples were big as bullets and twice as dangerous.

Quimby turned away to shield his eyes. But no man alive could resist those seductive suck-melons.

"What's the matter?" she asked, moving in for the kill. "Don't you like girls? I hope you're not queer."

"Absolutely not!" he roared.

She turned around and salaciously swiveled her hips for him. She backed into him to grind her ass into his crotch. "I think you're right," she said. "I think you are glad to see me."

72

She turned around and draped her arms around his neck to pull him between her bodacious breasts. Smothered in tits, Quimby rolled his eyes to heaven. His lips quivered as he prayed for strength.

Pepper's hand slipped into his fly and found his pink hard-on. When she wrapped her fingers around his member and squeezed, he was done for. He had a weakness for well-endowed women -- just like every other red-blooded American.

He looked around to make sure they were alone.

"Just between you and me," he chuckled as he began to unbuckle his belt, "it's okay to spit in the devil's eye when you're already in hell..."

There's one of these holy hypocrites in every town. And if I know anything about Bible-thumpin' bellyachers, it's that the ones who holler loudest got the most to hide.

I raced into the tent. The dunk tank was sad and empty. The crowd was silent.

"What's goin' on?" somebody asked.

"No time to explain," I said, and pointed to two burly men. "You and you -- drag those speakers outside."

On the dunk tank was a microphone. I ripped it loose and began to carry it back to the trailer. One of my girls pulled me aside. She was nearly in tears.

"That horrible man said he was gonna shut us down. But I need money for college!"

"Don't you worry, darlin'," I promised, looking into her moist doe eyes. "That moralizing motherfucker's gonna get his."

"How?" she asked.

"When I give you the signal, crank the speakers."

73

I returned to the window. Quimby wasn't wasting any time. He was already between Pepper's spread legs, eating her out but good. He looked like a hog at a trough.

Pepper and I made eye contact as she grabbed his white hair. Her mouth curled into a devilish smile. I hung the mike though the window and waved my hand to the blue-eyed co-ed.

"I do declare, Roy Quimby!" Pepper cried. Her voice cut out of the speakers and echoed up and down the midway. "YOU'RE THE BEST PUSSY-EATER IN WEST TARWATER! YOU MUST EAT A WHOLE LOTTA PUSSY TO GET THIS GOOD!"

He got to his feet and dropped his drawers. His pink cock stuck out at an angle under his pot belly.

He held his hands next to his head and made two horns out of his index fingers. "AH'M HORNY AS HELL," he cackled, "AND AH'M GONNA RIDE YOU LIKE THE DEVIL HIMSELF!"

The Ferris wheel ground to a halt. A hush fell over the carnival. The only sound was Pepper shouting a blue streak: "C'MON, BIG BOY, FUCK ME HARD!"

"YOU'RE GONNA FEEL EVERY INCH OF ME, YOU BEAUTIFUL WHORE OF BABYLON!" he yelled as he screwed her for all he was worth. About a dollar ninety-eight, by the look of it.

"OH, OH, OH MY! GIVE IT TO ME, QUIMBY! RAM IT HOME!"

Nothing draws a crowd like sex. Quimby's bawdy broadcast was no different. Gathered around the rocking trailer was a mob twenty bodies deep.

74

"THEY DON'T CALL ME A FUNDAMENTALIST FOR NOTHING!" he yelled. "AH'M GONNA FUCK YOU UP THE FUNDAMENT -- UP THE ASS, THAT IS!"

Fucking her butt was as tough as squeezing toothpaste back into the tube. Her asshole put up one helluva fight. But that unrepentant pervert stuck two fingers in and pried it open.

"I'M PARTIN' YOUR CHEEKS LIKE MOSES PARTIN' THE RED SEA! SAY MY NAME, YOU HOT BITCH!" he screamed at her as he shoved it home. "SAY MY NAME!"

"ROY RAYFORD QUIMBY IS FUCKING MY ASSSSS!"

"AH'VE SCREWED MANY A WHORE'S ASS IN MY TIME BUT YOURS IS THE TIGHTEST! H'IT'S EASIER TO FIT A CAMEL THROUGH THE EYE OF A NEEDLE THAN TO SHOVE MY DICK UP YOUR BUTTHOLE!"

The rat bastard couldn't even fuck a butt without turning it into a sermon. Pepper was like, "SHUT UP AND SCREW ME HARDER, FAT BOY! HARDER!"

"GET READY FOR THE CUMBATH OF YOUR LIFE, YOU HUSSY! AH'M GONNA DOUSE THE HELLFIRE IN YOU WITH MY RIGHTEOUS SEED!"

He came with a groan and a grunt. Then he pulled out and used his own hand to pump the final creamy squirts across her cheeks.

In triumph he shouted, "YOU'LL THINK TWICE BEFORE OPENING YOUR BIG MOUTH AGAIN, AH GUARAN-DAMN-TEE-TEE-TEE-TEE..."

His hard-on wilted as he heard his amplified voice echoing out of the loudspeaker. "WHAT IN TARNATION!?-ATION-ATION-TION-TION..."

Shocked and horrified, he bolted from the trailer. He didn't even think to pull up his pants first.

Old women fainted at the spectacle of his shriveling dick. Schoolgirls giggled. Babies cried.

Good thing Sheriff Billy Grimes was there to protect the good people of Sheepskin from that penis-parading pervert. "Okay, you sick-o," he said. "Show's over. Let's go."

"No, wait," he pleaded to Grimes's stone cold face. "It's not me you want. It's *him*. It's him, I tell you!"

Sheriff Billy just shook his head and cuffed him. "Hey, Quimby!" I called. "Didja know today's nun and orphan day at the carnival?"

Quimby sagged his heavy shoulders and started to cry like a faucet. "Ah have sinned," he blubbered to the crowd. "Ah was in the grip of Satan!"

"You mean the grip of her *ass!*" a smart-aleck heckled. The spectators started to laugh. Some pelted Quimby with garbage as Grimes led him away.

I stepped inside the trailer to see Pepper. "Oooh," she said, rubbing her tender behind. "I'm gonna feel that tomorrow. It was worth it, though."

"Baby," I said, "you gotta kick these hypocrites where it counts --"

"Below the belt," she finished. "*Ah guaran-damn-tee!*"

* * *

Somebody check my back for me. There must be a sign on it that says *CRUCIFY ME.*

Not one hour after I took care of Quimby, the power went out at the dunk tank. No more lights, no more microphone. No more money.

I thought the generator had gone down again. But outside, the rest of the midway was still going strong.

I ran and found Teddy the juiceman. He was shooting the shit with the blind ticket seller for the World's Largest Rat single-o.

A tape-recorded come-on spieled outta the speakers, over and over and over till you wanted to puke: "YOU MUST SEE THE RAT...THE WORLD'S LARGEST RAT..."

"Get off your ass, Teddy, and fix my juice!" I yelled.

"There's nothing to fix."

"You mean you *turned* me off?"

Teddy shook his head sadly.

"GOLLY, IT'S BIG...YOU MUST SEE THE RAT...THE WORLD'S LARGEST RAT..."

"You got the wrong one in there," I told the blind man. "I'm looking at the world's largest rat right here!"

"Don't blame me," Teddy said. "I just do like I'm told."

"RATS DON'T COME ANY BIGGER THAN THIS, FOLKS..."

I've seen more rats than I wanna think about. Take a look around you -- this whole world's full of 'em. But of all those greasy, flea-infested rodents, there was only one ratbastard who had the power to pull the plug on me -- Peanut Gaines.

"THE WORLD'S LARGEST RAT...YOU MUST SEE THE RAT..."

He'd been pushing me for weeks but this time he'd gone too far.

Let Peanut spill the beans to O.B. Krass! Let him say I balled his wife! Let him say I banged his mother and sister, too!

I didn't give a flying fuck about anything but getting some justice around here.

* * *

I was so mad I was actually spitting the whole way to the management office. It was a pea-green trailer propped up on cinderblocks and 2-by-4s. I barged in without knocking.

"Hello, Randy," said O.B. Krass in that way of his that made you wanna beat him like a red-headed stepchild.

He looked small and weak as he sat behind this enormous gun-metal gray desk. The nub of an El Cheapo cigar was wedged in the corner of his mouth. On his pinkie was a gold ring that looked too big for his bony, raw, red fingers.

He had watery, red-rimmed eyes and a cheap black wig with glued-on black eyebrows to match. The fur was matted and mussed like a possum scraped off the underside of a car. It flapped in the breeze from an oscillating fan.

"I guess you win, Peanut," he goes, carefully counting out a hundred in twenties. His yellow false teeth were too big for his mouth -- he was always grinning like a skull. "That did get his attention."

"What gives?" I hollered. "Why'd you let Peanut cut me off?"

"Back off, cowboy," Peanut growled as he trapped me in a bearhug from behind and pulled me away from the old man. I fought his iron grasp but it was no use.

"Goddammit!" I hollered, sick of all this fucking around. "Let's have it out once and for all!"

78

"Peanut," O.B. said coolly, "Let him go."

"You sure, boss?"

"He won't make a scene. Will you, Randy?"

The big ape loosened his arms and I shrugged out of his grip and straightened my clothes. I noticed Bunny in the corner, painting her nails. She didn't even look up at me.

"You see?" O.B. said. "He's all right. Just a little confused, is all."

"The hell I am! I know exactly what's going on."

"You have no idea," he said. "Have a drink, Randy."

"I don't wanna drink." My brow was sweating and prickly heat went up and down my arms and back.

"He ain't *asking* you," Peanut said. "He's *telling* you."

"And *I'm* telling *him*, I don't wanna drink."

"A man who knows what he wants," said O.B. "I like that."

"You mind telling me what the hell I'm paying you for?" I asked, giving him by best glare.

"Skin shows always draw some heat," O.B. goes with a shrug. "You know that."

"I know I gave you a grand to take care of it."

"But sometimes it takes more than money. Take a guy like Quimby, for instance."

"So I'm fired, is that it?"

"You got it ass-backwards, son. You're hired."

"Whaddaya mean, *hired*?"

"I like the way you operate. You got brains to think with. Ain't he a bright boy, honey?"

"The brightest," Bunny answered without looking up from her nails. "Everybody says so."

"I'm always on the lookout for bright boys like you."

Like most hayseeds, O.B. talked a country mile around what he wanted to say before he actually got there. I was like, "What's your point, Krass?"

"We're more than a carnival --"

"Yeah, yeah," I bitched, "we're all one big happy family around here."

O.B. cracked a smile that made me shut up and listen. He goes, "The Riot's part of an underground pharmaceutical enterprise."

"Drugs," I said, playing it cool. This was ten times better than what I thought he'd say. Suddenly I was interested.

"Methamphetamine."

"You into distribution, or what?"

"Not exactly," he answered. "Ever hear of the Sons of Satan?"

"Surely."

The Sons were one-percenters -- motorcycle outlaws, the worst. But their meth labs were legendary. Crank got them where they are and keeps them there.

"The Riot handles the money laundering for their Mid-West market. It comes in dirty and we clean it through our rides and joints. Occasionally we'll hold the product for 'em, too. But mostly we do the laundry."

"What about the heat?"

"That's the beauty part. We already got the fuzz greased for the crooked games and shabby rides. We just turn around and use it as a cover for the laundromat."

"That's a helluva racket," I said, nodding in appreciation. Anybody who double-crosses the cops and gets away with it gets my respect any day of the week -- even a dirty little fucker like Krass. "Enough about you, though -- what about me?"

"We need a new courier," he said. "Somebody to take the money back and forth. A go-between cuz I don't like the Sons on the lot. The cops feel obliged to put on the pressure."

"So what happened to your old courier?"

"Boo Lavender?" he goes.

"Good ol' Boo," Peanut drawled.

"Good ol' Boo," Krass echoed wistfully. Then the edge was back in his voice: "Good ol' Boo started acting up. We had to let him go."

Something sinister there -- a warning. Come to think of it, it'd been some time since I saw good ol' Boo around the carny circuit.

O.B. looked at Peanut and snapped his fingers. "Get the money," he said.

Peanut jumped up from his chair and went for the door. I kinda enjoyed seeing the big ape do what he was told. Nice to see that shitbag cut down to size.

"You got a piece to carry?" he asked me after Peanut left the trailer. "Just in case you get jumped by a nigger or something."

He opened his drawer and pulled out a snub-nosed .45 and a .38 double-action revolver, laying them on the table one by one. I liked the look of the .38. It was the kind of gun that made you feel like a real big sonofabitch.

O.B. saw me admiring it. "Go ahead," he said. "Pick it up. It ain't loaded."

I gripped the .38 and aimed it off to the side. Nice balance. I squeezed the trigger until the hammer fell with a satisfying click.

"No paperwork on that one," O.B. said. "So if you ever use it, drop it."

I set the .38 back on the table just as Peanut returned with a blue nylon duffel bag that made me cringe. It said *DAN CHECK FITNESS* but screamed *LOOK INSIDE ME.*

He tossed it on the table before O.B., who zipped it open to show me the contents. I couldn't help whistling. Bricks of bundled twenties stuffed the bag.

"One hundred fifty large," O.B. announced.

"How much of that belongs to me?"

"Ten grand per delivery. Not too bad for a day's work."

I couldn't help smirking. "What if I make off with it?"

"You makin' a funny, boy?" Peanut asked in the background.

Krass ignored him, studying me for a few seconds and then he said, "You ain't the type."

"What's that supposed to mean?"

"It means you're a coward, asswipe," Peanut sneered.

"You're just the fucking life of the party, ain't you?" I cracked over my shoulder.

"Shut up, the both of you," O.B. snapped, "bitching at each other like a couple of pantywaists. What I mean, Randy, is you're too smart to fuck up an easy ride like this."

"Don't say yes right now," Bunny suddenly said and I jumped at the sound of her voice behind me. I'd forgotten she was there. "Think it over first -- right, honey?"

I thought she meant me with that "honey" business. But when I looked at her, she was looking at her husband. And then her blue eyes slowly slid to me and did all the talking for her.

Take the job, they said: *Take the job and we can stay together.*

"I don't got to think it over," I said at her. I looked at O.B. Krass as I slid the gun into the waist of my jeans so the butt stuck out. "I'm your man."

And then we shook on it as if that meant a damn thing to anybody anymore. Lord knows it didn't mean anything to me. Never did, never does and never will.

* * *

Peanut and I left the trailer together.

He handed me the bag with the money but didn't let go of the handles until he had his say: "Just so there's no misunderstanding, flattie. I didn't want you on board. I told Krass we couldn't trust you."

"Trust is overrated, apeshit. Nobody ever went broke thinking the worst of people."

He used a matchstick for a toothpick. The red end was bobbing up and down as he teased it with his tongue. "You know all the answers, don't you?"

"I even know some of the questions."

"You're a real smartass alright," he goes, spitting out the matchstick. "A real smartass."

"And that just kills you, don't it?"

A smile crept into the corners of his mouth. "No hard feelings, eh?"

"Never."

He stared at me. His tongue played along the gum and inside of his lower lip, like he had a wad of chew there but he didn't. Finally, he thrust the bag at me, turned around and walked away.

* * *

A few days later, I found myself somewhere south of Salt Lick, Alabama.

I stuck around this roadhouse with these wagon wheel chandeliers, killing the afternoon with this bottle of low-rent whiskey I knew.

It was just me and a handful of locals in the Char-K. At that time of day it's your professional drinkers -- shell-shocked vets and parolees and down-on-their-luck types. All of 'em with that haunted look in their eyes.

The only thing they were waiting for was the next drink. Not me. I was waiting for my connection to show at the appointed spot. I was early and he was late.

So I got up to take a piss. I was a little tipsy as I walked to the men's room. Must've had more than I thought.

Behind me, somebody came into the restroom but I didn't think anything of it. But as I'm standing at this crusty urinal, pissing onto a cake of pink fragrance, this somebody shoved me.

I threw my hands up to keep from crashing into the wall. But that didn't change the fact that I was pissing all over myself. My dick whipped back and forth like a wild fire-hose.

The guy who knocked me, he started laughing: "Har har har!" Like this is the funniest thing he ever saw. Maybe it was. What the fuck do I know?

Once I start whizzing, I can't stop on a dime. So I just turned around to confront this guy, still pissing like a race horse on the floor. It wasn't just one joker -- it was two.

Shit smells. And I smelled shittown all over this gruesome twosome. I would've finished what they'd started with the .38, but instantly I knew that they were my connection.

Laughing boy had a big, fucked-up face that looked like it was drawn by a three-year-old. He wore aviator shades with yellow lenses. His curly hair was dark brown, big on top and long in back.

But his beard didn't match. It was red and scruffy like desert scrub. His red T-shirt said *I'm So Happy I Could Just Shit* with a cartoon frog on the john.

As bad as he looked, the guy who was with him looked ten times worse. He was a human skeleton, shirtless, in a black biker jacket with fringe. He had a sunken chest, protruding ribs, and skin that was fish belly white.

He was full of blue prison tattoos, hearts and swastikas, and wore tight black jeans. His chunky black motorcycle boots looked funny on a pair of skinny bow legs that made me think of a wishbone.

His fingers were like maggots writhing on the underside of roadkill. Tattooed on three knuckles were the letters F-T-W for *Fuck the World*.

He had an evil, pointed gray beard. Two greasy, black pigtails trailed down his back. "Carnival boy," he goes, stepping back from the piss puddle that was inching toward his boots. "Outside."

I finished my business, zipped up, and then followed them out into the lot. "Where's your bikes?" I asked, looking around and not seeing any.

"We only ride for pleasure anymore," said Shades. "We take the pickup on jobs."

"Speaking of," Pigtails said. "Let's get it on. I wanna get this shit over with."

His pupils were dilated. His eyes were dull black holes. A real snake-in-the-grass. The kind of jack-off you don't want as either a friend or an enemy but if you have to pick one you'll take him as an enemy. I was glad to have that heater tucked in my pants.

"Okay by me," I said as I opened the Menace and unbelted this three-foot stuffed dog that was sitting in the back seat. I sat it on the hood.

"What the fuck?" goes Pigtails. I winced from his bad breath. It was like some small animal crawled down his throat and died there. "Some kinda joke, carnival boy?"

I whipped out my pocket knife and slit the plush toy from belly to throat. The bundles of cash appeared in the gaping wound. "That nylon bag was a goddamn sore-thumb," I said. "You wanna count it?"

"Do we need to?" Pigtails asked.

I shook my head. It was all there. Maybe I was a coward or maybe I was just playing it smart and maybe there's no difference between the two, but I hadn't fucked with their money.

"Didn't think so," he goes like an insult.

Shades returned from the pickup with another nylon bag. A yellow one this time. *COURTLAND-CLEGG JR. HIGH* it said in black letters with a cartoon bulldog.

"One hundred fifty," he goes as he handed it over. Black grease was caked under his fingernails.

"What about the ephedrine?" Pigtails asked.

I was like, "What about what?"

"The ephedrine, motherfucker, the *ephedrine*. We told Peanut we wanted the ephedrine this time."

I knew that ephedrine was some kinda controlled substance they used to cook up crank but I didn't know I was supposed to deliver some of that, too. "Peanut didn't tell me nothing about any ephedrine."

"Well, you tell that motherfucker something for me --"

And that was when Shades hauled off and punched me in the face. I went down but he stayed on me, pummeling my face and guts -- whatever he could reach with his fists. We rolled around in the dirt and I went for my piece but it'd fallen out during the scrap.

I reached for my knife but froze when I heard the unmistakable sound of a gun being cocked. Shades and I stopped scuffling and held on to each other as we listened to the silence. Blood leaked out of my nose and I sniffed some of it back and tasted the rest of it on my lips.

"Playtime's over, kiddies," Pigtails announced. I looked over my shoulder and saw him standing above me, aiming my own damn gun at my own damn head.

We slowly got to our feet. Pigtails said, "Don't let what happened to Boo Lavender happen to you, carnival boy. Dig?"

What I dug was that that part about the ephedrine didn't just slip Peanut's mind. He was just making more hell for me. Miserable motherfucker.

I wiped the blood with the back of my hand as I watched them get into the pickup. Shades drove. It made a big circle around me as it pulled out of the parking lot. It rolled past me and stopped about ten feet away.

Pigtails stuck his head out the window. "We meet here again," he hollered. "Two weeks. And don't forget the goddamn ephedrine."

Then he unloaded my gun and tossed it out the window as the spinning truck tires fired dirt and stones back at me like buckshot and I had to cover my face.

* * *

PART TWO: STEWED, SCREWED & TATTOOED

"Randy," Bunny begged, "lemme play with the dirty money."

"Again?" I said, making like I was annoyed.

Every time I had a bag of laundry, she had to fuck around with it first. It was a crazy little game we played -- the kind where I always won.

At last I was like, "Okay, but you know the rules. Say pretty please."

"Pretty please?"

"With sugar on top."

"Pretty please, with sugar on top?"

She got down on her knees and gazed up at me. No man could ever say no to those blue eyes. Her dreamy stare drifted down to my crotch and lingered there.

I'd sprung my hard-on from its prison. My pants were down around my ankles. I was cocked and loaded.

"Wow," I said, "wouldja look at that?"

"What?"

"My dick's grown an extra inch, just for you."

Before going down, she gave me a wink. Her eyebrows arched like we were conspirators in some dirty deed. Her mouth was nothing short of a miracle.

She brought me to the edge before backing off. My orgasm rose and fell like a Fender twin-reverb. Her head bobbed in my lap as she gobbled me like candy.

"No doubt about it," I groaned, chuckling. "Your mouth and my dick go together like country music and NASCAR."

I felt heavy and dull. Everything was numb except my red-hot stiffie, which felt everything. When Bunny blew a cock, it was like being shot into space and buried in the earth at the same time.

When a girl on coke sucks dick, she sucks dick. There's no messing around. She's all business. Won't stop till she gets you off -- not even to take a breath.

"Wanna cum?" she asked, lifting her face up to me and panting. A bubble of spit glimmered like a genuine Diamelle in the corner of her mouth.

That was a helluva thing to ask. I was torn between wanting the pleasure to last forever and wanting to get it over with right this second.

"You're the driver," I said.

"I'm gonna take you there..."

She ducked her head back down and began sucking and jerking frantically to get me off. She two-fisted and tongue-whipped me over the brink. I reared back and suddenly it was payday.

I recovered from the recoil, and she was still holding me between her lips. My dick slowly melted in her mouth. When I was soft, she let me go with a sad and delicate kiss.

"Know what?" she asked. "I'd suck your dick even if I didn't have to."

"Jeez, babe, that's the nicest thing anybody's ever said to me."

I opened up the nylon bag and started taking out the banded stacks of bills. She ripped off the bands and scattered tens and twenties all over the bed.

We laughed and tossed the bills around like a couple of kids with confetti. It was like midnight on New Year's.

She was still wet from her shower, and the money stuck to her all over her body. It was the most beautiful damn sight I've ever seen.

"See this?" she said as she lay back on the green carpet and spread her legs wide. "This pussy's got your name on it."

"Where?" I go. "I don't see it."

"Right here. Look harder. See it yet?"

"No. Where?"

"You're not looking hard enough. Come closer..."

I dropped to my knees and nestled my face between her moist thighs. The skin was still flushed from her piping hot shower. Staring into her cunt was like looking down the barrel of eternity.

My tongue went to town. She melted like sweet cream butter on a hot biscuit. Bunny was squirming from all the lovin'.

"Mmm, I'm all yours," Bunny gushed, eyes closed and grinning.

I got into it, using just my mouth. My hands roamed up over her body. I grabbed tit and nipple as my head bobbed and burrowed into her crotch. Bunny clutched handfuls of tens and twenties as she moaned.

My hand groped for her soda cup. Tiny ice cubes sloshed around the bottom as I lifted it to my mouth and up-ended the cup. Ice slid between my lips. I felt out a decent-sized piece and, holding it with my tongue, spat the rest back out.

"Don't stop," she murmured. "Don't stop..."

I hid the ice under my tongue as I frenched her fuckhole again. What I lost in reach, I made up for in technique. People can say lots of things about me but they can't say I don't give as good as I get.

Concentrating on her clit, I knew she was on the verge when it was tipped with a tiny diamond, like the stylus on a record player. She was teetering. All she needed was a little push to get her over.

And that's when I spat that ice chip right into her pussy.

She screamed and her cunt seized up so quick, the muscles shot the ice back at me like a bullet. I saw it coming in slo-mo and I thought I could duck away. But I was moving in slo-mo, too. It ricocheted off my cheek and nearly put out my damn eye.

It was dangerous but worth it. She came in a second. Her back arched like she was riding a wave of ecstasy that carried her away.

"Oh, oh, you're killing me!"

Just let that be a lesson to you fellas who wanna try this stunt at home. Wear some eye protection -- goggles or something.

"God, Randy, that was unbelievable" she sighed, lying in a pool of ecstasy. "You got so many angles you're a circle."

"C'mon," I said, "help me get this money straightened out."

"I bet this is enough dough to lam to the West Coast -- Los Angeles or Vegas, wherever. I bet we could live the American dream off of this."

"Sure," I said, "until somebody fingered us and the Sons blew our heads off."

"So what if they do? You gotta take a chance sometimes."

"Chance is for rubes. I belong to the Church of the Sure-Thing. And ripping off the Sons goes against my religion."

I thought that was the end of it.

Stupid me.

* * *

It was an all-night haul to Decatur. We hit the road jacked on bennies and cocaine with black coffee chasers. We were sweating bullets of caffeine.

We passed a fatty back and forth to take the edge off. Speed and weed. Two great tastes that taste great together.

Bunny did a line off the dashboard with a rolled-up hundred. Then she pulled down the visor with the mirror and started touching up her makeup like a crazy person. I didn't know what the hell for. She couldn't look more gorgeous if she tried.

The coke made her talk too much, too. Racing on uppers, she couldn't stop yapping about nothing at all. Like a broken record, over and over. Not enough weed in the world to chill out her rush.

The rhythm of the wheels came up through the soles of my shoes and legs. I kept one eye on Bunny and one on the road. Her foot was on the dash, cotton balls stuck between her toes as she painted her nails.

I swerved the Menace to make her goof it up. The fumes were getting to me.

"Stop it," she goes.

"What?"

"*What?*" she shot back, aping me.

"There was a bag in the road. I had to hit it."

She dead-panned, arching her eyebrows.

"You should always drive over a bag in the road," I explained. "There might be a puppy inside."

She made a face. "You are so sick."

I changed the subject: "So what'd you tell the S.O.B.?"

That's what we'd been calling O.B. -- the S.O.B. Like a pet name, except we didn't mean it in a nice way.

"About what?" she goes, sniffling.

"About riding with me."

"I told him I was riding with one of my girlfriends."

"And he bought that?" I laughed.

"Of course he bought it," she goes, her voice cracking like she took some offense. "Why wouldn't he?"

I took a good, long look at her. She did that bikini top justice. I was like, "A girl like you doesn't make girlfriends."

She shot me a mean look.

"Hey, don't get me wrong," I said. "I mean that in a good way. Women take one look at you and they hate you for it."

"I know the girls talk shit about me," she goes. "But it's just cuz they're jealous."

"And that's what I'm saying. There's a lot to be jealous of."

After a while she started to fidget. Maybe all the benzedrine was making me paranoid, but being with Bunny felt like hanging around a convenience store. The longer you stuck around, the better your chances of getting offed during some holdup.

I pushed off with my feet, hitting the accelerator hard. The needle quivered around one-ten. The engine became a droning whine.

Leisurely I smoked. Cigarette after cigarette, flicking each butt out the window. In the rearview mirror it hit the road in a burst of orange sparks.

She gave a long, drawn-out groan. "Gawd, I hate driving!"

"I love it," I told her. "The highway is my home. The road goes on forever so you never have to stop."

I figured it wouldn't do any good to tell her how, if you drive long enough, your eyes blister from the road. Your feet catch fire and your teeth start humming. Your ass goes numb and you swear your head will explode.

And that's when you slip into it. *Nirvana*. You're not coming or going anymore. You're nowhere and everywhere at once. You don't feel anything but the road caressing your soul.

But I didn't go into it. I wasn't put on this earth to change anybody's mind. I'm only here to get paid and laid. Just like the tattoos across my knucles say: *P-A-I-D* on the left hand and *L-A-I-D* on the right.

"So what's your philosophy?" I asked, challenging her.

"I get horny at the wrong times," she goes.

"That's not a philosophy."

"It is for me."

I was like, "You horny right now?"

"Yeah. Whatcha gonna do about it?"

"Not a damn thing. I'm gonna keep going."

"That's what I mean. I get horny at the wrong times."

"This is America, sweetheart. If you've got an itch, scratch it."

She spread her legs wide, wedging her right foot in the corner of the open window. She planted her left on the dash. Her knees were level with her chin.

"Mmmmm. Scratch it for me?" she asked. Her blue eyes were big and pleading.

"What're you, a commie? Scratch it yourself."

I didn't have to tell her twice, either. She reached down between her legs and eased the bucket seat back. She pushed her mini skirt up and touched the crotch of her red thong.

Two fingers under the elastic. With the other hand she stretched the crotch down. She ran her fingers through the lush curls.

Her eyes were shut and a contented smile played on her lips. Wind whipped her blonde hair across her face. Still in her reverie, she lifted her butt and tugged her panties down.

If there was one thing Bunny was dedicated to, it was pleasing herself. She was her own best turn-on. A real self-service kind of girl.

She drew lazy circles around her clit with the tip of her finger, taking care with the long nail. I could smell the excitement from here. A crystal clear string stretched from her fingertip. It looked like a white-hot filament.

We came up on an eighteen wheeler and passed him on the left. High in his cab, he couldn't miss seeing Bunny's free show below him. That cracker pulled his horn in appreciation.

"Always give the truckers some!" I laughed.

I let him keep pace with us for a second or two, to give him something to talk about for the rest of his life. Then I punched the gas to pull ahead, swerving back to the right too soon to piss him off.

A long horn blast rattled the Menace and split our ears. High beams filled the interior with blazing white light. I poured it on, dusting the pigfucker. Soon his headlights were only pinpoints in the rearview mirror.

Finally her fingers found their way into her hole. She fucked herself excruciatingly slow. One, two, and then three fingers were fed into the velvet folds.

I could hardly keep my eyes on the road. The Menace swerved recklessly. We were all over the road. What did she care? Orgasm was at hand.

She came with her whole body, and she was still cumming long after we rocketed past the Wigwam Motel in Weedowee.

* * *

You'd think it'd take a while to blow twenty grand. But you'd be wrong. Throwing money at Bunny LaFever was like throwing it on a fire.

She'd upped the ante on everything. She wanted nothing but the best -- the fanciest restaurants with the lobster and the champagne, the name-brand motor lodges and piles of coke to snort.

But even the best wasn't good enough for her. She always wanted more. And like a damn fool I kept reaching into that stuffed dog like it was bottomless.

I was playing a dangerous game but I couldn't help it. I'd do anything to keep those tits. I'd blow myself to hell before giving up that ass.

Okay, so maybe I was acting dumb, but I wasn't altogether stupid. I knew whatever I took out of the Sons' money I'd have to put back sooner or later -- more sooner than later. I was in the red, and there was only one way to get back in the black.

I sat in the diner booth, flipping through the latest Carnival Call. It's a trade weekly and the showman's bible, full of carny news and play dates and help wanted ads. You can buy it on every lot.

I opened it to the classifieds in the back and started looking. Suddenly Bunny reached across the table and pulled down the paper.

"Whatcha reading?" she goes, making these korny little pixie eyes at me.

"Some show wants agents. *Good money*, it says."

"Where's it at?"

"West Tarwater. Only ten hours away."

She screwed up her face like she was tasting a sour lemon. "Ten *hours*," she whined. "West *Tar*water? That sounds just awful."

"Maybe West Tarwater ain't good enough for you, princess, but it's an honest hustle and that's good enough for me."

"I don't know what you're worried about when we already have like a *ton* of money."

98

"Whaddaya mean, *a ton*? We're practically broke, sweetcakes."

"The *dog*, bright boy. We got that stuffed dog."

"Not that again," I said. That woman had a one-track mind, and for the past few days she'd been gunning for the Sons' cash. "I told you a million times already -- it ain't ours to spend."

"Aw, what're you scared of?" she goes, mocking me.

"It ain't the money, see? It's the principle of the thing."

"Money *is* the principle of the thing. I wouldn't think I'd have to tell you that."

Easy for her to say. Women never worry about spending other people's dough. They think they can wave a little tit around and everything'll be alright for them.

I was like, "Yeah, well, I got a thing against getting shot. I'm funny like that."

"O.B. shaves a little off the top, ya know. Five hundred here, a thousand there -- and they haven't shot *him* yet."

"Russian fuckin' roulette," I said. "That's what that old boy's playing."

She shrugged her shoulders and gazed out the window. I knew she was dreaming about being with some other man. Some ace hustler who wasn't afraid to rip off the Sons.

I should've kept my mouth shut and let her dream all she wanted. But I didn't. I had to open it and make excuses and explanations that sounded like shit even to me.

Bunny listened patiently for a while and then she said, "Randy, honey, you've always been honest with me. So I kinda feel bad that I ain't been completely honest with you."

99

I didn't say anything but let her keep talking: "There's a reason the Sons don't mind when O.B. takes a grand or two. It's like they're kinda too busy to care."

Too busy? I didn't get it and said so.

"Too busy with me," she said. She turned her face away.

Oh, I got it all right. I got it in fucking Technicolor. It was suddenly so goddamn obvious it hurt my head and turned my stomach.

Bunny was O.B.'s whore.

My hands tightened into white-knuckled fists. I wanted to ring his neck and choke the life out of him. That bastard was lower than a snake's belly.

Bunny LaFever was one helluva woman -- the best I'd ever known -- and he pimped her ass for a goddamn kick-back. Her pussy was like this top-of-the-line hot tub in the Hollywood hills, and there he was pissing in it. Some guys can't have nothing nice but have to turn it all to shit.

That $2.95 breakfast special sat in my belly like lead. I wanted to puke bacon and eggs, buttered toast, greasy home fries and hot black coffee.

"Didja hear what I said?" she asked.

My jaw ached I clenched it so tight. "I heard it. You don't have to say anymore."

"I'm sorry," she said.

"He's the sonofabitch who's gonna be sorry."

"But I'm sorry, too."

"Stop saying that, goddammit!"

"Okay. I'm sorry."

"*Listen!*" I barked so loud the joint got real quiet. Some of the other diners looked up at us, their forks poised before

100

their mouths. Green beans and mashed potatoes hung in the air.

I lowered my voice, but it trembled with anger: "You don't have to apologize to me -- *not ever*. The past is over and done with. Whatever happened, we left it all back there behind us and that's where it stays."

"You mean you still want me? After everything I told you and all?"

"What, are you crazy? Baby, I want you seven ways from Sunday!"

"You can have me, too. Any way you want me, I'm all yours."

"I want you all to myself. I'm through sharing with O.B. From now on, you're *mine*."

"Let's run away together," she said. "Let's never go back to the Laff Riot."

"That's a promise," I said, throwing some money down on the table as we got up to leave.

* * *

We didn't need the Riot and we didn't need the Sons. Me and Bunny didn't need anybody but me and Bunny. We roared through West Tarwater just before nine o'clock the following night.

The neon midway flickered in the twilight on the outskirts of town. It was set up in the vast parking lot of the Shop-A-Lot. They can pave over the farms till Kingdom Come but the carny's forever.

I could smell the hot dogs and grilled onions from here. I was like, "Smell that smell? Know what that is?"

"Mm-hmmm," she purred. "The smell of money."

"Sure as shit, babe. It's like a homecoming in your sweet momma's arms."

The wheel of the giant SkyDiver towered in the sky. In the daytime it was all washed out but at night it was bright and beautiful, like Christmas Eve on the Fourth of July. It was all freedom and salvation and big, fat promises.

By that time of night, the only joint left for us to work was the Penny Pitch. It's strictly a nickel and dime operation unless you've got a dame like Bunny busting her hump on the inside.

She was a living, breathing come-on with a smile like Las Vegas at night and an ass worth hollerin' about. Her T-shirt said *Me So Horny* in gold, glittery letters. But you didn't have to know how to read to get what she was selling.

Stuffed in a T-shirt so skin tight it was nearly transparent, you could hang a picture on them nipples. Tied in a knot at her midriff, it showed off her stomach. Flat and hard and deeply tanned after spending all day on the road in the sun.

Men were lined up three and four deep around our joint to get in on that action. She had those chumps throwing quarters and half dollars and even wadded-up ones and fives at the Lucky Strike decals stuck to the floor.

Any joe'll tell you it's better when you pay for it. And she had those simps paying all night. She sold them a chance to goose her buns as she worked the perimeter of the joint. Making change and small talk, she pretended not to notice when a stray hand squeezed her thigh.

She wasn't above giving a little back, neither. There was a helluva lot of grateful bulges around. Silver pieces fell like rain on the shellacked floor. And there wasn't a damn one of them mooches looking to see if he'd won anything.

It was so easy I was almost ashamed. She did all the work. I didn't have to do a damn thing except keep the push

102

broom moving across the platform, sweeping money into the trough.

We worked our routines for the next couple days. Everything was going great. But for some reason, deep down I got a bad feeling about all of it.

I couldn't tell you why. There wasn't anything I could point to. Deep down, I just knew that we couldn't go on like this forever.

* * *

After West Tarwater, we moved on to Ypsilanti. Late in the afternoon I was getting dressed to go out and hit the midway. But Bunny just sat there on the edge of the bed, watching some fuck with a haircut on the color TV.

"Up and at 'em," I said. She gave me a look. I was like, "We gotta go to work."

Suddenly she started bawling her pretty little eyes out. "It's even the same motel rooms!" she cried.

"What're you talking about?"

"I'm sorry, Randy, I tried -- honest I did. You saw how hard I tried. But I just can't take it anymore. I want out."

"Outta what?"

"Outta the carny -- outta The Life. I want something better than this. I wanna start over."

"What's wrong with it? It's a damn good ride."

"Yeah, if you don't mind going nowhere fast!"

"Whaddaya mean, *going nowhere*?"

"I mean we'll never make it this way. We're poor and I can't stand it."

"You don't like it, go back to O.B. and be a rich whore again."

Yeah, it was a rotten thing to say. But I said it and I wasn't sorry. Not until she started to cry her eyes out again, anyway. I can't stand that and I'll say or do practically anything to stop it.

"Aw, baby, don't cry -- I'm sorry, honey, I didn't mean it."

"Don't touch me!" she screeched, shrinking from my hand. "Maybe I am a whore. But at least I know what I am!"

"What's that supposed to mean?"

"It means you're no different than the marks. You're a goddamn rube, same as them!"

"Watch your mouth or I'll slap it right off your face."

"Go right ahead!" she yelled. "I know you won't, you coward! Look at yourself. You're a loser hustling for table scraps. You don't fool me."

If anybody else would've said that to me, I would've killed them. But coming from Bunny, those words stung. They hurt cuz it was true.

I couldn't deny it. I was a bullshit artist and I had the whole world conned, even me -- everyone except Bunny. She knew me better than I knew myself.

"Look at us," she said. "We're always running away but we always wind up where we started. It's a different carny but it's the same grease and grime, the same hot dogs, the same cows and pigs. It's the same shit in a different place is all. We're trapped."

"All we need is some time, darlin'. Everything'll be great. You'll see."

"I wasted enough time with you already. At least with O.B. I had some nice things. With you I got a whole lotta nothing."

I was in no mood. I'd be damned if I was gonna sit around and listen to her piss and moan all night. Somebody had to make a living.

"You gonna be here when I get back?" I said. But I slammed the door behind me before she could answer. I didn't care if she was or not.

* * *

So I went out alone with something to prove. And if felt great -- better than great. It was incredible. What a night! I'd never had such a string of suckers.

I was on Lloyd Dixon's Dixie-Doodle-Dandy midway. I was under the blue, and I don't mean under a great big beautiful sky. I was hustling without a fix.

When the cops're paid off, I can play it as hardcore as I want. My criminal ass is covered. But Lloydie-Boy don't pay off the fuzz. He don't need protection.

His midway's so squeaky clean it's what us flatties call a Sunday school show. No 'rooking allowed. It's seen less action than a nun's panties.

I felt naked letting it all hang out like that. But I was out for blood. And the danger just added to the thrill of the score -- like walking a tightrope without a safety net.

I ran circles around those simps. Build-ups, Razzle Dazzle, even a little craps in the back ass of the midway. Those rubes didn't know what hit 'em.

As if grifting that lot wasn't bad enough, around midnight I was also twelve inches inside another hot property, Kitten Dixon.

Kitten was Lloydie-Boy's barely legal daughter. She was stuck selling ice cream Brrr-itos all day when she should've been starring in a titty show all night. Her double-Ds were like a double dose of prescription painkillers.

105

I was nuts to be dicking that bodacious, brown-haired babe in her Roll-A-Long trailer -- right under Daddy's nose. But I was so fired up, I was gonna fuck the owner, fuck his carny, and then fuck his darling daughter, too. That'd show the bastard what's what.

Hell, if you knew Kitten like I knew Kitten, you would've been doing her, too. That talent could take a cock like nobody's business.

She had *FUCK ME* written all over her. Like a billboard, in great big screaming yellow letters. She was an ad for screwing.

My hips ground against her in slow, tight circles, screwing her till those big brown eyes rolled to the back of her head. Burning mountains of love rolled and pitched as we slammed together, sweating like barnyard animals. Her boobs shuddered with our fiendish fuck-quake.

I couldn't get enough of her. I couldn't get too deep. Each frenzied stroke was better than the last.

Her back arched sharply as she climaxed with a series of yips. Butt-bouncing waves of ecstasy washed over her as the convulsions raced through her body.

Coming to, she got on her hands and knees. I lay back with my arms crossed behind my head. My solid-state shaft reared its head. They were seeing eye to eye, snake to snake charmer.

She rolled out her tongue like the proverbial red carpet. I got the royal treatment all over. Several times she brought me to the brink of oblivion, but then held back. She squeezed the base of my shaft until the explosive jizz lost its fizz.

It was time to give her the stick from behind. Still on her hands and knees, curvaceous Kitten turned away. She reached around to spread those chubby cheeks wide.

106

There's nothing I love more than a sure thing. And Kitten was the easiest mark of the night. I slid inside like it was nothing at all.

I didn't need Bunny LaFever to get my kicks. I was getting along fine without her. Kitten was getting along, too, closing in on another of her famous orgasms.

She moaned uncontrollably, swaying her head from side to side with my quickening thrusts. Her long brown hair swept across her back. I pulled it like the reins of a horse and drove the two-bit hussy hard.

We were both on the verge. Everything was a blur. I no longer heard her but felt myself explode. I kept banging away till I was too soft to do any more damage.

* * *

She was tucking my spent member back inside my pants when there came a loud knock at her trailer door.

"Oh, no!" she cried. "It's Daddy!"

I peeked through the frilly curtains over the window. "It's worse, kiddo. It's Clifton Suedene."

"Who?"

"The sheriff."

"You know him?"

"You could say that."

The sonofabitch always wants a cut of the action. And he'll sniff around like a dog after a bitch in heat till he gets it. He smells graft wherever it lies.

"Kitten," I said, "go wait in the bathroom."

Everybody's gotta get his ass kicked. Even me. The sooner it's begun, the sooner it's done.

When she was safely away, I opened the door. Suedene sauntered in, cool and casual. "I heard you were in town, Randy. Long time, no see." His voice poured out like oil.

"Not long enough," I said.

He gave a little chuckle as he hiked up his belt. All the humor left his grin until all that was left was evil and emptiness.

"Now you know I can't let you up and leave," he goes, "without making a contribution to my favorite charity."

He wasn't gonna come right out and ask for my money. He'd make me glad to hand it over. Cops're like carnies that way. We're cut from the same piece of dirty canvas.

"Favorite charity, huh?" I said. "Lemme guess. That's you, right?"

He liked that one. He actually laughed.

"You know the rules, son," he said, removing his hat to scratch the stubble on his shaved head. His eyes were black beads set too close together. "You got to pay to play in Gatling County."

"Play with this, why dontcha," Kitten bubbled. I turned around just in time to see her drop the fluffy pink towel. She gave me a wink as his greedy eyes ate her up.

Lucky for me she knew the score. It was either give up the gelt or give up the goldmine between her legs. Better to use the one than lose the other.

That girl was one in a million.

But that only meant there were 999, 999 others with that something special between their legs. Poor little thing! She was peddling her pretty ass for nothing.

I'd be long gone by daybreak. And she'd be a little bit wiser. No matter how smart you think you are, there's always somebody smarter: *yours truly*.

* * *

I spent the night in the back seat of the Chevy, parked behind the Shop-A-Lot. I started out feeling damn pleased with myself but then Bunny's words came back to poison me.

She'd planted that seed of self-doubt. The kind that sneaks up on you like cheap liquor. It finds you in the middle of the night when it's just you against your head and somehow the head always wins.

What happened with Kitten and Suedene was only more proof: I was your garden variety jerk hustling for table scraps and nothing would ever be any different. A bottle of Hit & Run later, the sting was gone. Shit was straight lighter fluid.

* * *

I woke up the next morning with a mean motherfucking hangover. On the way back to the motel, I passed a gas station where a fat woman with a beehive hair-do and legs like tree stumps had set up shop.

She sat in a sagging beach chair with a red-lettered sign next to her. *Starving Artists Sale*, it said. She was hocking velvet paintings out of the back of a van.

Propped up in a line were Jesuses, sad clowns, Bruce Lees, rainbow unicorns and a ton of fat Elvises. $19.95 for each, frame included.

Next to some topless Polynesian beauty with ruby red nipples and a smile for every sailor in the South Pacific was an Elvis priced at forty bucks.

"Why's that one twice as much?" I asked the lady. A fat plug of tobacco made her lower lip bulge.

She spat thick brown juice into a Styrofoam cup and said, "It's a Fontaine."

"A what?"

"Leo Fontaine," she goes as if that's all she had to say.

I shrugged and shook my head. It didn't mean shit to me.

She was like, "Nobody does sweat like Fontaine. He's like the Da Vinci of Elvis perspiration."

"You don't say," I said as I took a closer look. Silver sweat ran down his cheeks like a doiley. It was impressive all right -- damn impressive.

She spat into her cup again. "Wanna buy it?"

* * *

"Back already?" Bunny said when I walked in. She was in the middle of touching up her toenails and didn't even look up. But as far as I was concerned, it was too damn early to start something.

"I got you something." I held up the velvet painting.

She turned around to squint at it. "What is it?" she goes.

"It's a Fontaine."

"A who?"

"*Leo Fontaine.*"

"Who's that?"

"Only the pre-eminent practitioner of Presley perspiration." I set it on the chair and took a step back to admire it. "Go 'head and laugh, but this'll be worth something someday."

110

"That's our ticket outta this dump," she said, sitting down on the edge of the bed. "All we gotta do is find somebody dumber'n you to buy it."

The woman had a mouth like a loaded gun -- just itching to shoot you down. But I was just waiting for a crack like that.

I pulled out my wad from the night before. A tight roll of bills wrapped in a rubber band. I snapped the rubber off and fanned the bills before her eyes.

"Nice wad," she said, unimpressed. Her tone was like a knife in my heart, and she was just twisting it in deeper. "But money's got a way of running out on you. A girl needs someone she can rely on."

"What're you saying?"

"Ain't it obvious? I love you, honey, but the season's over."

I couldn't believe she was giving me the blow-off with that old line. It was carny talk for *So long, sucker!*

"Oh, yeah?" I shouted. "That's fine by me, but *I'm* keeping the Fontaine!"

* * *

We hit the road as hard as we could stand it. Eleven hundred miles in twelve hours -- a personal best. For half the night we had the highway to ourselves and the radio relay towers blinking like lazy red fireflies.

Between the both of us I'll bet we didn't say half a dozen words.

By four a.m. we made Big Chimney, where the Laff Riot was playing a still date. I pulled into a dark, deserted parking lot.

111

"I guess this is it, doll," I said. "The part of the movie where we kiss and say goodbye."

"No kisses. It'll be easier on you."

"At least tell me you intended to run away with me. Give me that, at least."

But she silently piled out of the car and was gone. Just like that, it was over. I couldn't believe it. She'd sooner be with O.B. than with me. She'd rather be treated like dirt than gold.

Stunned, I sat there for a few minutes wondering if there'd ever been anything there at all. At last I turned to the Fontaine in the back seat. "Women," I bitched. "Who can figure 'em?"

* * *

When you ain't got money, that's all you can think about. It was the same way with Bunny LaFever.

I couldn't turn around without smelling her on my clothes or in my car. That mix of shampoo, hairspray, perfume and cigarettes haunted me like a ghost.

I missed her something awful. And I tried to put that something to sleep with a binge of bourbon, barbiturates and bimbos with big boobs. I carried on like a country song. I wasn't myself but some stranger who was trying to kill himself in my body.

But when I came to with a tattoo on my dick that said *ACTUAL SIZE*, it was crystal clear that I couldn't go on like this. Not if I wanted to live to see another day. I had to pick up the pieces of my broken life while I still had enough dignity left to put it back together.

Try with all my might, I couldn't figure how I wound up with that ink job on my johnson. I tried to remember the night before. And the night before that. And the one before that.

But everything was a blank -- a black hole where my life had been shot down the shitter.

Come to think of it, I was thankful I couldn't remember anything. I didn't wanna know what I'd done. A man can sleep nights with an empty head. It's as good as a clear conscience.

Hell, it was hard enough to look at myself. In the bathroom mirror, all I could see was my own sorry-ass face looking back at me.

I was unshaven. My hair was a mess. One eye was swollen shut with a helluva shiner. Fuck if I knew how I got *that*, too.

I cupped my hands under the cold running water and splashed it over my face. I drizzled it over my hair and ran my fingers through it like a comb, smoothing it down as best I could.

* * *

I reached Toby Tyler's Fun-4-All after midnight -- too late to do anything but check out the lot.

The show was a permanent fixture a mile north of Port Goshen, a naval installation of something like 25,000 seamen. The lot was lousy with drunken jarheads getting into fistfights over nothing.

Like all crooked carnies worth the name, it had a real wild nudie show. *GIRLESQUE!* screamed the signage: *SIN-SATIONAL!! SKIN-TILLATING!!! ALL-NUDE REVUE!!!!*

On the bally stage outside the tent, one cocktease after another was shaking it to some scratchy swamp boogie to lure the men inside. Strings of lights criss-crossed overhead.

White bulbs clung to the shivering wires like drops of water on a spider web.

Everything about this raggedy den of sin and corruption said home. Too bad it was too late to score a decent joint. I promised myself to get up early tomorrow and get something going.

*   *   *

By 11:30, it was like fifty thousand degrees outside. The heat from the asphalt came up through my shoes as I made my way across the busy lot. Over all the joints and rides hung a thick haze of patchouli, charcoal smoke and gasoline fumes.

But something about that skin show caught my fancy.

Where there's pussy, there's money. And where there's money, there's pussy. One takes your mind off the other.

I peeled back the tent flap and went inside.

It stank of beer. The red canvas glowed from the sunlight. They'd thrown down straw to cover the mud. Colorful spangles and loose feathers were mixed in.

It was too early for the first show of the day so the joint was empty. The only soul inside was the owner, piss-drunk. He slumped in a wooden folding chair with his knuckles scraping the ground and his legs stretched out far and wide.

His sleeveless undershirt showed off hairy, meaty arms stenciled with Navy tattoos. Leather suspenders held up a pair of pants that were snug around the middle and baggy everywhere else. His steel toe work shoes were spattered with white paint.

He was nodding off, his chin pressed to his chest. I thought he was about to pass out. But then he opened his yap and started talking.

114

"I know what you're thinking," he said without opening his eyes or lifting his head. "But it ain't too early t' be drunk when I'm shtill drinking from lash night."

He took a long pull of bourbon and then offered me his bottle. I took a swig myself and felt that smooth sour mash whiskey burn all the way down to my belly.

"Brownie Jarboe," he said, introducing himself as he held out his meaty paw. I grabbed it and he pumped my arm for like a minute straight.

"Randy Everhard," I said.

"What's your joint, Randy?"

"Nothing right now. I'm a flattie without a store."

"Flattie, huh?" he goes, scratching his stubble and arranging his thoughts as best he could. "You any good?"

"Best you ever saw."

"Maybe I could use you in here."

"Maybe," I said. "What's your cut?"

"Nuthin'."

"*Nuthin'*?" I asked, suspicious. "What's the catch?"

"It's my wife, Butterfly. She's running around on me. All I need is the proof."

"So if I catch her in the act with this other dude, I get to operate inside."

He threw a smile full of gold bridgework. "From the minute I laid my eyes on you, I says to myself, now that right there's the sharpest knife in the kitchen."

"What about the heat? I don't want any run-ins."

"S'all taken care of," he boasted with a sloppy wave of his hand.

* * *

Later that night, it was dark, smoky and steamy inside the Girlesque. Standing room only, too. The crowd of men jostled and jockeyed for position in front of the stage. Moths swarmed in the pale spotlights.

The show was running strong. The featured stripper was sticking a long fluorescent lightbulb up her snatch. Like a sword swallower in reverse. The light made her shaved crotch glow red. Craziest damn thing I've ever seen.

A strip show's the best place to score. Ask any flattie, he'll tell you. Everybody at a hootchie-kootch is drunk and horny -- nobody thinking straight, keeping one eye on the stage and the nakedness parading back and forth. The sons of bitches just walk right into your trap and never know what hit 'em.

"Here, friend," I said, passing a free ticket to the chump who'd just dropped a bundle on the Razzle and wasn't too happy about it. "Don't go away angry."

Carnies got a word for those special tickets -- ducats. We use 'em to chill out beefers. You know, give the sore losers a little something for their dollar.

"What good is this? A ride on the merry-go-round?"

"It's your meal ticket."

"A hot dog?"

"Not a dog -- pussy."

He didn't get me.

"See that girl on stage?" I go. "Give her this ticket and she'll let you eat her out."

He didn't say anything.

I was like, "Whaddaya think I'm lying? You want me to prove it to you?"

116

"Yeah," he goes. "Prove it to me."

I spotted a skinny kid in the crowd. A recruit that looked too green to be in high school, much less the service.

"Hey, sailor," I said, pulling him aside. He must've thought I was gonna toss him out cuz he fought me. But I held fast. "Take it easy, son," I said. "I just wanna ask you a question."

"Sir, I didn't sneak in here, sir!"

"That wasn't the question." He looked at me nervously, his eyes darting left and right. "Ever eat out a cunt?"

"S-sir, no, sir," he goes, too scared to lie.

"Well, here's your chance to put some hair on that chest." I stuffed the ducat into his fist. "You know what to do?"

He shook his head no. By damn, the kid really didn't know! Can you imagine -- in this day and age? Where have we gone wrong? I blame the school systems, personally.

"Give this ticket to the lady on stage," I told him, "and she'll take it from there."

He took it in his damp, trembling fingers and walked to the rickety stage. It was nothing but pine planks on saw-horses.

The stripper traipsing across it couldn't have been more naked. Not without turning herself inside out. She tried that, too, when she squatted down at the edge and plucked the ticket out his hand with her cunt.

She butterflied her snatch. She had the biggest pussy in the whole damn world, and it was right there for the taking. Just dive right in, like a pink swimming pool.

But sailorboy didn't wanna take the plunge. So she grabbed the back of his head and pulled it into her crotch.

117

She pulled off his sailor cap and put it on her own head, winking and laughing with the crowd as she held his head in place as his arms were flailing.

"Now where's mine?" the beefer goes.

"Huh?" I said, turning away from the show.

"My ticket," he said. "Where's _my_ ticket?"

"You gave your ticket away. One to a customer. That's the rule."

"That's the shittiest rule I ever heard of!"

"Sorry, pal. Rules are rules. I don't make 'em, I just follow 'em."

Truth is, those ducats didn't come free to me. I had to pay Brownie back for each one, for services rendered. Just goes to show that even when you think you got a sweet deal, the bastards will still find a way to stick it to you.

I searched the mob for my next victim. Instead I noticed a pickpocket working the crowd. She was a hot property to boot.

It was a brilliant routine -- I had to hand it to her. She was a stripper who'd been on the stage a few acts before. And now she was mingling and making nice with the crowd.

She was topless and in a g-string. Buttfloss cleaned her crack. But its only purpose was to hold dollar bills around her waist. She had a skirt of greenbacks.

Nobody thought anything of it when her right hand went for their happy hard-on. Meanwhile her left went for their pocket, relieving them of their wallet. Nobody but me, that is.

I strained my eyes to see the hand-off. Her partner was a scrawny dude in a greasy denim jacket and camo pants. He

118

wore a Shur-Fire Sparkplugs cap with the bill pulled down low over his face.

As he edged by, the tart passed him the wallet, which he stashed in one of his pockets. Smooth and seamless. Couldn't have done it better myself.

Too bad I saw the whole thing, start to finish.

Too bad for them, I mean.

I grabbed the pickpocket from behind. "Make it look good," I told her. I held onto her hips and rubbed my pelvis against those solid chunks of buttcheek.

"Fuck off," she snapped, pulling away. Her violet eyes burned back at me. "I'm working."

"I'll say."

"You some kinda cop?"

"Nope. Just a common criminal, same as you."

"So cut me some slack."

"What, outta the goodness of my heart?"

"Don't narc on me, I won't narc on you. I seen you working your routine over there."

"Brownie knows all about me, baby. Does he know about you and your pal?"

She didn't say anything and then she said, "How much you want."

"How much you got?"

"Two-fifty and you go away forever."

"Business is that good, huh?" I asked, holding out my hand.

"*Not here*," she hissed. She had lustrous blue-black hair down to her shoulders with bangs cut straight across her forehead. "Talk to my associate. Meet her in the funhouse."

"Her?" I asked, thumbing at the one in the denim jacket and red cap.

"You know, as in a woman?"

That's when I started to get that feeling I get when I'm gonna get laid.

* * *

The funhouse was called *Bump in th' Dark*.

"Fun my fat ass," I bitched.

We were all alone in there -- us and the broken down gimmicks and gizmos. The only thing that worked was the funny mirrors, and even they were cracked.

"Your problem is you ain't fucked up enough," she said, helping herself to the joint in my mouth. Primo Kentucky bluegrass.

She pulled the smoke deep inside and held it there, letting it fill her lungs and poison her bloodstream. She exhaled. Her sugar-coated smile glowed purple in the blacklight.

"Naw, that ain't it," I said. "I have always believed that people got to make their own fun."

"You got any ideas?" she asked.

Before I could answer she pulled off her grimy cap and shook out her long, double platinum blonde hair. She unbuttoned her jeans jacket and threw it in a corner.

She wore nothing underneath. Her tits knocked together like two Skee Balls. They were fake as a hooker's orgasm but they got the job done.

120

That shameless hussy's finger traced the outline straining against my pants. "You got what I want," she gushed. "A great big hunk o' love."

"Now about my three hundred scoots," I said. "Before we go any further."

I was stoned but I wasn't stupid. She pouted her lips and made the cutest boo-boo face. But I wasn't buying the act.

I told her I was serious and she said okay and dug out a handful of bills and counted out three hundred in fives, tens and twenties. I was prepared for the worst, half-figuring that the dickplay was just a diversionary tactic. But once she'd paid me off, she dropped to her knees and pressed her face against my crotch.

I was thinking that this was pretty all right as she tugged the zipper down. I could hear the click of every tooth.

It sprung out like a jack-in-the-box. She jumped back, staring as it uncoiled and stretched. My midway monster swayed and stiffened before her wondering eyes. They were as big as saucers.

She made nice with my nads. But I was too shit-faced to feel it until she really started cranking. Arousal cut through the weed.

Words magically appeared like on an inflating balloon. Up and down my twelve inches was that crazy tattoo that said Actual Size in big block letters.

"Nice ink," she goes as she gripped my shaft. Her fingers didn't reach all the way around. "Where'd you get it?"

"Dunno," I go. "I was stinko at the time. But I been thinking about adding a little pinstripe."

"Oh no," she said, shaking her head. "Too slimming. A girl likes to see some girth."

I gave her some girth all right -- I was as big around as a beer can, at least. She wasn't intimidated by it. On the contrary, she leaned in and inhaled.

When she popped it out again, it was fully inflated. My tattooed letters looked like the name on the side of a blimp above the Superbowl.

"I love to feel it blow up in my mouth," she goes.

She started to massage me again. I thought she was gonna twist it like a balloon animal. I was gonna wind up with a goddamn poodle for a prick and I didn't give a shit.

"By the way," she said. "My name's Penny. Penny Happening."

"Baby, you'll never know how pleased I am to meet you," I said as she bent forward to engulf me again. "Not in a million years."

I leaned way back to give her multi-talented tongue room to work. That's when I noticed the psychedelic blacklight poster on the wall, curling up at one corner. *Ass, Gas or Grass*, it said, *Nobody Rides for Free*.

There are as many ways of giving a blowjob as there are women, but her voracious technique was unmatched in the history of head. She was a real slut about it. Which made it all the better.

What enthusiasm! She pulled out all the stops. She did all the work. A blowpop never had it so good.

I checked us out in the funny mirrors. My tiny head was stretched out way up here and her huge head was way down there. Really freaky.

The succulent O of her lips bore down on my dick. It was like the Elephant Man, humongous and obscene, like a nightmare.

Most women won't go down on you before knowing what's in it for them. But she blew me like I was the last dick on earth, and it was all hers. Her clit must've been in the back her mouth, she liked oral so much.

That golden throat was too good to be true. You couldn't put a price tag on her kind of cocksmoking. She had that ESP -- Extra Sexual Perception. She knew what makes a man feel good.

"Whatever you got," I groaned, "put it in a bottle and sell it at the mall."

She breathed harder through her nose as she sucked the living daylights outta me. I knew she was gonna to take me there. She was gonna see this blowjob through to the end.

Enough was enough. The floor dropped out from under me. I came forever, like I was falling head over heels to the center of the earth.

My hands were still gripping the greasy steel walls when I snapped out of it. She was still guzzling the entire load. I felt like I was going down with it.

That stupendous suck-off would've been enough to make any other man go home happy. But not me. I thought I'd get some valuable information out of her.

"While I've got you here," I said, "tell me something, babe."

"Mmm," she purred, licking her lips. "Anything."

"Hanging around the strip show, you must hear a few things." She looked up at me expectantly, waiting for the question. "What's the word on Butterfly?" I asked.

"You mean Brownie's wife?"

"Where does she go, who with, all that."

"What do you care about that dried-up old whore for?"

"Let's just say I'm the curious type."

"Well, I don't know anything about Butterfly."

"Really? That's funny. Cuz I know a little about Brownie. Like, for instance, I know he don't appreciate cannons in his joint."

"Blackmail is sooo tacky," she said. "It's such a turn-off."

"Skip the sermon and tell me what I wanna know -- or else."

"After I blew you and everything," she griped. "Okay, have it your way. Butterfly goes to this motel, mostly."

"You know where it's at?"

She nodded. "It's this shitty little dive off the interstate."

I was like, "Looks like me and you are going for a little drive."

"Oh, goodie," she cracked, rolling her eyes.

* * *

We took the divided highway and drove ten miles south of Shanahan. Another five or so miles north on the interstate was the Shangri La-Tel. It was a single-level dump across the highway from the truck stop and the smut shop.

Nine windowless rooms ran along the front. Gray paint was chipping off the cinder block exterior. Doors the color of dried blood.

On the far end was the office, an ancient pick-up parked out front. In the window was a cardboard sign with *Vacancy* scrawled in red magic marker. No shit. There were no other cars in the lot.

"Try around back," Penny said.

124

I cut the lights and turned the corner, letting the car creep on its own momentum. Loose gravel crunched and popped under the wheels.

Nine more rooms were in back. Parked in front of three of the doors were cars, invisible from the road.

"That's hers," she goes.

"Which one? The Casino?"

"Uh-huh."

The Olds Casino was a 2-door deluxe convertible. With the top down, it looked like a swimming pool on wheels. The white leatherette interior practically glowed in the dark. I whistled between my teeth in genuine appreciation.

"What're you doing?" asked Penny.

"Parking," I said as I rolled to a stop in front of a room six doors down from number 18.

"Why?"

"To make it look like we belong here."

"You mean we're staying?"

"Hell, yeah. We're gonna stake out the joint. See what's what."

"Dammit, Randy! I made plans for tonight."

"Wash your hair some other time," I said.

Penny made a big harumph about settling in, wiggling her ass impatiently and crossing her hands over her chest. She blew away the strand of blonde hair that had fallen in front of her face.

"Get used to it," I told Penny without looking her in the face. "We might be here a while."

"Can I turn on the radio at least?" she asked.

125

"Be my pest," I said, waving at the dial. I clicked the ignition and the dash lights glowed green. Penny tuned something in.

Old metal whispered out of the speakers. Insects droned in the weeds outside. I hung my arm out the window and drummed my fingers on the door.

Nobody said anything for the longest time. We passed a bottle back and forth in silence. I stared at the red door, memorizing it until it blurred and then disappeared and I was staring through the motel and at the road.

Penny said something, breaking my spell. I looked at her and was like, "What's that?"

"Any fries left?"

"I dunno."

I reached into the back seat and shook the Scooter Burger sack. Loose curly fries rustled inside. I tossed her the bag.

"Thanks," she said and started plucking them out, one by one. "Lordy, I'm gonna eat every one of these fries. You mind?"

I shook my head. "You know," I said, "I don't even know what the hell this Butterfly person looks like."

"Well, here's your chance to find out."

My eyes shot toward the door just as it was opening. "Fuck! Get down!" I hissed, pulling her head into my crotch. "Make like you're giving me head."

Penny didn't need to be told twice. What a girl! A genuine national treasure. Her fingers were at my fly. She wasn't just going through the motions, either.

I slid my eyes to the left to spot Butterfly and whoever she was with. But I was too late. They were already in the car.

Its engine roared to life. High beams flooded the inside of the Menace. I flinched at the bright light, turning away so no one could get a gander at my face.

I heard a woman laughing drunkenly. As the Olds tore past, kicking up dust, she yelled, "Get a room, cheapskate!" A whiskey bottle smashed against the side of the motel like an exclamation point.

"Fuck," I cursed.

"Mm-hmmm," Penny mumbled on the end of my dick. Her tongue ran around my royal crown. She sucked in her cheeks as she concentrated on the sweet spot on the underside of the head.

The best feeling in the world is a fat roll of twenties hanging in your pocket. But she felt better than even that. She had it beat by a mile. I was gonna feel her lips on me for weeks afterward.

Even so, I didn't wanna waste my wad on another oral. I could only imagine the magic act her cunt put on. If it was half as talented as her mouth, it was gonna dance circles around my dick.

Besides, her patient pussy deserved nothing short of twelve inches. I'm generous like that. Every woman deserves my dick at least once in her life.

My hand slipped inside her pants and was all over that tight ass. "Don't go looking for what you don't wanna find," she said.

I didn't get her at first.

And then I did.

She was a he.

127

The whole world screeched to a halt.

And it was just me grabbing hold of another man's hard-on. His was tied up and wedged in his asscrack. It was the worst feeling in the world.

I let go like it was a live wire. A real shock to the system. I was sober like that.

I should've tumbled her angle sooner. I was an idiot not to see it. A girl who doesn't ask for something in return can't possibly be a girl.

I opened the door and fell to the ground, puking my guts. I wanted to die. Nothing makes you wish for death more than being on the bad end of a gender bender.

Penny tried to help me up but I pushed the she-male away. "If I had my gun," I said, wiping barf and slobber from my mouth, "you'd be dead."

"What's your beef, baby? Didn't you have a good time?"

I struggled to my feet. "Gimme one good reason why I shouldn't smash your face in."

She rolled her eyes. "Now don't even try and tell me that wasn't the finest blowjob of your life cuz that would be a lie and we both know it."

It was true, of course. That was the best BJ of my life -- and that's saying a lot. But that wasn't the damn point and I told him so. A guy like me just can't go around getting his dick sucked by another man, pre-op TV or not.

"Don't worry, sugarfoot," he said. "You ain't queer if you thought I was a girl."

That didn't make me feel any better. But like they say, no use crying over spilled cum. Especially when he conned me fair and square.

I climbed back in the Menace and started the engine. I leaned over to the passenger side and opened the door. "Get in," I said.

Penny stuck his head in. "You mean you ain't gonna just up and leave me here?"

"No," I go, looking straight ahead, "I ain't gonna just up and leave you here. Cuz I know you're gonna keep your damn mouth shut about all of this. Like nothing ever happened."

"I won't say nothing to nobody," he said as he sat down and shut the door. "And my partner won't say nothing to nobody neither."

I knew a goddamn threat when I heard it. I tumbled the set-up pretty quick. If I knew their dirty little secret, they were gonna get one, too.

"Blackmail's such an ugly business," I said.

"You oughta know," he said matter-of-factly. "If we paid you off once, you'd only want more money not to go to Brownie. This way we're even."

What could I say? Penny was right. Heartless bastard that I am, I would've demanded a pay-off each and every night.

But now we were locked in a Mexican stand-off, aiming secrets at each other like loaded guns. There was no way out except to lower our weapons. Nobody wins and nobody gets hurt.

Looking at him by the dim dashboard lights, I saw a woman even though I knew better. It was like an optical illusion.

"What're you chuckling at?" he asked as we sped back to the carny.

"I hate to admit it," I said, "but you're more woman than most cooze. It's a damn shame you're a queer."

"Who's a queer?" he goes, mad as hell. "I ain't queer! I'm a woman trapped in the body of a man. I'm pre-op now, but someday I'll be real."

"Alright already -- you're a woman. You got the mouth for it, that's for damn sure."

She was like, "I'll take that as a compliment."

* * *

It was after three a.m. The Fun-4-All was closed for the night. The marks had split. The carnies that were left were at the G-top.

I was cutting out of there, on my way to the parking lot. I was alone and wasn't watching my back. That's when I got grabbed from behind.

I closed my eyes and cursed the day I ever set foot on the Laff Riot and met Bunny LaFever. I didn't even have to open my eyes to know who it was. Sooner or later they'd catch up with me.

When I turned around and opened my eyes, I saw I was right. Standing there were my two favorite people in the whole world.

Shades and Pigtails, the Sons of Satan. The Gruesome Twosome. Creature Double Feature.

Shades was in a black T-shirt that said *I'm as Confused as a Baby in a Topless Bar*. Somehow I didn't doubt that. Pigtails was in his same stinking black biker jacket with fringe.

I wondered which lousy rat-fink fingered me. It could've been anybody.

You hear all sorts of romantic gobbledygook about the brotherhood of carnies. But there ain't such a creature. I've never had any problem making my share of enemies on the sawdust circuit.

"Hey, fellas," I said, "I was just thinking about you."

Shades was like, "Really?"

"No, not really," Pigtails growled, wincing like it hurt his head to say it. "Did you figure we wouldn't track your dumb carny ass down?"

"I'm gonna level with you," I said. "It just slipped my mind."

"One hundred fifty *grand* slipped your mind?!" Shades sputtered.

I was like, "Hey, I got a lot on my mind, okay?"

"Everybody just shut the fuck up," said Pigtails, massaging his throbbing temples now. "Carnival boy, just give us the fucking money."

"No problem, Ace. I got the scoots in my car."

* * *

I popped the trunk and pulled this wool blanket off the toy pooch. "You and that goddamn dog," Pigtails bitched. And then he reached in and pulled it out.

"I had a dog once," Shades goes. "A real one. And then my step-dad fucking shot it."

"Aw, fer crissakes," Pigtails bitched, "here come the waterworks. Look what you gone and done, you dumb peckerwood."

"What'd I do?" I said.

"Hold the puppy," Pigtails said, thrusting it into Shades' hands.

"Thanks, man." He caressed the dog and rubbed its head against his cheek. "You're all heart."

This scene was a fucking greeting card. But the bitch was, the pooch was still fifteen grand short. I'd managed to put most of it back, here and there. But when you're a Son of Satan, *most of it* is what's known as a good reason to whack somebody.

"*You* --" Pigtails said to me. "Let's go for a ride."

"Naw, that's okay," I go, stalling.

My momma told me never get in a car with strangers. My momma didn't know how right she was. I had to give these shits the slip and fast.

"C'mon," he said, opening his jacket just enough to let me see the butt of the revolver wedged in his crusty jeans. "Let's go for a ride."

"Okay," I said, "I know a good one."

I started walking and heard the hammer cock behind my back. I gambled that he wouldn't shoot me out in the lot where somebody could come along at any minute.

But that didn't stop my scalp from tingling and the sweat dripping and the nausea oozing in my belly like hot, black tar. My legs were shaky but I kept going and didn't stop till I reached the midway.

Lucky for me, Buddy Dula was still on the lot, fine-tuning the Zipper into the wee hours of the morning. The Zipper's like a Ferris wheel gone bad, with cages that spin all the way around. It's one crazy motherfucker.

So was Buddy Dula. His name decorated a handful of warrants for assault and battery and armed robbery. He knew I knew it, too. He couldn't do me enough favors.

I was like, "How 'bout a ride, Buddy?"

"How 'bout it," he goes.

The three of us piled into one Zipper car. I didn't wanna get sandwiched between them, so I got in first and slid all the way to the right. Pigtails squeezed in next to me and Shades next to him.

"Hold your dog, guy?" Buddy asked Shades.

"Fuck, no," he goes. "Rex is gonna ride with me -- ain'cha boy? That's a good doggy."

Buddy looked at me and shrugged. He was like, "You boys better empty your pockets."

"The fuck we will," said Pigtails.

"Suit yourself," I said as I handed Buddy my wallet and car keys.

Buddy shut the cage door, pinning us inside. The black vinyl seats were cracked with age and crusted over with sweat. My head fit in the dent from everybody else's head.

The padded bar pushed against our bellies to hold us in place. It was real intimate-like. Like being in a cage crowded with unwashed animals. Pigtails' ribs were poking me like sharp sticks.

The ride started up. "Every been on a Zipper before?" I asked as the cages got up to speed. "Cuz Buddy's gonna take your ass to school!"

When you ride Buddy's Zipper, you really know it. You hit 3 Gs and experience weightlessness. The world turns upside down and you come off it a changed man.

It's all in the operation of the thing -- the execution. Buddy Dula made that machine an extension of his body. He could sling that bitch something beautiful. Like some jazzbo singing through his saxophone or trumpet or whatever -- more than a ride, poetry in motion.

"Pretty good, huh?" I hollered to Pigtails above the grinding hum of the motor. His lips peeled back from his mouth. He had teeth like an old graveyard, tombstones going every which way.

As we flipped over and over, knives and brass knuckles and loose change slipped out of their pockets and rattled around the cage. Pigtails was squirming uselessly. He spat curses as everything fell to the ground below.

There's no better way to disarm a man than a spin on the Zipper.

"Let it go, baby!" I laughed. "You gotta let that shit go!"

I felt him worm his arm down to his jeans. I knew he was going for his gun -- it was wedged in his jeans too tight to fall out. There wasn't a damn thing I could do about it, either.

"I'll shoot you right here, asshole," he said, working the barrel of that gun my way. Between his bloodshot eyes and that freaky-ass goatee, I knew he wasn't shitting me. "And I'll shoot your boy down there, too, if I have to. Makes no difference to me."

If a piece of machinery could cum, then that ride was ready to shoot its load. We were really humming now. The engine made a high-pitched whine as the Zipper tossed us around.

I heard Shades moaning. He must've had a weak stomach. The poor bastard wasn't made for these spin-and-barf rides.

Suddenly he retched a colorful flood. A sickening rainbow of half-digested junk food and drink spewed from his mouth. Straight onto Pigtails.

"Aw, Jesus H. Christ!" he bitched.

134

Barf splattered him from his face to his lap. Chunks of hot dog stuck to his goatee. He tried to squirm away as Shades convulsed with more upchuck.

"Fuck!" Pigtails hollered. "The gun! I lost it!"

You could hear the fully-cocked revolver as it bounced and slid around somewhere inside the cage like a rattlesnake or some other wild animal you wanna keep your eyes on. But it stayed just out of sight, mocking us.

The cage turned over itself again. Suddenly the gun seemed to float before us in mid-air for an instant, like we were on a rocket ship in zero gravity. Pigtails and I made a grab for it, but just like that it was gone again.

"Sumbitch's got a hair trigger!" Pigtails yelled.

It knocked and tumbled around the cage like one of those lotto balls. Sooner or later, somebody's number was gonna come up. I closed my eyes and all I could see was Bunny LaFever.

The gun went off. The explosion was deafening. Sparks flew where the bullet ricocheted off the front bars.

I heard Pigtails shrieking. His voice was somewhere below the ringing in my ears. It sounded garbled, underwater-like.

"Goddamnmotherfucking -- it got me!"

"Where!?" Shades yelled.

"My *foot*! Owwww! Fuck! Fuck! *Fuck*!"

I reached down and blindly felt along the floor.

My finger was there when the gun slid by. I hooked it by the trigger and got hold of it. I pushed it through the bars of the Zipper cage, and it dropped to the ground.

* * *

When the ride was over, Buddy let us out.

Pigtails tumbled out of the cage and hit the dirt. He grabbed the heel of his boot. The leather was blown away and blood trickled through his fingers.

"You got all yer money now," I lied. "Take it and go. I'm through with you and Krass."

"Think this is over?" he croaked up at me. "Nothing is *ever* over! You hear me?! *Nothing!*"

I walked away and Shades was in no condition to stop me. He was on all fours on the ground. Puking his guts all over again.

"You didn't see me with those guys," I told Buddy Dula as he returned my wallet and keys.

"I don't know what you're talking about," said Buddy. "I don't know you from Adam."

Secrets are like money around here.

And I'd just bought myself some time.

* * *

The following afternoon, alone this time, I took Butterfly's advice and got a room at the Shangri La-Tel. Tied up out front was an ornery, three-legged pit bull.

"You wanna room in back?" the manager asked. He was old with fuzzy tufts of hair like some kind of fungus growing on his liver-spotted head. I smelled liquor on him.

"I want 17," I said. 17 was the room next to Butterfly's. "It's sorta my lucky number."

"And you wanna get lucky," he said, winking a rheumy, red-rimmed eye. A game show was playing on the color TV behind him. Somebody just won a brand new car -- lucky fucking them. "Ten bucks for an hour or fifty bucks a night."

136

I slid him a five-spot. "Room 18," I asked, "they here for an hour or the whole night?"

"That's special. Them two took it for a week. We'll make you the same deal, if you want -- two hundred up front."

"You take cash?" I asked as I took out my wallet. I meant it as a joke. But he thought I was serious.

"That's *all* we take, sonny."

* * *

I unlocked the door and tried the light. The wall switch didn't work. I had to screw the damn bulb in by hand. The naked bulb was weak, throwing a dim glow over everything.

It was a little slice of heaven, all right. Blue shag wall-to-wall. Puke green bedspread. Dangling from the ceiling was a dried-out fly strip like a lower intestine.

Nobody came there for the looks. Or the smell of stale beer and cigarettes. From the sound of it, they came to screw. The walls were paper-thin.

Right that minute, Butterfly and her backdoor man were making with the humpy-pumpy pretty good. The noisy rhythm of screwing was unmistakable. Grunts and groans galore.

They were giving that bed frame a workout, really testing its springs -- *squeak! squeak! squeak*! The headboard knocked against the wall -- bang! bang! bang! It sounded like a drunken band parading down the street.

You couldn't help listening in on them. She didn't give you a choice. Talk about a broadcast! I felt dirty just listening to her go on and on about her pussy and his dick and his dick in her pussy.

I put my ear to the wall to hear better:

"Unnngh," she moaned, "I'm so full of your cock I can't hardly stand it!"

"How you want it? You want it like that?"

"Yeah, I want it harder -- give it to me harder! Yeah, baby -- stuff it! Shove it in me!"

I didn't need to see what was going on. Not with that filthy fucker filling in the blanks. In between the thrusts, she gave the pornographic play-by-play.

"I'm so wet for you, loverman."

"You like to be on top, don't you?"

"That feels soooo gooooood!"

"Talk to me, you cheatin' slut -- tell me what it feels like."

"I'm stretched so tight around you. You got me maxed out like a credit card!"

She had a real knack for description. Word images burned into my mind. It was downright dick-raising.

The guy was like, "Your husband fuck you like this?"

"No! No!"

"Does he fuck you this good?"

"He don't fuck me hardly at all!"

"I'm so hard for you, baby! You ever had a dick this hard?"

"No!"

"Ever have a dick this big?"

"Never ever! I can feel it in the back of my throat, it's so long! It's touching me everywhere -- you're driving me crazy!"

"Your ass is in-fuckin-credible!"

138

"Oooh, that's it -- grab my ass, spread my cheeks. Stick your finger up. Like that, baby -- *Ohhh!*" she screeched, "You make me feel so cheap! I wanna be your whore! Tell me I'm your whore!"

"You're my whore! My special whore!"

Take it from me -- dicking is all in the delivery. So that fella must've had one helluva magic wand. She stopped speaking English and started speaking in tongues -- some weird mumbo jumbo sex jive. Babbling in the universal language of *fuck-me-baby*.

She wasn't making any sense but any fool knew what that low moan meant. Building inside her body, overflowing her mouth. She was going over to the other side.

What started out as a moan ended as a high-pitched screech. Like a whistle. And then it shot into the upper registers which no man could hear. Hound dogs started howling in the distance.

Butterfly was a screamer. An open-mouthed, lung-emptying, ear-splitting shrieker. She was having the orgasm of her life and she wanted the whole goddamn world to know it.

Her ecstasy subsided, ebbing against the cock that was still going like no tomorrow. I stood there listening to him screw her. He hadn't cum yet but was on his way.

It was only a matter of time now. The headboard thumped, the mattress groaned. Harder, faster. It was like waiting for the other shoe to drop.

"I'm gonna cum!" he finally cried. We were all relieved.

"Cum inside me!" she gasped.

"You sure?"

"Yes! I want you to!"

"I wanna cum inside you!"

"Yeah, baby! Fill me up! Please, I need it to live!"

Christ-a-mighty, she was melodramatic. But he didn't mind. I imagined Butterfly riding on top.

He came with a cry, moaning as he poured into her body. They fucked some more, bed springs squeaking. And then I didn't hear anything.

I lay back on the bed, smoking and waiting, smoking and waiting. That's when I fell asleep.

* * *

A couple hours later, there was some commotion. Sounds of waking up, getting dressed, bullshitting around.

"Baby?" she called. "What about your thingy?"

"Leave it," he told her. "We'll be right back."

I heard them leave the room and drive off. I had to act fast. Back in the front office, I handed the manager ten bucks to loan me his key to room 18.

"Wait a cotton pickin' minute," he said, holding the key out of reach. "You her husband?"

"Nope."

"A bedroom dick?" he asked, squinting. "Cuz we had it up to here with all y'alls funny business."

"You got me all wrong," I said. "I'm just your garden variety panty sniffer."

He scratched his nose as he thought this over. Flakes of dead skin fell like snow. He wore a western-style shirt with mother-of-pearl buttons buttoned all the way up to the neck.

"Well, hell," he drawled as he dropped the keys into the palm of my hand, "Why'nt you say so in the first place? We got to stick together!"

140

* * *

Inside 18, I took a look around to see what was what. What it was was ugly as 17.

On the wall above their unmade bed was a picture of wild horses. When I took it down, it left a clean square on the grimy wall. I hung the velvet Elvis in its place.

Call me a psychic, but I just knew that Fontaine was gonna come in handy someday.

I whipped out my pocket knife and sank the tip of it's blade through Presley's eye and into the wall. I pulled out the knife and then lifted the picture off its nail. Plaster crumbled as I dug at the mark in the wall.

Lucky for me, whoever built this shack was thoroughly half-assed about it. Within a minute I'd broken through to the other side. I kept cutting until I'd made a hole big enough to fit my index finger.

Next I used the tiny scissors in the knife to snip a neat hole around the eye. I hung the Fontaine back on the wall, lining up the holes. When I put my eye to the peephole, I was looking straight into my room next door. Perfect-o.

I brushed the tell-tale crumbs and flakes off the pillow and got the hell out of there.

* * *

Half-asleep, I heard the car as it pulled in and parked. "Oh, you!" she called playfully, laughing over the noise of slamming doors.

I shot up out of bed and pressed my left eye to the peephole as they unlocked the door. Butterfly came in first, hugging a paper barrel of Finger Lick'n Chick'n.

She didn't look like I thought she would. That bleached big-ass hair-do was more tarnished trophy wife than ex-carny stripper.

141

But don't get me wrong. Butterfly was a long drive from over the hill. That woman could still do a lot without doing anything.

Teetering on a pair of glossy white pumps, she wore a thigh-length white patent-vinyl coat that was belted at the waist. She set the fried chicken down and untied the belt.

The coat opened to reveal a little red silk Japanese kimono. It was short enough to show the black panties when she bent over the bed. The fabric was stretched so tight across her buns it gave off a high sheen.

The man who came in behind her was thin but muscular and half her age -- a strapping young stud with a headful of brown curls and a movie star tan. He wasn't wearing a shirt. In each hand he held a bottle of La Pierre Rosay to wash down that fried chicken.

"Don't eat in bed," she said as she stripped the thin puke green blanket off the bed. "That's what my momma used to tell us kids."

Holding one end by the corners, she whipped it up and let it float to the floor. When she bent at the waist to smooth out the wrinkles, he ground his groin against her backside.

She stood up and he slid his arms around her waist, pulling her close. His hands cupped her breasts as he kissed her neck. She took his groping for a minute before stopping him.

"C'mon, baby -- suppertime. You gotta keep your strength up."

He placed her hand on his bulge. "I'm a growing boy," he said into her ear.

"So that's where you put it all," she said, turning to admire his package inside the tight pants. They were striped in shades of brown and yellow.

142

He got down Indian-style on the blanket. Around him, Butterfly fussed with paper plates and containers of biscuits and mashed potatoes with gravy.

He unscrewed the bottles of pink wine and filled two plastic cups as she finally settled herself on the blanket. She lay on her side with her legs bent, facing him. Her upper half was propped up with an elbow.

"Dig in," she told him, waving her arm over their spread.

"First things first," he said, lifting his cup of wine. "To us."

"To us," she agreed, raising hers to touch his. She knocked it back in one gulp. "Oh, my," she giggled as he refreshed her cup. "That La Pierre goes straight to my head."

He grabbed a breast out of the bucket and tore into it. She delicately held a drumstick between her fingers as she nibbled the tender meat off the bone. Every few bites she'd delicately pat the corners of her mouth with a paper napkin.

I could smell that fried chicken from here with its 7 Secret Seasonings. My empty stomach was bitching and moaning as they stuffed themselves. My guts were growling so loud I swore they'd hear me through the wall.

"Lemme butter y'alls biscuit," he said, grabbing one out of the carton.

"Honey," she cooed, "y'all can butter my biscuit anytime of the day or night."

She wrapped her lips around the bottle neck and tipped it back. Her eyes closed. The muscles of her throat tensed and relaxed as she finished off the sweet wine.

"May I please have a napkin?" he asked politely, holding up his greasy fingers.

143

She took his hand instead and began licking the grease off. He held hers and returned the favor. His tongue darted between her digits as she sucked the savory juices off his index finger.

They pulled each other closer until their mouths met. Tongues intertwined. He broke the kiss and leaned closer to french her ear. She sighed, gushing. He licked the back of her knee and she gasped. He kissed her toes and she nearly died.

That's what you call a fool-proof woman. There wasn't a spot on her body he couldn't touch without giving her pleasure. She had more erogenous zones than Nebraska's got cornfields.

"I hope y'all saved some room for dessert," she said, opening her eyes.

"Why, heck," he mumbled as he nibbled her neck, "there's always room for dessert."

"Is that so?" she purred. She rolled on her back and spread her legs as she pulled aside the crotch of her panties. Hot pink pussy glowed inside the dark mass of curls. "C'mere and lick my skillet, honeybunch."

He planted his face squarely between her legs and didn't stop until she came, flopping like a fish out of water.

Suddenly his head shot up like some prairie dog sensing danger. "Something's not right, babe," he said, all concerned. "It feels different."

"No," she said, all flush and drunk, "it feels wunnerful..."

He stood up drunkenly and stumbled about, checking out the scene. The Fontaine caught his eye. He examined it closer.

144

We went eyeball to eyeball in a staring contest. I tried my damnedest not to blink. I wanted to scream in pain as my eye dried out.

"That's just The King, honey," she called behind him.

"I swear it weren't there before," he said. I smelled sex and cheap wine on his breath.

"Why sure it was. Why wasn't it?"

"I dunno. Something's different."

"You're drunk is what's different. Come back and show me how much you love me."

Reluctantly, he finally turned away. I could breathe again, and started to rub my sore eye. When I put the right eye to the hole, I could see stud-boy was aiming to please.

Butterfly's red nails strafed his back as he entered her. Her legs were locked around his waist, and she violently pulled him down into her body.

She whipped her head back and forth, transported. Her mouth was a lipstick blur of ecstasy.

No doubt about it -- the lady liked big dick. And from the look of it, big dick liked her. He kept bouncing on that tramp-o-line like she was the best lay in the world.

And maybe she was. It looked like a helluva good time from here. My dick was getting jealous.

Tits rolled back and forth and side to side as he rammed his rigid rig deep inside. The dark brown areolas were as big as silver dollars with nipples you could hang a hat on.

His cock plunged down again and again, disappearing into the forest of her fuzz. Her bush was a rug of thick, black pile. Droplets clung to the fur like glitter.

I would've killed to be him, driving deep inside her hot little hole. I did the next best thing, under the circumstances. I undid my pants and started flogging the log.

He pulled out and she got down on all fours. "Fuck me from behind, baby -- pretty please?" Wiggling her ass at him, she was just begging for it.

Her body writhed and undulated out of control as he doggied her pussy. My hand was the grip of her insatiable cunt, flying up and down my cock in time to the rhythm of his thrusts. I wanted to explode with her.

She came with a scream. His cock was still planted in the clutches of her pussy as spasms rocked her world in waves. The sound of her ecstasy drove me over the brink.

* * *

When they left their room, I quietly slipped out the door and followed them. They'd walked a few steps when I came up behind her.

"Ma'am?" I asked.

She turned around. "Yes?" Her voice had that guilty, defensive sound to it.

"Your husband hired me."

"My husband?" she asked. All the color drained out of her face. She fanned herself with her pocketbook, slowly composing herself. "Donny," she said to her stud, "Go to the car."

"Yes, ma'am," he said shyly.

She opened her purse. "I trust that you won't find it necessary to tell the Senator."

"The Senator?"

"My husband. Senator Royce Boydell."

146

Well, shut my mouth and call me cornpone! I'd been peepin' on the wrong cheatin' wife. They do know how to carry on down here, don't they?

"Oh, yes, right, right," I said, covering up my goof as she handed me a wad of cash. "I'm certain we can keep this between us, Mrs. Boydell."

"Good," she declared. "Husbands and wives, they have to have their secrets."

"That they do, Mrs. Boydell, that they do."

"He thinks I'm visiting my momma's people," she said with a wink. "C'mon, loverboy," she said to Donny, taking him by the arm. "I don't know why Justice Wheeler insists you're a homosexual. I mean, really, you are straight as the day is long."

"Well," he said sheepishly, "the judge pays me extra."

They drove off, leaving me all alone with my naked thoughts.

* * *

I worked the Girlesque the next day and night. All in all it was an average score. I couldn't complain.

It was well after midnight by the time I was pulling out of the carny lot to head back to my motel.

That's when my headlights caught the woman, less than fifty feet before me. She was directly in the path of my car. She stood defiantly with her legs spread and hands on her hips.

I cursed and slammed on the brake. Wheels slid over the loose dirt like ice. The Menace jerked to a stop, nudging up against her body like a lovesick puppy.

She pounded her fists on the hood. Her miniskirt and black fishnets and a billowy, transparent top showed what-

147

all she brung to a party. She had the best set of tits I'd seen all day. Big, bold and spicy in a black brassiere.

My heart was still in my throat as she came around to my side and yanked open the door. "I'm driving." She insisted.

"Goddammit," I hollered, "I wet myself!"

She lowered her gaze to glare at me. "Shut up and shove over."

Yeah, I knew I knew that voice. It was the same woman who'd yelled at me to get a room the other night. "So you're Butterfly," I said as she got behind the wheel.

"There's one thing you're gonna learn about Butterfly -- she don't like snoops."

"What'd you expect? Running around with another man and all."

"Is that what Brownie told you?" she said and then she laughed too long and loud with a mouthful of teeth.

She tore out of the lot. We hit the road in a cloud of dust, fishtailing for a good hundred feet before she straightened it out.

I figured there was a whole lot else that Brownie didn't know.

* * *

Miles away, we screeched to a halt in the parking lot of the Shangri La-Tel. Butterfly got out, unlocked the door to room 13. I followed behind her.

Water was running in the bathroom sink. The door was closed. Behind it, a petite feminine voice called out, "That you, baby?"

"It's me, lover," Butterfly goes. "I brung a friend. You know Randy, don't you?"

148

"Only Randy I know is buried in a pet cemetery in Oskalossa."

Butterfly snorted in amusement. "That girl! Teenie Martini's a hoot and a half." She sat on the bed and patted a spot on the mattress next to her. "Keep Butterfly company till Teenie's done putting on her face."

I made small talk. "So you were in the hooch."

Between those tits and that ass, she had the kind of body a man would pay good money to see. No shit. She had what it takes to make a dick stand at attention. Fuckability in 48-28-36 dimensions.

"Those were the days."

"Why'd you quit?"

"Nobody wants to look at granny shake her shit."

"You got more now than most ladies ever dared of dreaming."

"You lie like a rug but I love you for it."

"This dick don't lie. I got a bona fide boner just sitting near you. Feel it -- hard as a rock."

She took me up on the invitation and reached into my lap. Her hand stroked and squeezed me through my jeans.

"I wonder how big I can make it."

"Take off your clothes," I said, "and let's see."

"You can't touch me while I'm dancing, though. House rules."

"Okay."

"Twenty bucks is my going rate."

"Okay."

"But it's thirty if you cum."

She stood up and began grinding those hips to this transistor radio she had. She'd quit the biz years ago but you wouldn't know it. She wasn't a damn bit rusty.

Her whole body undulated and writhed like a well-oiled sex machine. She teased to please, giving me tantalizing promises of the flesh beneath her clothes.

"Go, baby, go!" I yelled. There was never a more appreciative audience than me. "You really know how to sell it!"

"Damn right I do. The tease is everything. Girls today -- they just strip it all off and swing it around. Like those twats Brownie's got stripping for him," she bitched. "What does he care about art for? He just wants to fuck some fresh meat."

"Some jerks're never satisfied with what they got. The grass is always greener."

"But somebody's gotta mow the lawn!" she laughed.

Button by button she undid her blouse. It was like opening a curtain on those big tits. They sure as hell don't make 'em like they used to.

She tripped the lock on her front release bra. The black, satiny cups clung to her mounds.

She pushed them apart. I nosed my way between them. She pressed those fleshy globes together in a bosomy embrace. My head disappeared. I could've stayed there forever.

She sprung me, and directed my eyes lower. I eagerly anticipated the spectacle to come. She kept me waiting, too. When she finally lifted her skirt, I saw bush. No panties to get in the way. My cock lurched forward.

She spun around and shook her lusty butt in my face. Grinding away, the milky flesh of asscheeks strained against the criss-cross network of her stockings. I tried to cop a feel but she wiggled her finger at me.

150

"Hands off the merchandise," she snapped. "Take it out for Butterfly. I wanna see it get big and strong."

I lay back on the bed. My cocktower swayed and stiffened for her. Every hard-on I'd ever had was just a warm-up for this one.

"*Actual size?*" she said, arching an eyebrow as she read the tat on my dick. "Now that's what I call truth in advertising!"

She straddled me, gyrating inches above my swollen head. She reached down and dug her long red nails into the crotch, piercing and stretching the thin threads. They snapped, pulled past the breaking point.

I've seen some pretty good snatch in my time but hers takes the cake. I mean it. She had a pussy worth a thousand words. I can't go on enough about it. It was the Cadillac of cunts.

I was transfixed, hypnotized. My eyes were all over her. I could practically feel her cunny just by looking. My cock was so hard, the slightest breeze wafting over its head would've made me explode. It was literally crying for mercy. A tear slid down the side.

She slid three fingers up her snatch. In and out they went. I was never more jealous of anything in my life.

Her hips rolled in raunchy circles, faster and faster. She lowered herself to my aching cock, teasing me. She lifted it away, and then lowered it again. So close and yet so far. I felt the heat radiating from her furnace.

She was daring me to thrust myself into her butterfly. My dick was a randy rocket, red-hot and ready for take-off. Through sheer force of will I kept it down.

"Come on, baby," she taunted. My body trembled. Sweat poured off my face. "You know you want to. Hmm?"

I wanted to soak that sweet snatch from top to bottom. I wanted to cover it in cream. I wanted to drown her in a deluge of dick dew.

"C'mon. C'mon. C'mon. Shoot it all over me. Won't it look pretty, like a string of pearls?"

Yeah, that would be nice. But it'd look even prettier buried inside. Nothing could stop me from caving. I would've killed to fuck that pussy.

I reached behind her and grabbed ass. I pulled her down, thrusting upward at the same time. Our bodies smacked together. I couldn't get any more inside her if I tried.

"How much for a lay?" I grunted.

"Nothing," she gasped, getting used to my bone. I was touching her in places she'd never been touched before. "I ain't a whore. I strip for money but screw for free. Now get that big thing of yours working --"

With some girls, the tits are all hype. There's nothing beyond the tease. The show starts and stops with the come-on. When the curtain goes up, all you get is an empty stage. You wind up feeling gypped.

But not Butterfly. Hell, no! She delivered.

She took you straight to the promised land. Between those legs was paradise on earth. The land of milk and honey lay between those supple thighs.

I was full tilt and to the hilt. My cojones were swinging like bells. Her cunt was jumping. My plunging poker kept her exploding non-stop.

"Baby," I said, "you fuck like you invented it."

"I did," she smiled. "Well, the best parts of it, anyway."

And then she did something with her cunt that was beyond belief -- beyond words, even. I can't say what it was

152

but before I knew it I was exploding for what seemed like forever.

Those powerful pussy paroxysms kept my pump primed. We slowly humped and bumped as I went soft inside her.

* * *

"Now I know why you're such a popular guy," Butterfly drawled in her syrupy voice.

"What makes you say that?"

She pulled away from me and crossed the room.

"Take a look --" she said, dropping the latest Carnival Call on my stomach. It was folded open to the classifieds in the back. One ad stuck out:

RANDY EVERHARD

or anyone knowing his whereabouts

Contact B.L. c/o Carnival Call

Butterfly pulled out a couple of cigarettes and lit both in her mouth before handing me one. "Who's B.L.?" she goes, lying on her stomach on the bed and propping herself up on her elbows.

"Bunny LaFever," I said, trying to sound cool while my heart was jumping for joy.

"Bunny LaFever," she goes, pronouncing the name with a smirk.

"Sounds like you know her," I said.

She shrugged. When she spoke, smoke curled out of her mouth: "We worked some shows together. I seen some things. Heard a few stories."

"Like what?"

"I don't know what you think you know about Bunny," she goes, "but I know she ain't a real carny."

153

"What is she then?"

"That girl's got circus blood."

"*Circus*! I don't believe it!"

"Believe it, Randy."

She was dead serious but I refused. You see, carnies and circus people hate each other from way back when. We're two different tribes. Like Hatfields and McCoys. Nobody even remembers how or why the feud started but every year there's a dead body or two to keep it going.

"No way Bunny's circus!" I said. "I can smell circus from half a mile away. And that girl is carny through and through."

"I ain't lied to you yet," she said.

"But she told me her folks were carnies."

"I bet she told you lots of things. But I know for a fact she was married to this fleabag circus owner, and you know how they stick to their own kind. And that ain't the worst of it, neither."

"There's more?"

"I'll save you the gory details. Let's just say guys got a way of dying around her vagina."

"What's that supposed to mean?"

"The circus owner woke up dead the morning after his honeymoon night. He was old and all, but some say she killed him with her cunt."

She wiggled her eyebrows provocatively. Just thinking about Bunny's pussy made my cock stir despite myself.

Butterfly continued, "But that circus owner? He wasn't the first." She took a deep drag off her cigarette and then slowly let the smoke out. "Clowns and aerialists and lion

154

tamers -- she got 'em all. She was smart, too, for a while. She jumped from one big top to another so nobody got wise. But then she got cocky. She tried to cash in on that owner. Them circus folks caught on."

"Then what?"

"She left the circus cuz she had to lam. You don't wanna know what circus people do to traitors. So she went underground, to the carny."

It's the right world to disappear in. A hideout of grit and neon for people who don't want to be found. Lamsters, parole jumpers, runaways, you name it.

"When circus folk go bad, they go bad in a big way. That girl's nothing but a cold-blooded killer, Randy. She's got enough badness in her for *two* Bunnies."

"But the *circus*," I said with a shudder. I still couldn't get over it. I never would've guessed. Not in a million years.

Here I thought I knew too much to forget Bunny LaFever. Trouble was, I didn't know the half of it. All I was sure of was I wanted to get to the bottom of that girl -- or die trying.

* * *

My head was still reeling from the lowdown on Bunny when Teenie Martini appeared from the bathroom like a shot of whisky or a slap across the face.

"Where's your new clothes I bought you?" Butterfly cried. Sure enough, she couldn't get any more naked if she tried.

Teenie Martini was just 21. But with the face of a 16-year-old. And the body of a 12-year-old.

She had no tits to speak of. That girl must've been in the john when they were handing them out. But I'll take a cunt with nothing on top over nothing any day.

155

"Clothes and me are like oil and water," she said. "We can't stand each other."

That was fine by me. A hardbody like Teenie's was better off naked. She leaned coyly against the wall, arms crossed to punch up what little bit of cleavage she had.

"Teenie, this is Randy," Butterfly said. "Randy, Teenie."

My dick reached for her hand. She wrapped her fingers around it and squeezed. "I prefer the company of women," she goes. "But I got a real soft spot for hard cocks."

"It scares me when you say that," said Butterfly. "I'm afraid you're gonna run off with the first hard-on you meet."

"Whyn't you tie me down, then?" she giggled as she lay on her back on the bed. She brought her knees up to her flat chest, locking her hands behind her knees. The devilish position showed off all the pink.

"There's an idea," Butterfly said. She produced a length of red rope and bound her wrists. Teenie's lithe body was a knot of tight flesh.

I went south on her, slithering down that prepubescent-like body. My fingers combed her peach fuzzy pubes. Wetting my index finger between her lips, I drew it in lazy circles over the clit that was hardening into a candy red button.

"Isn't that the best, most wonderful pussy you've ever seen?" Butterfly asked behind me.

"It's all right."

"Whattaya mean, *all right*?"

"Take a chill pill. I'm just messing with you."

"Well, all right then," Butterfly snorted, amused. She snapped a thin leather choker around Teenie's neck. The band was studded with tiny rhinestones and such.

156

"Everybody should have a girl on a leash, don't you think?" she said, attaching a silver chain with links like dewdrops to her pet's collar.

"That's for damn sure."

"Well, what're you waiting for?" she asked as she pushed the back of my head into Teenie's crotch.

She was oozing in anticipation as my tongue reached deep into her musky box. I screwed her tangy twat for a minute or two.

"Hey, pal," Butterfly suddenly said, "you call that pussy eating?"

"Everyone's a goddamn critic," I griped.

"Never send a man to do a woman's job," said Butterfly, shooing me away.

"This I gotta see."

Butterfly's tongue was a blur as she savored the flavor of her girl's dripping cunny. She really knew her way around a twat. Teenie thrust her hips against Butterfly's ever-loving lips and the sticky fingers that plunged deep into her hole.

"So good, so good," Teenie cooed. "You feel soooo goooood."

Her moans became as short as her breaths as she verged on orgasm, suddenly screaming. The spasms rippled throughout her entire body.

I stroked my hard-on as Butterfly stood up and crouched over her pet's head. Slowly and expertly she lowered herself to Teenie's open mouth and out-stretched tongue. It slithered up and down Butterfly's crease.

Nothing gets a cock harder than two horny chicks getting it on. No mystery there. It's like two cunts for the price

157

of one. Four tits for the price of two. Any way you add it up it's two naked babes, no waiting.

"You know," I said, "you girls put on one helluva floor show!"

They were getting to me. I put my finger in Teenie's mouth. Her tongue twirled around it like it was a little prick.

With my free hand, I pumped my cockhead into a shade of plum. Blue veins bulged along my shaft. But as hard as I was, deciding which hole to screw was harder.

Butterfly opened her eyes. They were drugged with lust. Her auburn hair was a wild mane.

"Don't just stand there looking stupid," Butterfly goes. "Teenie's there for the taking!"

I positioned myself before her snatch, bullseye'd the target and dug in deep. She was most accommodating. My dick was in her cunt and my head in the clouds.

"Drill her!" Butterfly cried ecstatically.

Skin slapping, our three bodies blurred into a delicious delirium of grinding flesh. I'd hit the jackpot of jizz, slam-banging two nasty nymphos at once. In between her own moans, Butterfly made like the director of a skin flick: "Sink your meat! Fuck Teenie's pretty pussy!"

I went all out. I wanted to ram my bone up into Teenie's belly. I aimed to fuck my way clear through her muff-diving mouth and into Butterfly's hot little hole.

Harpooned two lesbians at once. Like pigs skewered on a barbecue spit. The thought of the both of them twirling on my pole was too far out.

My ball-bouncing frenzy drove Teenie's cunny crazy. It gripped me tight as a fist as I rocked her world. They screamed like down-home sluts through overlapping orgasms.

158

"Now cum!" Butterfly ordered: "Cum in her cunt!" Suddenly my body stiffened and the floor dropped out from under me.

When you cum, the whole world cums with you -- it's true! Teenie's puss spazzed up and down my shaft and I couldn't get the smile off my face. It was like carved in stone.

Semen flew everywhere as I pulled out. It was like quicksilver, dripping off hands, bellies, asscheeks.

"Now that you know our secret," drawled Butterfly, "we'll have to kill you."

"Or maybe we'll just eat you instead," Teenie said as she lowered her head to my cock. She blew on the tip, then blessed it with a kiss. The preliminaries had me standing at attention in no time.

"What're you gonna tell Brownie?" Butterfly asked.

I was like, "Who's Brownie?"

"That's what I like to hear," she goes. Her laughter sounded far away-like. "You just forget all about me and Brownie. You just go back to Bunny LaFever."

"Who said I was gonna go back to Bunny?"

"Nobody," she said. "Nobody had to."

Teenie swallowed me whole, lolling her tongue over the turgid tumescence. Occasionally she rolled her palm over the supersensitive head. I rolled my head back and that beautiful, shimmering road to ruin opened up before me.

Butterfly was right. I couldn't fool her. Teenie was on my dick but Bunny was on my mind.

I was like some junky who'd kicked the habit only to fall back into it. And then it was ten times worse. But you felt a hundred times better.

* * *

I beat it down to Zeleinople, where the Laff Riot was playing the tri-county fairgrounds. I hit the lot just in time for the after dinner crowd. I was just another face in the mob -- another neon-struck zombie.

That was the way I wanted it. The last thing I needed was to be found out by Peanut. Or recognized by anybody else.

From a hat stand I lifted one of those idiotic beach numbers -- the kind with a red celluloid visor. I pulled it low over my eyes. The tinted visor made everything look red.

I kept my head down as I slinked up the midway. I half-expected it to look different. But it was the same set-up as before.

The midway was a U-shape. The two horns were made up with one-way joints, placed side by side and facing in. Scattered up the middle were the four-way joints that get action from all four sides.

I felt like a mark as I ran the gamut of familiar flatties, avoiding eye contact as I heard their come-ons: "Yo, mister!" "Take a chance!" "Free shot!" "On the house!"

At the rear end of the midway were the same old rides and attractions. The same old merry-go-round. The same old Ferris wheel. The same old Flying Bobs with the girls' long hair flying behind them like streamers.

Bunny was right. Nothing ever changes on the carny circuit. Everyone just goes around and around in circles until they come out right where they started. Funny how I never noticed it before when it was so miserably obvious to me now.

I continued past the wall of port-o-sans and came out by the carny camp. The air felt charged with electricity. The

160

hair on the back of my neck actually tingled. Something big had gone down, and I just walked into what was left of it.

A few by-standers were at the far end. I headed their way to catch the buzz. "What'd I miss?" I asked these two metalheads in matching black Rükkus world tour Ts.

"Aw, man, you just missed it," the one goes.

The other looked at me and was like, "This old guy croaked. Took him away in an ambulance and everything."

"But didja see his daughter's tits?" the first asked the second. "Holy shit!"

"They were humongous!"

"Fuckin' humongous!"

"God*damn* fuckin' super-humongous!"

Old man and huge, young tits? On this lot, the only two who fit that description were Krass and Bunny. But what the hell happened? That's what I wanted to know.

"Didja see that dork's hat?" I heard the one headbanger say as I split for my car.

* * *

I drove around for a bunch of hours, smoking and thinking and polishing off a forty of Old Harlot.

My head was full of questions. But questions are cheap. It's the answers that cost you.

Two or three times, I passed the hospital. It was on the commercial strip outside of town. But I didn't go in.

I drove back to the carny, parking a few blocks away on a residential street and walking to the lot. At this time of night, the Riot was locked up tight. I poked around the outside of the fairgrounds looking for an in.

Razor wire was coiled around the top of the chain-link fence. But I found a spot where some juvenile delinquents had cut an opening at the bottom. Squeezing underneath, I caught my T-shirt and tore a hole in the sleeve.

I came out behind the Disco Dodge-Em bumper cars. The Riot was dark and quiet. Moonlight made the Ferris wheel, Zipper and Wild Mouse look like spook house skeletons.

I was creeping myself out pretty good as I slinked around, sticking to the shadows to avoid the rent-a-cops who patrolled the lot in between donut breaks.

I found Bunny's trailer. It was a silver Dyna-Flo, top-of-the-line. Shower, stove, toilet, waterbed -- the works.

"Oh, it's you," Bunny said when I walked in. Just like that -- like I'd never been gone. Like *I* was the one who placed the goddamn ad in the Call.

"Try not to look so happy," I said.

But that was Bunny for you.

You didn't know whether to kiss her lips or smack her mouth. Anything to shut it up. I had something she could stuff in it.

And that something was getting bigger by the second. She'd just stepped out of the shower. There weren't any clothes to get in the way of my eyes.

Yeah, everything was coming back to me now. Her tits were so big I could've fucked them from here. Nipples just begging to be sucked.

Sex parts jiggled as she towel-dried her hair and then twisted it into a turban on her head. She ran her fingers through her bush like a comb, fluffing the blonde curls.

162

She burned in my belly. The warmth spread out to my legs and hands. I was so hard I could've hammered nails through a two-by-four.

I knew what it was after. I wanted the same damn thing. The dick and I can always agree. We wanted to be rough and have our way with her.

She bent over to dry her feet. Her legs grew up into dimpled and chiseled asscheeks. High and tight, her butt pulled apart in a deep cleft.

"O.B.'s in the hospital," she said. "He had a heart attack." Her voice became a whisper: "I've been a bad girl."

"That's what I like about you."

"Not bad that way," she said. "I tried to kill him, Randy."

I was speechless. She kept talking. "I tried to screw him to death," she goes. "He's got that bad heart, you know. He takes nitroglycerin tablets for it. Well, I hid his tabs and then I came onto him. And I ain't the type to take no for an answer."

"Don't I know it."

"Christ, it was horrible screwing that old man. But tonight I almost got him. I was *this* close. His face turned white as a sheet and he started clutching his chest."

"Then what happened?"

"The dirty old man had a pill hid in his pinkie ring! Can you believe it? He keeps it there for emergencies. Like, how the hell was I supposed to know that?"

"So now he's in the hospital," I said.

"For now," she goes. "But not for long. O.B. don't trust hospitals."

"Why'd you do it, darlin'?"

163

"I guess I wasn't thinking straight," she said and hugged me tight. Her body was trembling so bad I could feel it through her cleavage.

It was times like this when I knew that she-devil routine was just a put-on and the real Bunny was nothing but a scared little girl who needed a guy like me to hold her hand and walk her through life.

She was like, "I think he's suspicious."

"I'll bet," I told her.

"I'm scared."

"You should be."

"I'm so glad you're back, Randy. You do all the thinking from now on. You're so smart and strong."

"I wanna be the man you want me to be."

"You are. You're the only one for me. I know that now."

Our mouths came together and we picked up right where we left off. I ran my tongue over her teeth and the inside of her mouth. She frenched me back.

She guided my hand between her legs. Her voice was husky, urgent: "Feel how much I need your cock. It's been too long."

Those lips didn't lie. There's only one thing in this world a man can trust -- a wet pussy.

She slipped down my body and opened my fly and that was that. There's no arguing with a woman whose mouth is on your dick. She's got you right where she wants you -- and vice versa.

She raised her eyebrows at my customized cock. "I ain't gonna ask," she goes.

"I ain't gonna tell you."

"Is it...permanent?"

"I dunno. Try licking it off."

Bunny ran her tongue up and down the length of my tattoo before sucking my cock good and long. Her pink tongue twirled around me like stripes down a barber pole.

When she stopped to take a breather, I turned her around. As I stripped, she got down on all fours on the floor.

She lowered her face and cheek to the pillow and lifted her ass high. The edge of the teddy slipped down her back. You could bounce a quarter off those buns.

"I am so ready for you," she gasped.

I stood up behind her and grabbed my shaft, guiding its head inside. It wasn't so easy, neither. She'd shrunk a few sizes since our last toss.

"Oh, Randy, you're killing me!" she cried. "Kill me! Murder me!"

I grabbed her hips as I angled my cock. If you wanna know the truth, no dame looks so good that she wouldn't look better with a cock in her cunt. And Bunny was no exception.

A woman without a hard-on in her is like a day without sunshine. A big fat dick is the missing piece. The finishing touch.

I pulled out and she maneuvered herself around. She lay back on the bed. My hands went for those boobs that could make headlines.

My fingers spiraled about the nipples. The areolas became taut halos. I lowered my mouth and took one between my lips. I sucked at one tit and pinched and squeezed the other until her legs were writhing.

Nosing around down there, my dick was destined to find her soaking snatch. I poked inside and worked the angles. *Hot damn*, that woman was the junk and the cure all at once.

"Do my titties," she growled as I sucked and tongued her nips. "Fuck my pussy." Her hot voice seethed in my ear as she clawed at my back. I thought she was drawing blood but I didn't care.

This was some reunion. I was fucking her in all the old, familiar places. Every stroke was its own reward.

But this was nothing. This was just for starters. We had all night to fuck each other's brains out.

She rolled away and stood up. I lay on the bed and freed my cock, ready for some righteous reciprocation. I swear, some days the only reason I get outta bed is to get back into bed.

She leaned over. Her tits hung over me. I inhaled the smell of fresh shampoo in her hair.

She took me in her hand and squeezed. Her fist fucked just the head. It was rough and dry. She broke a sweat. Her tits jiggled and swayed with her efforts. Then she reached over and pulled out the baby oil.

She poured on way too much. It slopped over my thighs and the sheets. She wrapped her hands around my member, coating every inch.

A hand-job might seem like a waste of a good woman. But not when you're in the hand of Bunny LaFever. That fist was as good as a cunt. Seriously.

She relaxed and tightened her grip. Relaxed and tightened, relaxed and tightened. It was like she was sculpting my hard-on. Shaping it with her squeezes and strokes.

"I love your dick," she cooed as she massaged my balls. "I mean, look at it. It's beautiful."

166

My cock and balls gleamed like a bowling trophy. She couldn't keep her hands off it. It scraped the ceiling. It poked through the clouds and bumped up against the moon.

At last she stopped jerking me and crawled up my body. Her slim torso slithered over me like a snake.

"Why don't we kill O.B.," she said as she nuzzled my chest. Her finger circled my nipple, leaving a trail of oil. "Why don't you finish him off?"

I laughed at that -- a good, long one. "I got a better idea. Why don't you finish *me* off?"

"I'm serious," she said, looking up at me to pout her swollen lips.

"Me, too."

"I mean it, Randy. Kill him."

I looked into her eyes, trying to read her mind. Suddenly I didn't know her anymore. She was a stranger to me and I'd never seen her before in my life.

"Kill him," she said again. It scared me how serious she was. I knew she meant it.

"Stop it, babe -- you're talking crazy."

"Kill my dirty, rotten husband for me. Oh, please -- *pretty please?*"

She pleaded just like when she was begging me to stick it to her from behind. I couldn't resist it then and it was damn hard to resist now.

"No," I said, "it's stupid."

"But he's rich. Imagine the score!"

"He's old, too. He'll be dead soon enough. Can't you wait?"

She was like, "Can you blame me for not wanting to wait for him to keel over? If we kill him now, it'll all be ours. Right now -- the whole show."

"I thought you hated the Life. Didn't you once tell me you wanted out?"

"I do! I did! But we'll sell it. All those joints and rides together." Her eyes widened to take in all the piles of money her greedy mind could imagine.

"All those joints and rides," I grumbled. "They add up to a whole lotta nothing when you're a lifer."

"Not a chance. Not if we do it right. We'll have enough money to do whatever we want. We can go anywhere -- we can do anything."

She rolled away and onto her side with her behind to me. I turned against her. My prick poked between her legs. She made a ring of her thumb and index finger and fucked just the head.

Her head turned to shoot me a smoky, bedroom gaze as she nudged my greasy cock against her slit. She lifted her leg for easier access and pushed me inside.

She gasped as I took over, driving my cock deep. She moaned, "It feels like you've been entering me forever."

We did it slow. Our bodies dropped into an excruciating rhythm. She thrust her hips away from me as I pulled out until the head was just inside. We held it there for a beat before coming together again.

"Save me from being his whore," she said. "I wanna be *your* whore. Yours and yours alone."

We read each other's body perfectly. It was second nature, as if we'd been screwing forever. I didn't even have to guide her with my hand on the smooth curve of her hip.

My cock was wired. I could blow my stack any second. We were barely moving. We didn't need to. She had that way of tensing up her cunt to squeeze my hard-on. I knew that pussy better than anybody. Better than my own hand, even.

"Kill him," she whispered as she tightened her grip on me. "Kill him so we can be together forever."

I must've been drunk off the impending orgasm. That's the only explanation. My defenses were down. I wasn't thinking straight. I would've promised her anything and everything.

I stick my neck out for nobody. But my dick -- that's a whole other bag o' donuts. "That bastard's a dead man," I said at last.

There was no other way to keep her. I was ready to lose everything over her. My money, my dignity, my freedom, all that shit.

I didn't care anymore. So long as I got what was coming to me. That sweet release.

"Oh, yeah," she said as she fucked me with just her cunt muscles. Her butt twitched as her sex kneaded my root. Its two dimples deepened just above her ass. "Tell me how dead he is."

"He is so fuckin' dead. He is so fuckin' dead."

I was surrounded. The tight walls closed around me. She was gonna make me explode just by squeezing me.

It couldn't have been more tight. I was locked inside. I couldn't pull out or push in, like one of those Chinese finger traps. I couldn't do anything but stand there and take it.

"Tell me what I wanna hear," she murmured.

My cock swelled even bigger with the build-up and made my hair stand on end. "He is dead, dead, *dead*."

169

"Cum in me, Randy. Cum deep inside me."

I erupted with a groan, full of relief and dread.

Afterwards, the smell of her damp muff hung in the trailer. Her tits rose and fell as she breathed. Still slick and chubby, my cock flopped back onto my belly.

I lit my cigarette off hers. We smoked Cactus unfiltereds. Fuck cancer.

Fuck *everything*.

* * *

Bunny and I planned to knock off O.B. Krass. Any square with his head on straight would've blown camp right then, but not my dumb ass. I wanted Bunny for keeps and I'd snuff anybody who got in my way.

She was what sex boiled down to. One hundred percent pure. A real shot in the arm. A genuine lift for the dick. The end-all, be-all drug -- upper, downer, and everything in between.

And me -- I was the addict who'd lost all sense of shame. I was the burnout on the street, the junky in the gutter, the loser in the sewer sleeping in his own piss. The jerk who'd sell his soul for his next fix of that girl.

When I pulled up in the Menace, she was already waiting for me on some street corner. Shrink-wrapped in a little red number with spaghetti straps. World's shortest dress -- she had to keep tugging it down over her ass.

Her blonde hair was piled up on top of her head. More paint than a circus wagon on that face. She looked like the kind of hooker you only see in the movies.

I was like, "That's your idea of inconspicuous?"

"I don't know what that word means."

"It means don't go out looking like that."

170

"What's wrong with it?"

"Not a damn thing -- that's the problem. Aw, hell," I said, revving the engine, "get in."

She bent over and looked into the passenger window. "I'm the one who's been here like half an hour. What's your rush all of a sudden?"

Even though we were three or four blocks away from the Riot, I was tense and nervous. I kept checking my mirrors to make sure I wasn't being tailed.

I clenched my teeth and spoke calmly. "If anybody tumbles we're together, we're fucked. Our alibis are shot and everything's over."

She rolled her eyes at me.

"I'm serious," I said. "Now I know a place we can go for secrecy. If you ever put your pretty ass on the seat here."

"You mean this pretty ass?" She spun around and peeled up her dress to flash a faceful of phenomenal fanny. She must've guessed I was annoyed and wanted to defuse the situation. But an ass like that was like throwing a match in a fireworks factory.

Her hot pink panties weren't much more than a shoelace that disappeared in the deep crack between those two humpworthy hemispheres. Cheeks like cling peaches in heavy syrup. She pulled them apart.

I wanted it so bad I could taste it. "Yeah, that pretty ass," I go. "Sit on it."

She knew there was no use arguing. She slid in and closed the door. I tore away from the curb.

* * *

I drove into this public park, parking near a picnic grove surrounded by pine trees. We got out of the Menace and laid

171

down in the grass away from the marks. Bunny picked these tiny yellow flowers and stuck them in her hair.

I smelled charcoal and lighter fluid. It was a good smell, and I wished I could be out there grilling weenies instead of planning to kill a man. But it wouldn't be long before the bad part was over and I'd be wearing Hawaiian shirts and hurrachee sandals with the best of them.

"Have O.B. and Peanut been talking about me?" I asked.

"Not anymore. They figured to let the Sons take care of you."

I smirked, remembering Shades and Pigtails. "I can take of myself," I said. "But that's good. I'm history, as far as anybody's concerned. Nobody would even think to connect me with this -- this thing that we're gonna do."

I couldn't even bring myself to say it out loud -- *murder*. But I didn't have to say it. All I had to do was pull the trigger and that would be the end of the whole thing. I'd lay low while she sold the carny and then we'd make off with a small fortune.

"Shit," I said, "I just felt a raindrop." Another hit my face. And then the sky opened up.

It was one of those crazy summer showers where the sun is still shining even as the rain is coming down. Everybody picked up their towels and blankets and scattered to escape the downpour. Most took refuge under the picnic grove.

Bunny squealed as we ran to the car and piled into the back seat. She straddled my lap facing me, draping her arms around my neck. Her dress was bunched up around her waist.

I was up to my ankles in empty beer cans and fast food wrappers. Her sweltering cunt pressed against me. It was like a radiator against my crotch.

172

That girl was born ready. The look on her face told me she wanted it right then and there but it was the wrong place and wrong time.

"C'mon, babe," I told her. "We gotta figure this out first."

"Fill in the holes, you mean?" she asked playfully. She looked great even with her hair plastered down, and runny eyeliner and mascara and all.

"That's right," I said, pretending like I didn't get her. When she saw I meant business, she made a boo-boo face but I kept on talking and she got over it. "I figure our best angle is to make this look like a robbery gone bad. You know, somebody shoots O.B. while heisting the dough."

She goes, "The Sons are making a big drop the night after tomorrow."

"Saturday."

"O.B.'s getting a room at the Fanta-C Motel."

"Sketchy motel, drug money, a homicide," I said. "Sounds perfect. With a line-up like that, you're just asking for it. What time do the Sons get there?"

"Midnight, supposedly. But they never show up on time. They won't get there before two or three, all lickered up."

"We could shoot O.B. and then let them find the body. Sic the cops on them and let the fuckers take the fall for it."

She shook her head. "Coroners can figure the time of death. It'd be better to pin it on some carny somehow."

"To make it look like an inside job," I said. "I like the way you think. With the Sons showing up and all, it'll just add to the confusion."

173

A shiver rippled through her body and she was like, "I suddenly realized that we're actually going to go through with this."

"You scared?"

"And excited."

"You know," I told her, "when you kill somebody, that changes everything."

"But we're different!"

"We'll see. I hope it won't come between us."

"Your dick is the only thing that'll come between us," she said as she undid my pants and finagled me free. "I promise."

I looked around. Rain ran down the steamed-up windows. Nobody was close enough to see us. I was like, "What's that you said about filling in the holes?"

I was up like the sun even before she pulled the crotch of her panties aside. I palmed each asscheek as she squirmed, rubbing my hummer against her clit. Our lips mashed together so frantically we forgot to breathe.

She leaned over me, planting her hands on my shoulders. She stared at me, biting her lower lip, as she positioned herself over my rigid upright. I thrust my shaft up as she lowered her body.

My cock slid in nice and greasy. A perfect fit. Like lock and key. I went deep. She took every inch of that invasion.

The prick expanded exponentially, filling up her hot-buttered snatch. I couldn't shove in any more if I tried. I felt her muscles grip me all around like a handshake. My root was sealed tight. She squeezed her thighs together to lift herself up and then relaxed them to impale herself on my pole.

174

"You have the best fucking cunt," I groaned, breaking our kiss.

"You have the best fucking cock."

We held each other tight and rocked back and forth. I rubbed the deepest reaches of her body. Journey to the center of a girl.

Her cleavage glistening with rain and sweat. I pressed my face between her breasts and sucked the water and salt. I took the top of her dress between my teeth and stretched it down over her tits. They were soft, like satin cushions. Her nipples were like thimbles.

She leaned back, placing her elbows on the back of the passenger seat to prop herself up. Planted on my pole, she rolled her hips in excruciating circles and thrust her pelvis back and forth. Her head tossed from side to side.

"Oooooo," she goes. Her eyelids fluttered. "Ooooooo, baby..."

I don't care how much pussy you've seen, the best cunt in the world is always the one that's right there in front of you. And hers really knew how to throw a party. It sucked my shaft in and grabbed me desperately, rhythmically squeezing my piece as I rammed it home again and again. My dick grew more sensitive with every plunge.

We were really steaming up the windows. Rain drilled the car roof. The windows were cracked open and droplets gathered along the frame, getting bigger and heavier and then finally falling off.

I heard respectable people talking outside, nearby.

"Somebody's coming," I said. Bunny kept on with it. "Baby, didja hear me? They're liable to call the cops."

"Fuck me," she said, biting her lower lip to exaggerate the F: "*Ffffffuck* me, killer."

"Slow down, honey." I tried to pull out from under her but she dug her nails in my back.

"If you don't fuck me, I'll cry rape -- I swear to God I will."

Her lip curled in that sneer of unbridled lust. The tip of her tongue ran across her white teeth. One tooth had a spot of lipstick on it.

Her body undulated, grinding her pelvis against me to draw me in and out of the wet warmth. I wasn't able to resist. I started bucking up while she thrust herself down.

She was like a machine gun when she came, humping like no tomorrow. I held on to her hips for dear life. She shook her head and those little flowers in her hair flew everywhere.

From head to toe she shuddered through powerful pussy paroxysms. I pressed my mouth against hers, smothering it to muffle her orgasm. She started to moan and was about to scream.

I stuffed my hand in her mouth to keep her quiet. She bit down hard enough to break the skin. I wanted to yell but held it in as blood trickled down the side of her mouth.

We pulled each other together tighter as her first orgasm subsided and another began to rise. She punched my back as each wave crested. Her dress was damp -- from sweat now, not rain.

Her body was climaxing all around me. It was too much for one man to take. The jig was up.

I felt my cock twitching, pumping its jizz deep into her body. When my throbs ebbed away, her cunt took over. Her powerful muscles squeezed the bottom drops out of my balls.

When I took my hand out of her mouth, the knuckles were scalloped with bloody teeth marks. Streaks of gore were smeared across her cheeks. She reclined backwards, letting me go soft inside her.

"Jeez, Randy," she goes, fitting her massive breasts back into her dress. "Sometimes you can be such a geek."

"That's it," I said, finally figuring it out.

"What'd I say?"

"Don't worry about it." She didn't need to worry her pretty little head about how I planned to pin the hit on some poor hapless carny.

* * *

A flattie spends half his life waiting -- for the perfect mark, the perfect opportunity. But this time, alone in my motel room, the waiting was the hardest part.

I was scared to kill a man for his money. But I was more scared not to. Fact of the matter is, when you got right down to it, I didn't give a damn about his money.

I wanted to be a big shot. For once in my life. Maybe I wanted that even more than Bunny LaFever -- to show the whole world that I was man enough to want something and get it.

But I didn't wanna dwell on it. I didn't wanna lose my nerve.

All I had to do was get through the next twenty-four hours. I hit the liquor hard. A bottle of Hell-Bent is as good as a time machine. It got me where I wanted to go -- Saturday night, eight o'clock.

* * *

Grease and potatoes is my sure cure for a bitch of a hangover.

177

I wolfed down a plate of home fries and bacon and eggs at a breakfast-anytime kinda joint, and then I made my way to the Laff Riot.

I wasn't worried about being recognized by anybody. I hadn't shaved in over a week and my beard was really filling in. A pair of sunglasses lifted from a convenience store, and I was practically invisible in the crowd.

I made my way to the back of the midway, stopping in front of the dope show. It was a walk-thru single-o housed inside a long trailer. Side panels opened up to make a show front.

Red lettering popped out of the white background:

SEE BUCKY REED

JUNKY! DOPER!! DRUG FIEND!!!

ONE TRIP TOO MANY! 100% ALIVE!

THIS EXHIBIT IS NOT ENTERTAINMENT

A tape recording barked out of the amplifier:

See the shocking truth of drug addiction and human degradation -- no expense has been spared to present this educational exhibit -- fathers bring your sons, mothers bring your daughters to see Bucky Reed -- junky, doper, drug fiend -- absolutely, positively one hundred percent alive....

Now a dope show ain't anything but the old geek routine dressed up for the war on drugs. Some stoner squats in a cage and bites the heads off of rubber chickens and snakes and what-not.

I handed my two dollars to this pregnant ticket seller who smelled like mothballs and went inside.

"Bucky Reed" lay in the corner of his cage, curled up in a ball in a pile of hay. He had a real cornball get-up -- a black fright wig and a shabby ape suit. There were gaping holes in the crotch and under the arms and at the elbows and knees.

Looking at the sorry-looking bastard, I ran through the murder in my head:

I was no longer a hustler on this lot. I was history, as far as anybody was concerned. Nobody would even think to connect me with this thing.

I'd disguise myself as Bucky Reed -- resident freak-show. After the show closed for the night, I'd blow O.B.'s head off with the .38, take the money bag, and leave that unmistakable ape suit as evidence.

I didn't feel too bad for Bucky. His life was nothing but wasted space. What did he care about prison for? Going to the Big House would just be switching one cage for another.

I reached between the rubber bars of the cage and poked him in the ribs till he came to. "Dude," he said groggily, blinking at me. His eyelids dripped black eyeliner like Alice Cooper.

"Take a powder," I told him.

"Huh?"

"Take a hike," I said, craning my neck to show him the way. "Am-scray. Get outta here."

"I don't get it."

"You get this?" I asked, waving a tab of acid.

"Sure, like, whatever, man." He squeezed through the bars and took the LSD.

"Leave the monkey suit," I said. He started stripping. "And the wig."

"What wig?"

"Never mind. Just leave the suit."

The tell-tale suit was the only thing I really cared about. Left behind at the scene of the crime, it was as good as Bucky's fingerprint.

That acid I pawned off on him was ten times your average dosage, too. Bucky'd be so blitzed when they nabbed him that he wouldn't be able to say who he was or where he'd been. Hell, he'd probably cop to the hit he'd be wiggin' so bad.

* * *

In that gorilla suit and ugly hat, I looked like hell. Smelled even worse -- this rancid combo of pot smoke, cheap beer and piss. But I couldn't get more incognito.

I laid low in the single-o, stalling for time. I even gave the marks their money's worth by jumping around and screaming and pawing at the nubile teenage girls through the rubber bars. I kinda liked that last bit about the nubile girls.

At eleven o'clock, I squeezed through the rubber bars and slipped out of the joint's side exit.

* * *

I was halfway to the Fanta-C Motel when the red lights of a state police car started flashing in my rear-view mirror. I figured it was my out-of-state plates. They're magnets for a trooper with a hard-on for transients and a ticket quota to make.

I pulled over to the unpaved shoulder. I cursed and drummed my fingers on the open window as I watched the cop approach in my side mirror.

To my surprise, it was a girl deputy. She gave new meaning to the words "arresting officer." I couldn't keep my eyes off her.

She made the uniform look good as she fleshed it out with more T-n-A than even stretch-polyester could contain.

180

Khaki clung to her every curve, and she had more than a mountain highway.

The top three buttons of her shirt were undone, no match for the glandular globes that overcrowded the crisp fabric. Giant breasts swelled beneath the skin-tight uniform. Lifted up and out, they made enough sweaty cleavage to put the Rockies to shame.

Her utility belt rode low on that slender waist. Her fingers just touched the butt of the big service revolver holstered on her hip. She was all police business.

"Is there a problem, Deputy Klench?" I asked, squinting to read the name off the golden badge pinned to her chest. *Elsa Klench*, it said. I tried to glimpse the beautiful face under the wide hat brim.

"I been on your ass so close I could've wiped it for you."

I gave a friendly smile. "You must have me confused with somebody else."

Her nostrils flared as she sniffed me. My ape suit reeked of pot and brew. "Step outta the car," she goes. Little blue icicles hung from her words.

She led me to the hood of the Menace where I assumed the all-too-familiar position. With my hands on the trunk and legs spread apart, she frisked me top to bottom.

My balls shrank up and away out of habit. Experience taught me that John Law could be a real nutcracker. Jane Law, though, liked what she found. On the second pass her fingers lingered at my bloating bulge.

"You carrying?" she asked. She'd found my piece all right, a fully loaded, double ball-barreled ladykiller.

"No, ma'am," I gulped. The long arm of the law was between my legs, fondling the length of my hardening cock.

She was like, "What's the big idea?" as she measured my pachydermic package with her fingers. Her voice was a hot hiss. "You some kinda pervert or something?"

"No, ma'am." Meanwhile she kept on carrying on with the offending anatomical wonder. The copper was copping a feel. Her fingers stroked and kneaded the inflated flesh until my ramrod was righteously rigid. I'd been pinched before, but never like this.

"What's with the monkey suit?" she asked. Before I could lie, she said, "It ain't Halloween. So you must be with the carnival. Ain't that right?"

"No, ma'am."

"You got the look of the gypsy about you. You been hustling tonight?"

"No, ma'am. Just trying to get where I'm going."

Before I knew it she had the bracelets locked on my wrists. She pressed down on my neck the way you do to an ornery junkyard mutt to break his spirit and show him who's who. My cheek slammed against the trunk.

"I know all about you carnies. You got sawdust in your shoes and larceny in your eyes."

She leaned into my back, and I felt the full weight of her overblown bosom molding their meaty selves to my shoulder.

"You think you can do what you want for free, scofflaw?" she whispered in my ear. Hatred dripped from every word.

I was thinking, this is when she asks for the payoff. Cuz everybody's on the take, I don't care who you are -- and that goes double for the law. Deputy Klench was asking for it all right. But not for the wad I thought.

182

She wrapped her left leg around my own, rubbing her crotch against my hip and purring deep in her throat. She straddled my cuffed hands and, with rhythmic pelvic thrusts, began to grind her snatch back and forth over my fingers and knuckles. The steam heat of arousal soaked her tight pants.

Suddenly she locked her arm around my neck and jerked me back. Simultaneously she kicked the back of my knee. My leg buckled and I dropped to my ass in a cloud of dust.

Laughing at me, she scootched her butt onto the hood of the car and spread 'em. She reached into her crotch and ripped. A panel of polyester tore away with ease. It'd been fastened with Velcro.

She wasn't wearing panties. From her pussy to the crack of her ass, her privates were public. She raised her legs high and wide. Those gorgeous gams went on like a two-lane highway. I saw the end of the road, dead center.

With some difficulty I got to my feet.

She unbuttoned her shirt to her waist. Popped from their polyester prison, her breasts ballooned to an even greater size. She pinched her erect nipples through the black satiny bra.

She removed her severe hat and out spilled a shower of impossibly long, lustrous blonde hair. Her eyebrows were severe black pencil lines. She beckoned with her finger.

"A badass like you is good for only one thing," she growled: "A long, hard fuck."

I shuffled toward her. She seized my belt and pulled me against her naked crotch. Her fingers flew over my fly, and then she finessed me out of my pants.

Around her waist hung her big gun. It was a black steel service revolver. I wasn't gonna try anything funny -- just something funky.

My pistol was drawn and cocked. A bead of pre-cum graced its tip. Staring down the long barrel of that gun, she instantly gave up. She held her thighs in place with the bend in her arms.

The car's hood was at the perfect height as my shaft easily slipped across the threshold. I piled inside, inch by glorious inch. She gasped and grimaced as her pussy surrendered to my gargantuan girth.

When I was completely in the custody of her cunt, I started with the ol' in-and-out. She had that lusty itch, and I ground and rolled my pelvis to scratch it from every obscene angle. Her twat was tied good and tight around my turgid tool.

"Faster," she ordered. "Fuck me faster!"

Upstanding, law-abiding citizen that I am, I obeyed.

"Harder, gypsy!" she barked. "Fuck me *harder*!"

I really put the slapstick to her. It's hard as hell to fuck a woman with your hands cuffed behind your back but I managed to drill her silly. We collided with the sticky smack of sweaty flesh.

My balls bounced off her ass as I drove deep. Her cheeks slapped against the hood. Her black brassiere galloped about like a suspension bridge in a hurricane. Turbulent titflesh threatened to spill out of those steel-reinforced D-cups.

She was one giant, shuddering cunt. I wished I could pour my whole body into her. And wrap that naked flesh around me like a big beaver coat.

"My ass," she gasped. I pulled out. My tool was greased enough to get the job done and done right.

Her arms were still in place around her legs. Fingernails dug into her milky white thighs. She pulled her legs higher

184

and closer to her body until her knees were on either side of her face and resting on the hood of the Chevy.

She dug her fingers into her cheeks and pulled them apart. I went in the hard way. Muscles gradually loosened their grip to take every inch.

The bozo who said sex is all in the head never had all of his dick up her wazoo. What's there to think about? I'm a man of action. So I acted, upping the tempo of my steely strokes.

Yippee-ki-yay and rooty-toot-toot! The slut couldn't get enough. I couldn't give enough. No matter how hard I tried.

Her back arched sharply as her screaming ecstasy cut across the middle of nowhere. Her tight, muscular stomach undulated with the waves of orgasm. She looked like a flag waving on the end of my pole.

I couldn't hold back any longer. With a grunt I gunned her down point-blank: bang bang bangity bang bang! until my chamber was spent.

When I pulled out my copper stopper, the bitch looked me up and down and said, "Looks like I'm gonna have to run you in."

"What for?"

"Sodomy's against the law in Tuscarora County."

What a set-up! But it was no use arguing. Cops don't hear anything they don't wanna hear. Believe me, I know.

* * *

Getting pinched is like getting crushed by the Ferris wheel if it takes a tumble off its cinder blocks. It's just another job hazard. You don't dwell on it. But if it happens, you deal.

185

I lay there on a lumpy mattress in a dark cell, worrying about Bunny standing there by the front gate not knowing where I was.

Would she be mad? Scared? You got me. I didn't even know what the hell I'd tell her when I got outta here.

But between now and then, all I could do was sleep off my piss-poor luck like a hangover.

Next thing I know, Klench was yowling: "Wake up, carnival boy!"

My eyes snapped open. I gasped out loud. That low-down, hyped-up hellcat was crouched above my head. She was down to her black vinyl bra, black vinyl crotchless panties and freshly polished black Gestapo boots. She was like licorice.

"I'm gonna straighten you out with some cruel and unusual punishment!"

Her naked crotch hung over me like the proverbial Sword of Damocles. Only it wasn't long and sharp but flaming red and raggedy like something out of a bad drive-in monster movie.

My hands instinctively tried to protect my face. But I couldn't move them. They were cuffed to the bed. I was helpless. I stared into that cunt. That cunt stared into me.

"Don't give me none of your lip, boy," she snarled. "Unless you want some of mine..."

She squatted down, lowering her big blonde pussy onto my face. She began thrusting her snatch back and forth, getting her sloppy wet petals and wiry curls all over me.

Suddenly she sat down on my face. She made her body go like lead. She settled in, adjusting her weight. Her bottom half fit my face like an iron mask.

186

This was pussy punishment to the nth degree. Naked flesh molded itself to my head. My nostrils were sealed. Mouth smothered. No room to breathe.

I was pinned under a penitentiary of puss. It was as dark as the grave. That cruel cunt had killed men before. And now the angel of death was knocking at my door. Panic set in. I started kicking for my life.

The face-sitting freak dismounted. I tried to scream but nothing came out. I finally caught my breath and wailed. "*Help meeeeee!*"

"*Aaaagggggghhhh!*" she yelled, drowning out my pathetic plea. "Go ahead and scream! Scream all you want! Nobody can hear you in here!"

My chest heaved as I sucked down great searing lungfuls of air. So close to death, I never felt more alive in my life. Every nerve was on fire.

She piled off me and stepped out of view. When she came back, she two fisted a dangerous-looking dildo -- shiny black and shaped like a monster cock. She stood above me and fellated its ten long inches. Her pink tongue flickering over the veins and nodules.

She raised one leg and planted her heel in my stomach, grinding it in place. She aimed the dildo at her crotch and inserted just its head. She rotated it to touch every delicious nerve.

She licked her lips. Her eyes gleamed wickedly. She clutched the dildo by its base and slowly eased it up.

She pulled it out to the tip. Immediately she drove the shaft in to the hilt again. Fingers fluttered over her clit as she screwed her hole faster and faster.

"Don't you just wish this was your cock, geek?" she demanded, staring me down. She drove her eyes like nails into my brain. Her heel dug into my gut. The pain became searing pleasure. "Suffer!" she cackled, mocking me. "Your cock isn't good enough for my pussy. But I'll let you lick my boot!"

She stomped her boot beside my head. I turned my head to face it.

"Lick it, dammit, or I'll crush your throat!"

I stretched out my tongue and tasted leather and polish. She groaned like I was tonguing her naked flesh.

"You lick good for a no-count geek. Let's see what you can do with this --" She shoved the dildo in my face. "Clean it good, carnival boy."

It was slick with her juices. My tongue traced the veins and ran over the nodules. I tasted her pussy.

"Looks like you've sucked dick before, geek! Have you been bu-fu'd, too?"

She pushed the dildo against my butt. My asshole locked up tight as a bank vault at four o'clock. I kicked her arm away.

"What kind of fiend are you!?" I hissed. "What do you want? I'll do anything! Anything but that!"

I begged, I pleaded, I cried uncle till I was blue in the face. And then I got a hold of myself, and started talking trash. If I was gonna go, I was gonna go with a shred of dignity.

"You loathsome, lowly geek!" she yelled. "Look at you squirming like a worm! I oughta squash you now and put you outta your misery! But then that wouldn't be any fun, would it?"

She straddled me on her hands and knees. Her cheek was pressed against my belly, her gaping sex mere inches from my face.

188

She reached between her legs and, with two fingers, spread her swollen lips. She picked up the phony phallus and bullseye'd it with a gasp.

"Fuck me," she ordered.

"How? You got my goddamn hands cuffed."

"Use your head, geekboy," she said. "Use your mouth!"

I lifted my head and grabbed the end of the dildo between my lips and got a good grip on it. Clenching it between my teeth, I began to thrust it in and out by moving my head.

Her body writhed and undulated out of control as I gave her the nastiest workout. I could feel my brain sloshing back and forth in my skull as I started headbanging faster.

Drool ran from the corners of my mouth. Snot flew from my nose. I felt like a dirty animal. I didn't let up even when she started to cum.

Her powerful cunt ripped the dildo out of my mouth. My head fell back, limp. In a daze I saw the dildo still planted in the clutches of her pussy. The end wiggled at me as spasms rocked her world.

"Lemme outta here, bitch," I groaned. "I done my time."

"There's only one way outta this jail," she cackled deviously. She turned around and straddled my face between her legs. "Eat your way out!"

Before I could take the law into my own hands, I had to take the law into my own mouth. I planted my face in her overheated puss. My tongue unfurled and then fluttered up and down her juicy crease.

Her aroused clitty rose out of its pink hood. I sucked it between my lips and pulled. It was a sucker move in more ways than one.

That's when Klench locked her powerful legs around my head. They were so long she could've wrapped them around me twice. I was crushed between the vicious vise of her thighs. She had me right where she wanted me. I'd fallen headlong for her iron trap.

"You break the law," she laughed cruelly, "the law breaks you!"

Those rock hard muscles flexed and churned, chopping my good looks into raw hamburger. My face felt like it was smeared on the inside of her thighs. The rhythmic pull of her muscles drew me deeper still into her smothering cunt. She wouldn't be satisfied till my whole head was holed up in her hooch.

"Whatsamatter, carnival boy -- cat got your tongue?"

She squeezed her scissors hold tighter and tighter until I thought my head would bust like a water balloon. But despite my tenderized face and the tangy juices that burned my eyes, I knew better than to stop quaffing that quiff.

"Eat my cunt, you dirty criminal! Eat it out good, you dumb sonofabitch!"

She was a gusher. Her sex oil tasted sharp as brass as it flooded my mouth, then ran down the crack of her ass. I followed its trail, licking lower. I tongued the sensitive patch of skin between her cunt and her asshole until she squirmed.

I traveled upward again to concentrate on her clit. I sucked the hard ball of nerves into my mouth and rolled it back and forth with the tip of my tongue. My nose burrowed in her carpet of curls as she pulled me deeper into her lunch box.

Her moans and groans grew louder and longer as she careened toward orgasm. "Lick it, geek boy! Lick it, lick it, lick it!" She was suddenly still, her body tight like a drawn bow.

190

Her muscles snapped. Her body bucked and writhed. But she kept her leglock tight, whipping me back and forth in her hurly burly bush.

That sadistic sexecutioner came so powerfully she stretched and twisted my neck between her thunder thighs until I thought she'd rip my head clear off. Her suffocating sleeper hold squeezed tighter. My limbs grew heavier and heavier.

"Dead man fucking!" she shrieked. "Dead man fucking!"

I couldn't breathe. I couldn't feel my arms or legs. I was nothing but a rag doll. Passing out, I saw silent pops of light and knew they were brain cells dying like stars. And then it was lights out for me.

* * *

I woke up in the back seat of the Menace. My head was pounding like the morning after but it was still dark out. It was a miracle I got out alive.

I couldn't move a muscle for the longest time. I checked my wallet, knowing that I'd find it empty. Elsa had kicked my ass and made me pay for the privilege. A thousand scoots gone.

The only thing she left me was my ape suit. Which I was still wearing.

"Bunny!" I cried, remembering everything. I crawled into the front seat and cut out for the motel. The dashboard clock said 3:46 AM.

* * *

Bunny sat shivering on the cement stoop outside the motel office.

She was wearing her gray sweatjacket with the hood pulled up and the zipper zipped to the neck. Her hands were

191

stuffed in the front pocket and she had the jacket tugged down over her knees.

Something was seriously wrong. When she turned to look at me, I saw that she had the beginning of a black eye.

"What the hell happened?" I go.

She burst into tears. "Where were you, Randy?! They raped me! They raped me!"

"Who?"

"Th-th-the Sons of S-S-Satan!"

"You said they were always late!"

"He just sat and watched them do it!" she sobbed.

I was like, "O.B.?" She nodded. "Which room is he in?" I said.

"F-f-forty-t-t-two."

"The Sons still around?"

She shook her head, looking up at me with her liquid blue eyes like I was God. And damn if I wasn't gonna exact some Old Testament revenge. I reached under the front seat of the Menace and pulled out the .38.

I wasn't thinking about getting away with murder. I wasn't thinking, period. All that went out the window with my sanity.

I didn't care about anything but killing that dirty sum-bitch.

I bounded up the iron steps first, Bunny following. She unlocked the door to their room. I eased it open.

The first thing I saw was a styrofoam head on the dresser. It was wearing O.B.'s ratty black wig and eyebrows. It looked like a shrine to roadkill. Beside it were his choppers in a glass of water.

192

O.B. was asleep in his wheelchair, withered and pale with a few long, wiry hairs sticking out of his head. He was in his plaid pajamas with a crocheted afghan across his lap, hooked up to an oxygen tank with tubes dangling from his nostrils. A line of drool hung from the corner of his mouth.

His chair faced the bed. The bare mattress was full of stains and cigarette burns. I could only imagine what had taken place hours before.

I pointed the revolver's business end at his head and cocked it. That sound of death cuts through even the deepest sleeps.

O.B.'s eyes widened as he looked at me and the barrel inches away from his face. I wanted him to know what was coming. I figured it'd be more horrible that way.

"Pull a gun on me, boy," he croaked, "you goddamn better pull the trigger."

The poor bastard thought I wouldn't go through with it. That was the last thing that went through his head. Except for the bullet, I mean.

* * *

Life changes just like that.

One second I was a carny grifter and the next I was a cold-blooded killer and it was too late to ever go back.

The power of the .38 had blown back the wheelchair, knocking it over. O.B.'s legs were in the air, still twitching. Where his head used to be, a gruesome geyser of gore spurted with every heartbeat.

The bullet had gone straight through and took out the TV on the other side.

On the bureau, untouched by the violence, was a Kooky-Kola bottle. But it wasn't filled with pop. It was stretched out and filled with layers of sand dyed in rainbow colors: red, yellow, pink, blue, green, purple and orange.

My ears were still ringing from the blast when I heard the toilet flush. Peanut stepped out of the bathroom, still zipping up his tight tan colored slacks. Crisp perma-press creases ran down each leg, and the flares just grazed the tips of his white loafers.

"Holy fuck," he goes. His voice was calm and oily.

I was like, "You didn't wash your hands."

"What the fuck've you done?"

"Sorry, man," I said, gesticulating at the dead TV set, "were you watching that?"

"Randy," Bunny said, quietly but sternly, "Give me the gun."

I handed it over without thinking. I touched this wet spot on my cheek and my fingertip came away bloody.

* * *

Seconds later, I was sober. And with a real bad feeling about all of this. I was like, "Uh, can I get that gun back, darlin'?"

"Let me think about it," she said. She screwed up her mouth as she considered it for a few seconds. "Hmmm -- *no.*"

She leveled it at my head. I was getting the picture now. I should've seen it coming a mile away.

"I smell a dirty frame," I said.

"And you didn't believe me when I told you he was a bright boy," she said to Peanut.

I looked from one to the other, tumbling to their set-up. I felt more used than a payphone in the bad part of town. "So I guess you two are an item."

Peanut shook his head sadly. "Christ, boy -- how can you live so long and be so dumb?"

"I'm kinda wondering that myself."

"You know what they say about geeks, boy," he said. "You don't find 'em -- you make 'em. Take a good look at yourself."

My eyes drifted down to myself dressed in that skunky ape suit and I felt like the biggest 'tard in the world.

"She geeked you, boy!" he cackled. "My baby doll geeked you good!"

This was a bad jam they had me in. But there's a way out of everything if you figure the angles right.

I had to come up with something. I thought so hard it was like this old rusty railroad spike of pain driving straight through my brain. "A-ha!" I said at last.

"I think el genius figured something else out," Peanut goes.

"Didja know she's got circus blood in her?" I asked him.

Peanut's jaw dropped. That apeshit wasn't laughing anymore.

"That's a lie!" she cried. She stood there with her feet planted firmly, her legs spread as she pointed the gun at me. "Don't listen to him!" she begged Peanut. But it was too late. Curiosity and fear and distrust were eating away at his head.

"Baby, is it true?" Peanut goes. There was a tremor in his voice.

"Of course it ain't true!" she cried. "Can't you see what he's doing, you moron? I am surrounded by fucking amateurs!"

She rolled her eyes in frustration, taking them off me. It was only for a second. But to me a second was as good as an hour.

I chanced it, diving for the .38. The explosion blew past me, blinding my eyes and nearly blowing out my ear drums. But I had my hands on its hot barrel.

We fought for it on the floor, our bodies twisting and writhing. Peanut was kicking me in the sides. I yowled in pain as Bunny tried to tear the gun away.

Pure animal instincts kicked in, and I grabbed hold of it for dear life and when it went off again the barrel was pointed straight up at the ceiling. The shot killed the light, dousing the room in darkness and raining glass. Bits cut into my back and up and down my arms.

Bunny screamed as I finally wrenched it from her hand and staggered over to the bathroom door. It was open. The light from inside made a sharp-angled patch across the floor.

"Don't make me kill the both of you," I said, wildly aiming it at first one and then the other and then back again. My shoes crunched on the broken glass. I went from wanting to puke my guts to wanting to spill theirs.

Peanut put up his hands in surrender. Bunny put her hands on her hips. "You won't shoot me," she cracked.

"I'd rather see you dead than with another man."

"Now, now," Peanut said with a weak smile, "let's not get ugly."

"It's already ugly," I said. "For your sake, let's just hope it don't get any uglier."

"Surely we can put our heads together and come up with something. What with sixteen ounces of crank and all."

My brain screeched to a halt. "How much?" I asked.

"Sixteen," he said. "One-six."

My mind started calculating. If I was up on my math, the street value of sixteen ounces of crank was sixty thousand white trash dollars, give or take.

"Where is it?" I go.

"Behind you," he said.

"Oh, that's cute. *Behind you.*"

"I'm serious. On the bureau."

"Sand art's on the bureau, asshole."

"That ain't sand, my friend. That's Satanic crank. The number one name in quality and value."

"You're shitting me."

"I never shit a man with a gun."

"Think about it," said Bunny. "We can split it three ways --"

"And we can forget all of this ever happened," Peanut finished.

"Forgive and forget?" I chuckled. "Fuck that. How 'bout if I take *all* the shit, and you lovebirds go to hell?"

"Don't be dumb all your life," he said. "The Sons'll come after you."

"Me and the Sons got an understanding now."

Greed got a hard-on. That shit was my ticket outta this craphole and every one like it. It was just like that bastard my daddy said: *No man is poor who's got money!*

"You're crazy!" Bunny goes.

197

"Crazy about you," I snarled back.

"You'll never get away with this," she goes. "I swear *I'll* come after you if I have to."

"I'll save you the trouble then."

"What do you mean?"

"I mean you're coming with me."

"What about me?" Peanut goes.

"What about you," I said.

"What're you gonna do to me?"

"Good question," I answered. "Guess I'll tie you up and let the cleaning lady find you with O.B. here. Turn around, ace." He did as he was told. "Got any rope or anything around here?" I asked Bunny.

She shook her head no, so I brained him with the butt of the gun. His body slumped to the floor with a heavy thud. I nudged him in the ribs with my toe but he was out of it.

Suddenly Bunny started acting like a different woman. "God, Randy!" she gushed, "That was so brilliant the way you played that! Didn't I do good, too -- pretending to be Peanut's lover and all?"

She smiled her best stripper's smile. You know, the kind she'd learned early on and didn't mean a goddamn thing.

"Shut up, Bunny," I snapped.

I couldn't stand hearing any more of her lies. Fooled once, you're no fool. But fooled twice, you're a *damn* fool.

* * *

PART THREE: LADIES LOVE OUTLAWS

I stopped at this spiffy new Gas-Up outside of De Kalb, a thousand miles away from the mess I'd made in Tuscarora County.

A haze of moths and mosquitoes swarmed around the flood lights that had the joint lit up like a football stadium. The Gas-Up was the most exciting thing to hit town since a twister took out the Wishy Washy laundromat in '78. All the kids were there, smoking butts and drinking warm beer and necking behind the dumpster.

I bought a Gas Guzzler of soda pop. 42 oz. of Diet Whatever. Outside, I pulverized a bunch of Quaaludes on the hood of the Menace and brushed the powder into the pop and then swished it all around. A car was parked on the other side of the lot, doors flung open, stereo pumping.

There comes a point when you stop asking yourself why you're doing what you're doing. Cuz you wouldn't have an answer anyway. You just have to see it through to the end, and maybe then you'll know.

* * *

I drove back to my room at the De Kalb Motel. A Do Not Disturb sign hung on the knob. I could hear the cranked

TV through the door. I cracked it open just enough to slip inside.

The only light came from the flickering TV. Blue shadows bounced off the walls. It took a minute for my eyes to adjust, but then I could see Bunny right where I'd left her.

She was hog-tied on the bed with nylon rope and bungee cords and whatever else I could lay my hands on. Duct tape bound her hands and wrists. Across her mouth were a couple strips to keep her quiet.

She heard me come in. Her nostrils flared as she twisted and rocked, testing the restraints that criss-crossed her body and pressed into her flesh.

She was scheming, plotting against me. I could see it in that burning glare of hatred. If she had a gun, she'd kill me.

I muted the television with the remote that was bolted to the nightstand. Then I had a shower and a shave and came back out wrapped in a towel.

I looked at her lying there on her stomach, helpless and pathetic. The ropes bit into her skin. She craned her neck to keep me in sight.

"Okay," I said, ripping the duct tape off her mouth, "tell me what a nice guy I am."

"That hurt, you bastard," she goes through clenched teeth.

"Poor baby."

She made a face, sticking out her tongue.

I was like, "You wanna drink or not?"

I raised the Gas Guzzler to her mouth. She took the straw between her lips and sucked. She stopped and glared at me, suspicious.

I stared back, wondering if she could taste the Quaaludes.

"Is this diet?" she goes.

"Sure it's diet."

"This isn't diet."

"You asked for diet, I got you diet."

"Taste it."

"I don't need to taste it. It's diet."

"It's not."

"Fine, whatever you say. But it's all you're getting so if you wanna dehydrate to death go right ahead."

She wasn't too happy about it but she sucked it down greedily.

"You can't keep me tied up forever," she said when she finished off half the cup.

"Why can't I?"

"Cuz you're stupid and you'll fuck up and then I'll make you pay for this."

"It's funny," I said, "but when I first met you, I used to like how you were always so sure of yourself. But now it just pisses me off."

"Oh, puh-leeze. You just can't stand it cuz I'm smarter than you."

"Who's got who tied up here, darlin'?"

"You got lucky, is all. But you've shot your load."

"Plenty more where that came from. Don't you worry."

"You'll need it to unload that crank."

"Don't need luck for that --"

"That's a laugh. Whadda you know about unloading speed?"

"I know some people."

"Oh, *some people*. These *people* got a name, bright boy?"

"If you don't talk nice I'll tape your mouth again."

"Fuck off, you rube. This ain't the carny. This is the big-time and you are so out of your league it ain't even funny."

The fact is, she was right. I didn't know anybody who could take the crank off my hands. The only fences I knew were in the carny, and I had to lay off that scene for a while.

Bunny sensed my predicament. She goes, "Sixty large is a big score to you, ain't it?"

"Ain't it?"

"Not to me it ain't. You're fucking pathetic. I actually feel sorry for you and *I'm* the one that's tied up."

Okay, that was it. Enough was enough. She knew she'd crossed that line, too. She saw it in my eyes.

"What're you doing?" she shrieked, suddenly scared, seconds before I grabbed at her.

"What I should've done a long time ago!"

She started to scream and roll around. I jumped on her and went for her panties. My hands grabbed the elastic waist and yanked so hard and fast I heard threads snare. I tugged them down to her thighs.

"Don't you touch me!" she hollered. "*Rape!* Bloody *murder!*"

"You wanna know who's boss, I'll show you who's boss!"

I scooped her up in my arms. Kicking and screaming, she was like a wild animal trying to make an out for itself. She could squirm all she wanted, but she was trapped.

"You play with me," I said, "you're playing with The Man!"

She fought me as I turned her over, screaming. "I'll kill you for this! I swear to God I will!"

I sat in the chair and laid her across my lap so her bare booty was up. I cupped my left hand and raised it high, holding it there. We both held our breaths in suspense.

Time stopped for a beat. And then, with righteous fury, I swung my palm against her trembling butt. A sharp clap rang in the corners of the quiet motel room.

I lifted my hand. Its mottled pink impression spread across her smooth white skin. Her reaction was delayed by the sheer shock of it.

"A-*how!*" she finally cried out in pain.

I raised my hand and let it crash against her naughty behind. The cheek was so firm it made a solid slap. How many times had I squeezed and pinched and otherwise manhandled that amazing ass of hers when all along what she really needed was a good spanking.

"You've been a bad girl, Bunny. A very bad little girl. And now you're gonna see what happens to bad little girls. You're gonna get yours."

I slapped her ass again and again. She cried out with each sting. The flesh jiggled with each impact.

My palm went numb but I didn't let up. Hell, no! That only made me whoop her butt harder. I alternated, slapping one cheek and then the other, to get them both good and red.

You've got to break a she-devil like Bunny. There's no other way to fix a conniving, double-crossing, back-stabbing bitch like that. For her own good, you've got to break her will and smash her spirit.

Each successive blow was another chip in the wall. I was going to knock her down and then build her up again. Start all over again, from scratch. Make a new woman out of her.

Before I was finished, her butt was beet red. Tears ran down her cheeks. My arm was aching and shaking. Her behind was burning from all the abuse.

And that's when I noticed the change in her. She'd stopped squirming. I'd spanked all the fight out of her.

But it wasn't sheer exhaustion that made her quiet. It was arousal. Her cries had become quiet gasps. I slipped a finger between her legs. She was soaking wet.

Unbelievable. She was actually turned on by this sadistic spankjob. I started in again, harder now, with less time in between slaps.

"This is gonna hurt me more than it hurts you!" I yelled.

That was the goddamn truth, too. All I was doing was spanking her behind but that bitch broke my heart and then shit all over it like it was nothing but something to shit on. Everything she'd ever said or done to me was a big fat lie.

She made me love her and want to kill for her and in the end it was nothing but a set-up that any rube would've seen from a mile away.

"This is for my mouth --" *Slap*!

"This is for my dick --" *Whap*!

"This is for my heart --" *Spank*!

"This is for my head --" *Swat*!

My hand was like an industrial machine, smacking her flesh over and over again, crashing against her buttocks. My

204

head began to spin in the monotony of it all. I was drunk off of it. I was a crazy person. Single-minded. Possessed by revenge. The room faded away until it was just my hand swatting those solid cheeks.

Her pussy came alive the more her throbbing butt went numb. Bunny had it coming all right. An orgasm, that is.

Her body stiffened in my arms as the burning consumed her soul. She writhed as agony spilled over into ecstasy. Bawling and shrieking mixed up in the frenzy of her flesh.

She came with one of her famous endless orgasms. The kind that kept her body pitching and bucking until she'd turned herself inside-out practically. By the time the waves subsided, she was beat.

She didn't know what hit her. A ton of bricks or an anvil or a piano. She didn't know anything -- her name or my name or which side was up, even.

Part of me wished I could be there with her. I slumped back on the bed with Bunny breathing hard on top of me. She was like dead weight once the 'ludes kicked in.

My heart was racing. My ears were filled with the roar of rushing blood. I was drenched in sweat. Right about now, that kidney-shaped swimming pool outside was looking pretty good.

* * *

I stripped down to my bare ass and let my toes curl over the edge of the empty, unlit pool. Still hard from the spanking, my cock jutted out over the black water. Moonlight dappled the little waves.

I cannonballed into the deep end. I stayed at the bottom for the longest time, letting the heated water surround me. It was as dark and quiet as the grave down there. I could pretend I was dead.

205

Finally I came up for air and shook out my hair.

"C'mere, baby," this voice goes, taking me by surprise. It was a woman's -- black. "I wanna make sure my eyes weren't playing tricks on me."

I looked at the other end of the pool and there she was with her cornrow braids and beads. Her back was against the side of the pool. She was almost invisible in the dark water but now I recognized her.

She'd been behind the desk when I checked in that afternoon, putting the afro in aphrodisiac:

I walk in the door and she's bent over in the shortest shorts possible and showing off what's on the menu. She stands up, black and stacked with a pair of tits that'd drive you crazy if you looked at 'em too long. She eats potato chips one after the other, picking them out of the bag between her long, lacquered fingernails.

I swam her way. Where she was, it was shallow enough to stand. She reached out underwater and grabbed my dick.

"Sho'nuff," she laughed. "It's all that."

"And if your fingers keep doing what they're doing, it ain't gonna be worth a damn to anybody."

"Then cut to the money, baby. Cut to the money."

I palmed her asscheek, expecting to get a handful of spandex. Instead I got a lot of skin. This lewd Nubian was totally nude.

I felt the flutter of one of the circulation jets gushing water back into the pool. She was standing there letting the powerful pump prime her pussy. I reached between her legs and felt her up.

"I can see you got yourself taken care of," I said. Next to her steamy cunt, the heated pool felt cool. She was so ready I could've slipped my hold damn hand in her like a puppet.

206

"My man Luther Fruitjuice be on the road," she said, grinding herself on my fingers. "He drives his own truck, know what I mean?"

"You mean it's only natural for a girl to get lonesome."

"Baby, I mean it's only natural for a girl to git some."

I wrapped my arms under her rump and lifted her a few inches out of the water. Her big tits broke the surface and bobbed around like a couple of pool toys. You could float all day on those inflatables, with a cocktail in one hand and a cell phone in the other.

She had nips like chocolate kisses. I fastened my lips on one as she locked her legs around my waist. She reached down and steered my shaft into her prepped pussy. It fit me like a glove.

In the water she was nearly weightless. It was like fucking in outer space. As I pushed in and out, the contrast between hot cunt and cool pool was incredible.

We banged together, slapping skin and splashing everywhere. Water squirted out from between her breasts with each crash. Hair beads clicked as her head jerked back and forth.

Still, I was worried.

Times like this, a bastard in my position can't help thinking about the front-door man. If I can kick his ass, I'll do his woman without a second thought. If he can kick my ass, I'll still do his woman -- but I'll make a point not to leave a mark.

I was like, "With a name like Fruitjuice, he's got to be one bad dude."

"Wouldn't you be?" she goes. Her dragon lady nails dug into my arms.

207

I could just see Fruitjuice now -- this black, badass mothertrucker in a plaid flannel shirt with the sleeves cut off. Muscular arms as big around as my thigh. Gold chain around a neck like a tree stump.

"He the jealous type?" I asked.

"Wouldn't you be?" the soul sista said again, suddenly seizing my steel with that special sumthin.

I tried to be cool about it. "So, when you expect this Fruitjuice back?"

"Chill, honey. We got *all* damn night."

We fucked from one side of the pool to the other. Back and forth, lap after lap after lap. Her eyelids fluttered as her eyes rolled to the back of her head.

"Lo' have mercy! Lo' have mercy!" she cried.

She was mere inches from orgasm. I had a short fuse myself. When I came, I could've filled the whole damn pool with it.

* * *

We chilled, recovering our senses at the side of the pool. My head rested back on the concrete as I looked up at the stars and wondered what to do next.

"What's your story, baby?" she goes. "Something's troubling your mind."

I told her everything.

Well, I left out the part about the dead guy and the tied-up girl but I kept the bit about having a ton of crank to unload.

When I was through, she was like, "Hoo, Lord! You white people're crazy, know what I mean? And I don't mean good crazy, neither. You-all're just plain *crazy*."

208

"So you can't do nothing for me?"

"Did I say that?" she goes. "Oh, baby, this be your lucky day! What you-all gotta do is talk to this friend of mine, Ulysses Homeslice. He knows how to handle these things."

"Where's this Homeslice at?"

"He ain't around here. He's out in Jasper-Purdy."

I knew it well.

Jasper-Purdy is at the intersection of two major Inter-states. It was more like an overgrown rest stop than an actual town. A neon oasis of gas pumps, cheap rooms and every fast food joint the bastards could dream up.

I was like, "He a fence or something?"

"Mm-hmm. Does pretty good for hisself peddling stolen speed to truckers and shit."

"I'll bet. Where's he stay at?"

"Some place called El Montero Motorlodge."

I knew of it. "Down at the far end of the strip," I said.

"But you gotta page him first, know what I mean? Cuz if Ulysses don't know you're coming, nigga won't open the door. Specially not to no strangers."

"Don't do me much good."

"Use my name, baby. Tell him, Sherronda Cherrybomb says I'm cool. Me and Homeslice go way back." Sherronda gave me his number and laughed: "You pretty okay for an ofay."

"Tell me somethin', Sherronda -- am I your first white boy?"

"My first white boy worth a damn. Sure you ain't got a little bit o' color in you?"

"I dunno. Got any white in you?"

209

She shook her head and tossed off a sly smile. "Naw."

"Want some?"

My dick was up and out of the water like a periscope.

* * *

Dripping wet and with my clothes in my hands, I walked back inside the motel room. Still hog-tied, Bunny was out of it.

I knew that I had to get my ass down to Jasper-Purdy, and that meant taking Bunny's ass along for the ride.

My fingers flew at the knotted rope and cords. The restraints fell away loose but she was too drugged out to try to squirm away.

* * *

Okay, get this crazy-ass scene:

Me, hauling ass in the Menace. Bunny LaFever in the seat beside me, all 'luded out. In the trunk, the twelve stretched Kooky-Kola bottles of crank dressed up like sand art.

"Gosh, don't it feel like old times, kind of, a little bit?" I go, not really expecting an answer from her in her state of mind. "You and me and the open road..."

It was already dusk and we were heading west into a storm. The clouds looked like an angry bruise. Red, black and blue smeared over the horizon.

I settled back and steered with my left wrist, cool as shit. My hand was curled loosely over the wheel. I was pushing ninety-five down this old two-lane that practically nobody used anymore cuz of the Turnpike.

I wanted to make Jasper-Purdy before those clouds burst. But we were still thirteen miles east of town when the sky opened up and all hell broke loose. It was a downpour of biblical proportions.

Rain hammered the roof. Drops like ball bearings clanked against the steel. Even Bunny covered her head and ears against the barrage of clinks and thunks.

Wipers swished back and forth like crazy, flinging away sheets of water. I hunkered up to the window to see the road. My hands were tense and close together on the wheel.

We hydroplaned at ninety-six m.p.h. Four wheels skated on the skin of water. Through sheer will alone I kept the rod on the right side of the highway.

And that's when we glided past her. I saw her out of the corner of my eye. She was a flash of wet T-shirt on the side of danger road.

I eased off the gas, glancing in the rearview mirror. I caught details as she shrank away. She was trudging along with her face down, defeated and pathetic. A red suitcase was in her hand.

The poor thing. Out there, soaked to the bone. I couldn't not pick her up. I mean, what kind of heartless bastard would I have to be?

I braked too fast. We spun out of control. The car began its whirling, swirling dance of death.

The wheel jerked left and right. The tires made a shushing sound as they slipped across the pavement. There was nothing to be done. I raised my hands, surrendering to the powers that be.

The rough shoulder tossed us high. I felt sick to my stomach when the radials left the road. "Oh my," Bunny said calmly, but it sounded a million miles away.

This was it -- the bitter end. What it all came down to. My whole life was meant for this moment.

We flipped end over end...

* * *

Birds chirping, blacktop steaming, the smell of wet grass and mud. Somebody knocked on the door. "Yeah?"

"Y'all okay?" the redhead asked excitedly. She wore a T-shirt with a gray fuzzy kitten with big blue eyes. "I saw y'all roll over!"

I looked at Bunny. She looked at me and blinked. Blood trickled from her nose. I looked back to the girl with the thick southern accent.

"We're fine here, thanks. You're awful wet though. Need a lift?"

"Y'all ain't going nowhere in that," she said.

"Says who?" I snapped. I was still in shock. Maybe it was the concussion. But nobody was gonna tell me what I couldn't do. "Get in," I told her.

"Y'all serious? Y'all are crazy."

I tried to get out but the door was stuck. I had to slide to the right, nearly into Bunny's lap, to kick at it a few times. It finally swung open with a painful shriek of metal against metal.

The Menace rested in a ditch. The windshield was laced with tiny cracks. Drizzling rain sizzled on the contorted hood.

Acting like nothing was wrong, I pulled some crumpled chrome away from the front tire. It came off easy. I winged it into the cornfield.

I pushed my seat forward and welcomed her into the back seat with an exaggerated sweeping gesture. She shrugged like what-the-hell-why-not and slid in with her red plastic suitcase.

212

I got in and turned the key. The engine coughed and sputtered, hanging on by a thread. The Menace wasn't what she used to be. But she still had some.

I shifted into forward and reverse to rock us back and forth, building enough momentum to get us out of the ditch. Finally we rolled over the gravel shoulder and lumbered down the highway.

The car undulated unevenly as she drove. Like a one-legged hooker hitting the pavement. Just doing the best she could with what she got.

I steered all the way right but the car kept drifting to the left. The hood was buckled, nearly folded in two. Between that and the pouring black smoke I had to lift myself off the seat to see clear.

The fan belt rattled. The body shuddered. Flat tires wop-wop-wopped as we crawled along slower than spit on an iceberg.

It took an hour to go three miles. We could've walked to Jasper-Purdy faster. But inside we were dry.

I asked the redhead her name. "Brandi Lustre," she said.

No shit, I thought. I thought there was something familiar about her. Instantly it all came back to me.

Brandi was that nymphomaniac we'd run into a couple months back. My dick sorely remembered, too. Like an elephant, it never forgets.

I probably would've dumped that noxious nympho on the side of the road. But I got a little nostalgic just looking at her again. She reminded me of a time before my life had gone to shit -- before I was on the lam. That was the only explanation for it.

Well, that and something else, if you know what I mean and I think you do.

She ran her fingers through her red hair, squeezing out the water. Freckles dusted her nose. She had long, delicate eyelashes that I could already feel tickling my belly as she deepthroated me.

"Where you headed?" I asked.

"Wherever," Brandi sighed, blinking these glittering green eyes.

She sat back, gazing out the window. She clutched her suitcase close to her chest. Her fingers nervously picked at the edge of one of the daisy stickers that decorated it.

"I'm disappointed in you," I said. She looked at me, confused and curious. "Don't tell me Randy Everhard was just another dick to you."

"Oh, wait," she goes, nodding. "It's coming back to me now. Y'all are the circus people, right?"

"*Circus*! Fuck that. All those candy-ass clowns and acrobats." Just saying those words made me want to spit. "Now Bunny here, that's a different story. But you won't catch *me* within a hundred miles of a damn circus."

"Oh," she goes, sounding sad. "Why not?"

"No money in it," I shrugged.

"She don't look so good," Brandi said, tilting her head at Bunny.

"Who, *her*? She'll be all right. She's just not feeling herself today."

"Looks like she ain't feeling anything at all."

"Where's Frank?" I asked, changing the subject. "You know, your husband."

"Up and left me. In the middle of the night. Took the car and everything. The only thing he left me was a couple hun-

214

dred dollars and a note that said he was sorry as all get-out but I was killing him."

"You got that effect."

"I know," she sighed. "But it's not my fault. It's just the way I am."

"Maybe so, but before we go any further, let's get one thing straight between us. When I say when, I mean *when*."

* * *

Jasper-Purdy. Gateway to the South. Crossroads of the Country. Convenience City, US of fuckin' A.

It was a town of nothing but motels, gas stations and fast food joints. Signs piled on top of signs on top of signs. It looked like every other place you've ever been to, times ten. Like Vegas without the glamour or the showgirls.

The place was full of truckers, travelers and transients passing through to all points south, east and west.

We gimped into town, backfiring every few seconds. Unhealthy blue balls of exhaust trailed us down the main drag. Every dumb chucklehead felt the need to stare and cat-call.

"Where should we stay?" Brandi wondered. There were too many choices and they were all the same.

The Menace decided for us, dying on the main drag just in front of the O.K. Motel. The rain had let up some.

I was like, "Everybody out. End of the line."

When I took a step back and looked at the hissing, creaking wreckage I almost cried like a woman. I'd logged a lot of memories in that Chevy. Shitload of jackpots. Best years of my life.

But it was a lost cause. She was a goner. Twisted beyond recognition. Crumpled up like the world's largest ball of tinfoil. It was a miracle we got out alive.

I slapped the roof like a fond farewell to a friend and then turned my back on it. "C'mon," I go. "We're abandoning it. We'll find ourselves a new car."

I threw Bunny over my shoulder and checked us into a room, signing under a fake name and paying in cash. I dumped Bunny on the bed, where she curled up into a ball.

"Why don't you get outta those wet clothes," I said to Brandi.

"I think I need a hot shower," Brandi said. Her teeth chattered. She shivered, still hugging that suitcase.

"Lemme get that for you," I said, "unless you wanna take it in with you."

She giggled nervously and handed me the suitcase. The wet shirt clung to her curves like paint. My dick twitched in appreciation.

Brandi's indigo hip-huggers were still damp. The cuffs were flared. Patent vinyl sandals peeked out from under the bellbottoms. Her toenails were painted pastel pink. She kicked off her sandals and padded into the bathroom.

I took off my own wet clothes and stretched out on the mattress in some dry underwear. The remote was attached to the nightstand with a wire. I flipped around and pretended to watch the free HBO on the TV bolted to the wall.

The better show was just across the room. Brandi kept the bathroom door open. She was so used to living with a husband, it didn't even cross her mind to shut it.

That's why I dig wives so much. They've forgotten the meaning of shame. They just let it all hang out like strippers backstage. Being naked means nothing to them.

216

She pulled off her tank top and showed off a couple of vine-ripened beauties that could do me a world of good. Big but firm. You couldn't ask for a better pair.

From where I was sitting, the only thing wrong with Brandi's boobs was my mouth and dick couldn't reach.

She absently touched her breasts while watching her face in the mirror. She cupped them while her fingertips grazed the nipples. Her head tipped to the side as she gazed deeply into her own eyes.

Her belly was curved. Smooth and tight as a drumskin. The top button of her jeans was undone. By now, my dick was double-puffed.

I shoved Bunny off the bed. She tumbled to the floor with a thud that brought Brandi out of her spell. Her head snapped up. I looked at the TV and watched her on the sly.

She glanced at me and smiled self-consciously. But she still didn't close the door. She wanted me to watch.

She bent over and reached into the shower. A spray shot from the shower head. Her tight, round ass wiggled as she fiddled with the knobs.

She stood up to get naked. My randy cock raised its hard self up as she wiggled her hips and worked her way out of the wet jeans. She daintily stepped out of the heap around her ankles, then kicked it aside.

She stepped under the piping hot pulse of the shower. Her tasty tushie was pink from all the effort of undressing. When she turned I glimpsed red bush. The rusty rings screeched as she pulled the curtain closed.

The clear plastic curtain was milky with age. The view was little better than an outline. A silhouette of pink and red, she stood with her back to the shower to let the water pulse over her head. Clouds of steam drifted to the peeling ceiling paint.

While she soaped herself up, I turned up the volume on the TV and reached for her suitcase. It was red pebbled plastic. The two fasteners had locks but they snapped open.

I lifted the lid and began rummaging. Cotton panties and bras and a string bikini, T-shirts and shorts, pink disposable razors, a can of shaving cream, makeup and a book of word jumbles.

Under all that was an arsenal of sex toys that would kill most women. Dildos and vibrators of different sizes and textures -- one for every hole plus three or four to spare.

Just then I heard her stopping the shower. The knobs squeaked as she turned them off. I closed the lid and snapped it shut.

I pushed it back to the foot of the bed as I settled back and looked at the tube. "Nice shower?" I asked as she stepped out, drying her hair with a white towel.

"Mmmm. Real nice. I'm *soooo* relaxed."

She stood in the doorframe, bending at the waist to tie the towel around her head like a turban. Her tits swung down and jiggled invitingly. When she stood up the turban teetered precariously.

"I can't tell y'all how grateful I am. For picking me up and all."

"Then don't."

Talk is cheap. Actions speak louder than words. But a naked lady screams loudest of all.

I gave her the once-over, over and over. She didn't mind. She didn't even try to cover herself. Which was good. Cuz that girl had nothing to hide.

218

Some girls got bedroom eyes. But she had the whole furnished suite. Bedroom eyes, bedroom lips, bedroom tits, bedroom hips and bedroom legs.

Her breasts were flushed from the hot water. The skin was mottled with pink splotches. Her belly glistened. Water dribbled down the spread of her hips. The red bush looked darker when it was wet. The curls were swept down into a point that dripped a steady trickle of water.

My dick got interested real fast. It poked its head through the fly in my tightie whities. I tucked it back inside. It rebelled, straining against the thin cotton.

Brandi approached the bed. Her fingers hovered above my blatant stiffy. It rose to meet them. A pink fingernail traced the bulging outline of my cockhead through the underwear.

"I need a change," she said. Water droplets hit my chest. They felt cool as they ran off.

"Who doesn't?"

"I mean right now." She released my cock and stroked me with her entire hand, ringing its thickness with her fingers. I thought I'd explode like a stick of dynamite and take three of her fingers off.

"You got something in mind?"

"Save me?" she goes.

"Hell, no -- I'm through saving women."

"Not *save*, silly -- *shave*! *Shave* me."

She took my hand and brought it to her damp bush. It was hot and humid. I didn't know if it was from the shower or the turn-on.

My fingers got tangled in her luxurious curls. She was like, "I brung a razor in my suitcase."

219

* * *

Lemme tell ya -- life does not get any better than being stranded in a cheap motel and shaving a runaway sexpot.

It didn't even matter that I'd killed a man not forty-eight hours before. That was a million years ago now. Like it was some other rube's life but this was my reality:

Brandi Lustre lay on her back on the bed with her feet squarely on the floor. I knelt between the spread of her thighs and got busy with tiny scissors.

The fuzz was too much for a razor. I had to trim her beard before I could shave it. Cut it down to size.

Two fingers made a comb. I pulled the hair straight and cut across. Red pubes sprinkled down. A towel caught the snips.

Once her bush was thinned and trimmed, I reached for the shaving cream. The can of Aloe-Sol was in the ice bucket. We'd filled it with steaming water.

I sprayed a fat dollop into my hand and gently worked it into her patch. The foam was hot from its bath. Hairs poked through the triangle of rich, white lather like grass through the snow.

I took the razor out of the bucket and drew the twin blades down from the top of her mound. Snippets and foam gathered on them.

I rinsed off the razor and started again, clearing another stripe as the blades quietly scraped the skin. It took several swipes before all traces of hair were gone.

Working this way, I shaved her mound from left to right. The hot shower had softened her fuzz. It came off pretty easy.

Getting around her slit was more difficult. The skin is thin there. Easy to nick by accident.

"Y'all sure you never done this before?" she asked as I carefully swiped the blade toward her thigh.

"I never said that," I said and glanced up to wipe my sweaty brow with the back of my hand.

The curve of her belly rose and fell as she breathed. I saw the flash of her easy, southern smile. She had big, white teeth.

I finished cleaning the bush away from the inner fold of skin where her leg met her crotch. My work here was just about done. A few more passes to scrape away the reluctant hairs.

I got up and went into the bathroom. I brought back a washcloth soaked in hot water to wipe away the stray hairs and spots of foam.

A cunt is a cunt is a cunt. But a shaved one is something else. It's a whole other animal. You can see everything. It's more naked than naked.

Her beautiful bald mound was slick to the touch. As smooth and white as porcelain. "Feel any different?" I asked.

"Yeah. Chilly."

I told her to touch it. She wasn't shy, either. Her fingers grazed back and forth.

"Like a cueball," she giggled.

Then she saw my cock. It stuck out in front of me. I'd been hard for who knows how long. I leaned into her like it was my destiny.

Brandi held her breath as tight pussy made way. Muscles grabbed at me. She gasped when my pubic patch scraped her bald mound.

221

"*Oooooooh*," she purred each time I eased out and then piled back inside. "*Oooooooh*, yeah. Fuckadelic, baby -- that's the way to do it. *Ooooooh*. Like that. Right there. Touch me there..."

I pulled out and pushed in, upping the speed until my balls were swinging. Her tits were shifting back and forth. Our sticky flesh slapped together.

I drove her ass halfway across the bed. I couldn't stop watching my cock disappear into that shaved pussy. I'd never get sick of looking at it.

"I wanna see, too!" she said. I pulled out. She stood up.

There was an armless chair in the corner. I pulled it to the center of the room and sat down. I could see myself in the full length mirror on the bathroom door.

Brandi had her ass to me. She planted her legs on either side of the seat. Bending her knees, she carefully positioned her open pussy above the raging upright of my pole.

I steered my cockhead inside her slit. Brandi hunkered down, impaling herself on me. Inch by inch until she got a whole foot of flesh inside.

"I'm so wet," she groaned, pleased with herself. Her thighs rested on my legs. "I'm totally stuffed."

"Look at yourself," I said.

She glanced up and gazed at the reflection of our bodies. We were joined at the sexes. Her spanking clean crotch was nestled against my gnarly bush.

"I look like a little girl!" she cried in glee. "I feel like a brand new woman!"

Her snatch was downright prepubescent. My cock looked huge and monstrous. Swollen flesh had her all stretched out. I was gonna tear her in two.

I reached around and found her joy buzzer. I played with it as Brandi began to bounce on my pogo stick.

Noises of pleasure gurgled in the back of her throat. Her green eyes were like slits as she rode my rig. It was like watching decent porno with us as the stars.

Her tits rippled as she plunged herself down on my prick. I grabbed the seat of the chair and began bucking in upward thrusts. My dick stabbed deep into her body.

She lifted her arms above her heads, lifting her titties. They bounced and swung in circles as our bodies slammed together. Her buttcheeks rippled as they bounced off my thighs.

She was so wet my cock was skimming across her cunt. No friction to ride. I increased my thrusts to make something happen.

Grunts and slaps filled the room. Her thighs flexed powerfully as she crammed me into the deepest reaches of her cunt. She started fingering her own clit.

Her hungry cunt spazzed up and down my shaft. Muscles gripped every inch of me. It was just what I needed to get off.

I grabbed her waist and bounced her up and down. She was like a puppet on my prick. I was jacking myself off with her body.

I was a long time coming. Building since the beginning of time. Orgasm hung over me like a heavy cloud, ready to burst and flood the whole world and the hell with it.

My body spun out of control. The floor dropped out from under me. The room was a whirl of swirling colors.

Brandi screamed. It sounded garbled. I threw up my hands, delivering myself into her pussy, sliding down to the inevitable end.

Semen boiled up and out in a slo-mo eruption. Time slowed to a crawl. It was like walking underwater. Dreamlike. Like syrup.

We had a couple more go's at it and then she had me crying uncle and I had her reaching for the nearest dildo.

* * *

The first chance I got, I slipped outside.

The rain had stopped earlier that morning. The sun was out. Jasper-Purdy was steaming like a sonofabitch. Stepping into it was like a sucker punch in the gut. It knocked the wind right out of me.

I stopped at a pay phone outside the In-N-Out quickie mart and called Ulysses Homeslice's pager.

While I waiting for his call-back, one of those old Ford Velociteers screeched to a halt alongside the curb. It was as big and black as a hearse. The store's plate glass windows shook with the lowdown idling of its souped-up engine.

Three punks in black sunglasses sat inside. Two greasy fuckups in the front. In back was a ghostly pale chick with short, raven-black hair and blood-red lipstick.

The girl got out of the freak mobile and sauntered into the store as I was dialing Homeslice. She wore big black army boots and a black slip for a skirt.

A slit up the side showed her white thigh. Pressed into it were bruises like fingerprints that made me think she liked it a little rough.

I read her skin tight T-shirt. A faded silk-screen of Jesus side-by-side with Satan. Above Jesus it said *Loves Me*. Above the devil, *Loves Me Not*.

The cotton shirt was so threadbare it was translucent. She had her sleeves rolled up. A ring of thorny barbed wire was tattooed around her scrawny left bicep.

224

She went bra-less. I fell in love with her tits. They were fist-sized balls of flesh with dark brown nipples.

My dick got interested real quick and followed her. But my brain took care of business when Ulysses' call came through. I stuck my finger in my ear to hear the man over their rumbling engine.

"Tell me what I wanna hear, yo!" he answered.

"Ulysses Homeslice," I said. "It's Randy."

"Don't know no Randy."

"Randy Everhard, bro."

"Where'd you get my number?"

He talked too fast. Like a machine gun, rat-a-tat-tat. Tense and wired. By the sound of it, he'd been sampling the merchandise.

"From Sherronda," I go.

"Who's Sherronda?"

"Sherronda Cherrybomb," I said as I rolled my eyes.

In his business, he had a right to be cautious. But I got no patience for speedfreak paranoia and cut through the bullshit: "I came into some crank, dude."

"Make it sound like you-all's daddy died and left you some."

"What do you want me to say?"

"Don't say shit. That's you-all's business. Ain't none of mine. All I care is, is it good?"

"*Is it good?* This shit is more than good. It's the best."

"Uh-huh," he said like he didn't believe me.

"I don't fuck chickens and I don't shit feathers, man."

225

"Say what? Listen up -- I'm gonna be square wit you-all. I don't know your white ass from Jack Frost."

"But you know Sherronda, and I know Sherronda."

"Bitch owes me money, I know that."

I thought that was the end of that. Homeslice didn't say anything for a while but then he said, "Awright, I'll give you ten G for it."

"You mean ten up front. How much after you sell it?"

"'Nother ten."

"*Twenty*!" I said, watching the punk rock girl through the plate glass window. She lingered at the back of the store. She picked a comic book off the wire carousel and flipped through it, looking bored.

I was like, "You're killing me here, Homeslice! This shit is *good*! This shit is worth like ten times that, at least!"

"Then sell it yourself, you greedy muthafucka."

"Aw, hell," I groaned.

"Fuck that *aw hell* bullshit. This be a free country. Find another buyer if you-all don't like it."

The passenger got out of the Velociteer. He swung a sawed-off at his side, clomping toward the door in his red-laced shitkickers. His shredded jeans flapping as he pulled open the door.

Goddamn armed robber. Not a careerist like me but an unprofessional punk doing it for thrills. Just another sucker at heart.

I watched the scene play itself out like I was watching a TV show I'd seen already. You know what's gonna happen but you look anyway cuz there's nothing else on.

The stickup man was pointing the shotgun at the skinny immigrant cliché behind the counter. He wore a bright yellow baseball cap with *Have a Nice Day* on it. A painful smile was frozen on his face as he pulled bills from the register.

He wasn't going fast enough. The punk was freaking out. Yelling and waving that shotgun around.

"I'm in a tight spot, man," I said, turning away from the scene inside the store. "It's a long story but the moral is, I need money *now* -- not later. Can you help me out? I mean, I'm begging you here. A finder's fee is all I'm after. Twenty-five up front and it's all yours. Can we make a deal or no?"

"I gotta think about it, know what I mean?"

Suddenly the sawed-off went off. I thought the punk had shot the guy. But it wasn't like that. The barrel must've been blocked, cuz the shot had blown back in the shooter's face.

I turned around in time to see the punk thrown backward into a cardboard display of Fancee pastries. It was an avalanche of cupcakes, powdered donuts and sticky buns. The sap's legs buckled beneath him and he was dead before he hit the ground.

The Velociteer spun its wheels as it peeled outta there. I smelled the sharp odor of burnt rubber. Exhaust from the dual pipes breezed by.

I was like, "Listen, Homeslice, I hate telephones. You mind if I stop by later on? We can talk about this some more in person."

"You do what you gotta do, but my word is solid. Ten G now -- ten G later. Face to face won't change shit."

"You said you'd think it over first," I bitched.

"I did. And now I'm done thinking. Ten now, ten later."

227

Inside the store, the clerk was losing it. Laughing and crying at once. He picked up the shotgun and held it out at arm's length and was actually talking to it. Like it was gonna talk back and tell him why the world's so outta whack.

"Fine," I go. "Whatever you want."

"See ya when I see ya," Ulysses said.

I slammed the phone down as the immigrant bolted out the front door. Shit stained his white pants. He was booking across the lot like he wasn't gonna stop till he got back to wherever the hell he came from.

I pulled open the door to the convenience store and waltzed inside. The smell of gunsmoke and fresh blood hung in the air.

The store was cold and awful quiet. I could hear the fluorescent lights buzzing and freezers humming.

I made my way down the first aisle and peeked around the corner. The gun moll was down on the floors on all fours, peeking around the corner. In her hand was a 9 mm.

There's something about a girl with a gun. Or maybe it's something about a girl with her butt up in the air. Her slip was hiked up over white cotton panties with yellow daisies.

I lifted a cap gun that looked real from the toy shelf and, sneaking up behind her, pressed the snubnose into her back. "Drop it, sweetheart."

"Fuck!" she hissed.

"Police." She lay the 9 mm down. I grabbed it and unloaded it, pocketing the cartridge and sliding the gun away. "Keep your hands behind your head!" I barked.

"What the fuck're you doing, pig?"

"I dunno. I'm just making it up as I go along."

"I mean between my fucking legs!"

228

"Oh, that." My hands were all over her ass. Talk about convenience! She was right where I wanted her. Down on all fours. I'd pulled away the crotch of her daisy panties and was stroking the soft folds of her pussy. "It's called frisking."

Her laugh was a snort. "I ain't got anything up there!"

"Cavity search, ma'am. Standard procedure." She loosened at my fingertips. I dipped inside her cunt. "Well, well, well -- what do we have here?" I asked as I found her bud.

"Fucking bastard," she said through clenched teeth. My hard jeans pinched my dick. I wasn't wearing any underwear -- freeballin' for the hell of it.

"Take it easy, baby," I said. "My backup'll be here any minute. Maybe the 10-7 was the only perp. If you know what I mean, and I think you do."

She breathed a heavy sigh. I had her and she knew it. "Make it fast, motherfucker."

Kneeling on the floor, I unbuckled my belt and undid my fly. I pulled out my cock and let it flop out. It swayed its fat head from side to side as it straightened out.

I tugged those panties down to her knees. Her ass was luminously white. Like it'd never seen a ray of sunshine. AC goosepimpled her skin.

I grabbed her cheeks, manhandling the firm flesh. My fingers left splotches of pink. My joint was expanding like the goddamn universe.

I guided my dick into her crotch, fitting its head into her hole. I started to squeeze inside. Her cunt seized up and closed in on me.

I wish you could've been there. Just to feel that snatch clutch every inch like she was gonna choke it. Unbelievably

229

tight -- like you could shove a lump of coal up there and ten minutes later it'd come out a diamond.

My hard-on swelled against her muscles until that uptight pussy finally began to succumb. It stopped resisting. It couldn't escape its destiny. It knew. It was gonna get fucked.

Hang a sign on her ass that says *Come In* cuz she was open for business! My stomach slapped her butt as I screwed her from behind. I grabbed her by the waist and pulled her back onto my raging ramrod.

I fucked her until she started to fuck me back. She rocked her ass back to meet my thrusts and push me in as far as was humanly possible. My balls banged her crotch.

My cock felt great but my knees were killing me. That tile floor was murder on my caps. Good thing there's more than one way to skin a cat.

I pulled out and stood up, knees screaming. I pulled her to her feet. She didn't protest as I picked her up and sat her ass down in a cardboard display filled with herbal shampoo.

She spread her legs as I positioned my dickhead at her cunt and pushed inside. My cock slid deep inside her body. There's nothing better than seeing your dick that far inside a girl. Our pubes scratched together.

I started off slow but was soon fucking faster. Her legs bounced with every thrust. Her army boots kicked the display as I kept up with the rhythm of the Blurpee machine endlessly churning cherry red slush.

Her tits rolled every which way. I pushed her shirt up to her neck. I covered one breast with my hand and squeezed. The flesh was cool to the touch. I played with her nipples, pulling them until she pinched her eyes shut.

Her red lips were open as we fought. We were fighting to get each other off. It was the war between the sexes down there, and her pussy gave as good as it got.

She stuck a finger in her mouth to coat it with spit. Then she reached down to her crotch and frigged her own clit. Her finger became a blur as she strummed herself to a climax.

She started to squeak. Her whole body tightened as she came. Her hands were white-knuckled fists. Her back arched. Her belly curved upwards. Her nostrils flared. I laid into her as pussy rippled up and down and all over my cock.

I fucked her like it was the end of the world. My dick was burning up her cunt. I was the nuke and she was ground zero.

My shuddering orgasm hit hard. It was like a beautiful mushroom cloud spreading against the sky. Windows and whole buildings blown to smithereens with the force of my blast. Civilization was a greasespot by the time we got through with it.

We were the last two people left on the face of the earth. It was Adam and Eve all over again. Naked inside a convenience store, with the fluorescent lights buzzing above our heads like fallout.

I helped her out of the display. The red outline of shampoo bottles and caps were pressed into the back of her pale thighs. She pulled her shirt down and looked for her panties. She found them snagged on the rack of Rope-a-Ronis.

"Can I fuckin' go now or what?" she bitched. She was the self-loathing kind of girl who resented you for making her cum.

"Or what," I answered, suddenly mentalizing something about sweetening a deal. "Around here, armed robbery gets you three to five, automatic."

"What the fuck's your point?"

"Come with me," I said. "I'll tell you all about it."

"Do I have a fucking choice?" she said, putting herself back together, but she already knew the answer.

* * *

We made our way to the El Montero. Bottle of rainbow-colored crank in my hand. "Sorry about your boyfriend," I said to the punk rock girl.

"Who, Andrew?" She made a face. "He wasn't my fucking boyfriend. Shit, I hated that loser. I hated him for loving me."

"Tell it to a shrink."

"I did," she said. "You must be one loser cop if they don't even give you a fucking ride."

"I already told you all of this -- I'm undercover."

"Yeah, yeah," she goes, bored out of her fucking mind. "And if I put out for this drug dealer so you can fucking catch him, you'll let me go. You guys are so sleazy it makes me fucking sick to my fucking stomach."

"You kiss your momma with that pottymouth?" She didn't say anything to that so I told her, "Lose the attitude. You'll enjoy it more."

I took a good look at her. Her momma gave her a pretty face but she managed to fuck it up all by herself. Three rings pierced her left eyebrow and one hoop dangled from her right nose hole.

But there was something there that rang a bell. It wasn't the jewelry so much as what she was trying to hide with it.

I was like, "Don't I know you from somewhere?"

232

She rolled her eyes. "Yo, asshole. You already fucked me so fuck the fucking pick-up line."

"It ain't a line if I swear I really know you."

"I fucking swear you don't," she shot back.

"Wait a sec -- I'll think of it."

"Would you please just shut the fuck up, please?"

* * *

We finally reached the motorlodge. It was a square stucco dive. Ulysses' room was in the rear on the second floor. We scaled the shaky iron steps.

I got ready to knock but stopped short. "Hot dang, I got it!" I go, snapping my fingers. "The Skyliner Diner outside of Kansas City. That was you brung me my apple pie, wasn't it?"

"If I say yes, can I fucking go?"

"Aw hell, she looked just like you, too --- only blonde."

"Listen, asshole -- I don't know who the fuck you are but I know you're completely full of fucking shit. If you're a cop, I'm a fucking nun."

"Great. We come all this way just so you can fucking tell me you won't fucking go through with it. That is fucking beautiful."

"Did I fucking say that? I'll do it, but only cuz I fucking completely hate myself."

"Well, thanks a fucking million," I said. "I'm gonna fucking knock now, if that's fucking all right with you."

"Knock or don't fucking knock -- think I give a fuck?"

"Fucking chill, punky." Silly bitch had more issues than National Geographic. "Just follow my lead and it'll go down like Linda Lovelace."

233

I rapped a few times. We waited. I knocked again.

"I got a gun aimed right at your head, motherfucker!" said the hyped-up voice behind the door.

"Aw, fer crissakes, Homeslice!"

The door was silent. I could hear the paranoid bastard thinking. "Randy?" he asked at last.

"No shit, Sherlock. I brung the stuff. And *a friend*."

"I don't like other people's friends."

"You'll like her," I promised. "Look for yourself, dude."

The door opened a few inches. His face filled the crack. When I saw it, you could've knocked me down with a feather.

Now I don't know if you've ever seen a black albino but it's a damn freaky sight. Ulysses had all the features of a black dude but his skin was white -- and not white like a white guy's but weird albino white.

His snow white fro was conked into shape. He wore it slicked back in greasy waves that pulled the skin on his face tight. His cheeks were sunken in.

Not only that but his pink eyes were too far apart. They were red-rimmed and crusty. Dilated pupils darted nervously from me to punky and back to me.

Nervous people make me nervous.

"Wassup?" he said, chilling out in front of the pretty lady. I relaxed a bit, glad she was there.

Ladies are a factor in every situation. Sometimes they make it worse, sometimes they make it better. With punky here, I figured the latter.

He shut the door to undo the chain and then opened it just enough to let us slip inside. He looked like shit but his short-sleeved shirt and long shorts matched. Turquoise rayon patterned with tropical flowers. They were like Hawaiian pajamas.

The unbuttoned shirt hung open. A drawstring cinched his shorts to his narrow waist. He was all stringy muscle, cords of rubber bands. He was wound up so tight he'd either spring or snap. His skin was covered in a sheen of sweat.

Did I say I was starting to calm down? Forget that. I noticed a scary new detail.

Fucker was packing a Glock. His bony fingers curled around the trigger and handle. They looked like they'd grown up around it like tree roots.

He closed the door behind us, killing the sunlight. The only light came from the six muted color TV sets placed around the room. Each one tuned to a different channel.

The walls were flickering blue with daytime television. Cartoons, soap operas and game shows made a nerve-wracking strobe effect that would send an epileptic into seizures in seconds.

I got the impression he'd been holed up in here a long time. The air was languid and ripe. B.O., bad breath and rotten food mixed with incense and roach fogger.

"Lights?" I asked, choking.

"No bulbs," he replied.

I shoulda known. Goddamn crystal meth fiends are resourceful as all get-out. When they forget their pipes, they use a lightbulb. They break off the metal screw with the filament and cook the ice in the bulb.

"How 'bout some AC?" I asked. "It's like an oven in here."

"Nah-uh. I'm fixing it."

In the flickering light, I saw that the window unit was gutted. Parts and components hung from wires like entrails. "Broken?" I asked.

"Fuck no. I took it apart. I'm gonna clean it and shit. Streamline it. Then it's gonna work better. Be a iceberg in here."

His Adam's apple was the size of a Red Delicious. When he talked it jogged up and down. He gesticulated, too, all loosey-goosey, waving that damn gun around.

"We're all friends here, man," I said. "Put the gun down."

"This be my German friend, Adolph," he said, pointing his Glock at me. I flinched at the barrel that wiggled inches from my face. "We like *this*." He crossed the index and middle fingers of his free hand.

My heart jumped into my throat and stayed there. I looked around, thinking, So this is where it's gonna end for me. This is where I'm gonna die.

"It's cool, man," I said. "It's cool." I nudged punky toward him.

Homeslice gave a big ol' grin and eased onto the edge of the bed. "Whyn't you come here and lemme whisper in your ear," he goes, this cool menthol cigarette twitching in his mouth. He lit it off a disposable and sucked in deep.

She came near and he pulled her into his lap. His lips moved close to her ear and she laughed. Her eyes drifted toward me, fixing me in a stare that chilled my blood.

Ulysses groped for a remote and aimed it across the room. Jazz fusion oozed out of the speakers in raunchy undulations. "Shit chills me out," he cracked as he pushed her out of his lap and into the middle of the room.

The fat-bottomed groove infected her like a disease. Punky started shaking her head and twisting her body. The flickering TVs made a slo-mo effect.

Her dance was a flood of shimmying sexadelic seduction. She simulated sex acts like she was channeling the ghosts of Sodom and Gomorra. Tits, hips and ass, everything was moving at the same time. It was like trying to watch all the acts in a three-ring circus at once.

"M-mm-mmm," Ulysses grunted, satisfied with the performance. "You make my dick stand up and sing."

He dug his free hand under the rumpled sheets, pulled out a flashlight and pointed it at her. Dust and smoke slanted through the pale yellow beam. He spotted her jiggling chest.

"C'mon, now -- let's see those tits that made you rich!"

She pushed her T-shirt over her breasts, feeling herself up. She stroked and massaged them one at a time. Then, simultaneously, she tweaked the brown nipples until they were hard. Her head rolled back. If I didn't know any better, I would've thought she was turning herself on for real.

One hand strayed to her slip and played with the lace along the bottom. She lifted the hem higher and higher to flash more and more of her thigh. She flashed her daisy panties, giggling like a naughty schoolgirl. What an actress!

She stretched the crotch of her panties, pulling it aside. She bent her knees and slowly burrowed the middle finger into her pussy. Her eyes were closed as she screwed herself.

Homeslice writhed on the bed: "Sweet Jesus, have mercy! I'd kill to be your finger!"

The gun aimed indiscriminately. I flinched and ducked. It was only a matter of time before he lost it and squeezed the Glock's easy trigger.

Her middle finger reappeared, glazed. Keeping her eyes on Ulysses, she stuck it between her lips. It was as if she was flipping him the bird and he didn't even know it.

She turned around and flipped up her skirt to flash some ass. She began to grind those cheeks in tantalizing circles. Clockwise and then counter-clockwise.

She slipped a finger under the elastic waist and tugged the panties down to her ankles. She kicked them off and bent over. Her creamy white ass was glow-in-the-dark.

Her feet were wide apart. She grabbed a cheek in each hand and spread her ass wide to reveal the full glory of her pink pussy. The brown eye of her asshole winked at him.

She inched backward to Homeslice. Her beauteous butt hovered over the enormous bulge in his lap. Big ol' mother-fucking dick pressed against the rayon shorts. It was liable to poke straight through.

Punky lowered her ass onto his lap. She thrust her naked cheeks over his cock. Her pelvis shot back and forth, rubbing his pop-up like a pro.

"Fuck that lapdance shit," he said, smiling as he pointed the Glock at her head. "Fuck that shit right now."

Punky froze. I froze.

"*Sike!*" he yelled and started to laugh. "I'm just messin with you-all. Look at the look on you-all's faces. Fucking comedic and shit."

With his free hand, he reached into his shorts and pulled out his tool. His cock flopped, thickening as it straightened. It was spotted like leopard skin.

Punky obliged with a little reach-around. She pumped his shaft. The cockhead poked in and out of the purple-gray sleeve of foreskin.

238

His dick got even bigger. It was the biggest muscle he had. It outweighed the rest of him.

She got down on her knees with her face in his lap. He was royally hard now, sticking up like a smokestack. She lovingly squeezed his stiffie in her fist, pulling down the foreskin. Pre-cum oozed from its slit like raw opium.

"Ooh, baby," she purred, her tongue sliding over her lips, "you look good enough to eat."

"You best be hungry. I got a full seven-course dick right here."

Her flickering tongue got better acquainted with his towering cock. Within minutes, they were best of friends. From knob to balls, he was slick with her saliva.

"Gaw-damn!" he cried as she stretched her lips around the head, swallowing it whole. He lay back and crossed his arms behind his head, digging the show. She really went to town on his petrified pecker.

She sucked him hard and soft, fast and slow, caressing every quivering sex nerve while cradling his nuts in her hand. When she wasn't making with the tongue action, she fucked him with her mouth. Every so often she sucked a ball into her mouth.

While all this was going on, I scoped out his hideaway. He had ash trays all over the place, spilling butts and ashes. I noticed a set of car keys buried in one heap. I pocketed it while he was off in Never-Never-Land.

Her head bobbed up and down as she drew his cock out until the head was just inside her puckered lips, then bore down again until she was kissing his balls. She was moaning and whimpering with a mouthful of black albino dick.

"C'mere," he grunted, pushing her mouth off his dick. She moved upward, licking his high-strung body the whole way. She lingered at his nipples.

"Hey, yo," he said, craning his neck at me. "Gimme a test drive."

"Come again?" I said.

"A test drive, a test drive, motherfucker! Gimme some of that crank."

I uncapped the bottle and poured a line of crank on the back of my hand. "Don't even have to cook it. Shit's pure enough to snort."

"What's with the rainbow sprinkles, yo?"

"That's camouflage, my man. Camouflage."

I held the crank under his nose. "Fuck that," he goes, making a face. "Sprinkle that shit on my dick. Gets all in her pussy that way. That's the part I want all jacked and shit."

"Sure, man, sure." I brushed the crank over his turgid tool. The powder melted in her warm saliva.

Ulysses palmed her asscheeks with one hand. His skinny fingers dug into the flesh. With his thumb on one cheek and his fingers on the other, he spread her cheeks apart to open her cunny.

Straddling his righteously rigid ramrod, she inserted the head. The way she squirmed on his prick, you'd think she liked it. Her eyes gleamed wickedly. Punky was a born performer.

"*Ooo-weee*, girl," he groaned, "you got a body a man can really sink his dick into."

She lowered herself, easing his fatboy up her snatch until she took it all. She lifted her hips until the knob bulged just inside. Then he pulled her back down on his dong.

240

She rode him forever. Like a cowgirl riding a mechanical bull in the worst kind of roadhouse. Her tits were bouncing in wild circles. He caught a nipple in his mouth and pulled. She leaned forward to french him as she lifted her ass in the air.

His dick had some serious reach. Ten inches, I figured, and thick as a baby's arm. He was only five in the hole. But that was enough to do a real number on her. His throbbing thickness had her wide open.

I wiped my mouth with the back of my hand and tasted the traces from the crank. It tasted sweet. That wasn't good.

Inconspicuous-like, I eased over to the crank bottles. I held my finger over the top and up-ended it. My fingertip came away with a sample.

I tested it with my tongue. No doubt about it. That shit was pure sugar. Sonofa--

I'd been had. I started to edge my way to the door. Everything was going from bad to worse.

"Where you goin', motherfucker?" Homeslice yelled. "Party's just gettin' started!"

"I forgot, bro' -- I gotta make this call. I gotta see this guy. I'll leave the shit here and be right back, 'kay?"

"Who you doin' business wit? That right there be im-polite! Fucking rude and shit."

"Sorry, dude," I said, not really hearing my words as I stared at the Glock aimed at my head.

My heart was thumping, pumping thick squirts of blood through my body. My only thought was animal instinct: get out alive. I didn't give a shit about the crank or money or anything but my precious life and I'd do anything to keep it.

He was like, "Ain't you-all gonna say goodbye to Adolph? Ain't your momma ever teach you some manners?"

241

"So long, Adolph," I heard myself say. The words echoed down a long nightmare.

"Mm-hmm," he said.

He squinted his left eye and took aim.

The blood was rushing in my head like a freight train with fifty cars of rolling stock. It was hard to hear him over all that noise: "Now Adolph gonna kiss you goodbye."

He squeezed the trigger. Time slowed to a crawl. My life was one long drawn out suicide.

Click.

Nothing.

"*Sike!*" he yelled, laughing way too loud and waving the empty gun like an insult in my face. "This is what you-all looked like!" he said, twisting his face into the face of white dread and then exploding into laughter again.

My legs were rubber bands. I felt like a jackass. Like a rube.

I was no better than that Punjab in the store. The whole world spinning out of control around him, and he couldn't do anything but stand there like a chump and take it. It was ten times worse than being shot dead.

"Gimme sixty, yo," Homeslice laughed. "We just getting started here. Come back later and we'll do some biz."

* * *

I ran down the steps of the El Montero like my feet were on fire and my ass was catching. Down in the lot, I tried several cars before I found Ulysses' ride -- a Plymouth Ambush, shit brown sedan.

The windows were tinted with cheap do-it-yourself decals. The dark, smoky film was full of creases and bubbles. A sweat-stained T-shirt was stretched over the back of the

242

driver's seat and about twenty Frootie-Tootie air fresheners hung from the rearview mirror making a godawful stink. Strawberries, grapes and vanilla all mixed together.

The engine roared to life and I stomped the accelerator. I laid some rubber on the main drag and rocketed onto the interstate. Jasper-Purdy couldn't disappear fast enough behind me.

Shocked, ashamed and shitting bricks, I cranked the window for some unscented air and screamed into the rushing wind till I tasted blood. I called myself names and beat myself over the head. My mind careened as I madly jerked the wheel left and right.

Who knows how or why the mind works the way it does but suddenly I remembered where I knew the punk rock girl from.

She was Angie Lumpkins -- little Angie Lumpkins from that sitcom *Strange Bedfellows*! You can't turn on the damn TV without seeing a rerun of it. Little Angie Lumpkins, the pesky, perky little girl next door.

She was all grown up now with a bad haircut and dyejob, but it was Angie Lumpkins all the same. And then it hit me: I screwed little Angie Lumpkins! Freakin-*A*!

I laughed out loud, drunk on the idea of it -- I felt a little sick, too. There's something deliciously depraved about defiling America's sweetheart.

Who knew she'd be such a killer lay? Just goes to show, you never know who's good in the sack until you get them there.

Poor Angie Lumpkins! Talk about taking a turn for the worse! From child star to gun moll in less than a decade. Would the madness never end?!

Hell, it wasn't me -- it was the rest of the world that was fucking nuts. I was the sanest jerk on earth. Compared to everybody else, I really had my shit together.

The more I thought about it, the more I knew that I had to see this thing through to the end. That meant tracking down Peanut to settle the score. He'd started it, but I was the one who was gonna finish it.

I got off at the next exit and then got back on, heading back to Jasper-Purdy.

* * *

When I walked in on them, Bunny and Brandi had nothing on but the TV. They couldn't have been more naked. Both on their backs with their heads at opposite ends of the bed.

Each girl looked like a part of the other. They were joined at the pussy by Brandi's fleshy double dong. Some kinda Siamese slut.

After all the Quaaludes I'd been slipping her, Bunny was too drugged to do much of anything. Brandi had to do all the work herself. She was propped up on her hands to get some leverage as she thrust her pelvis back and forth to drive the dong deeper into her delta.

Her cheeks were flushed. Her head was tilted back and a great big smile decorated her face. She was peaking again.

"What number you on?" I asked when the O subsided.

"Dunno," she panted. "I stopped counting at twenty-four."

Un-fucking-believable. Multi-orgasmic didn't even begin to describe it. They'll have to invent a new word just for her.

I cocked my head at their sordid sex scene. "Whoa," I said, "what's different here?"

244

"You'll see," Brandi goes without breaking her rhythm.

I came over for a closer look. "You shaved her," I noticed. Bunny's mound was now hair-free and carefree. She was as sleek as the finish on a new car.

"I was sick of waiting and got bored."

Brandi slid the double dong out of their pussies and got on all fours. She ducked between her legs and went south on her. With her mouth, that is.

I started at her shaved pud and tongued my way north, stopping when I hit her left tit. I began to suck it, inhaling nipple and areola.

Deep in the throes of Quaaludes and cunnilingus, Bunny grabbed the back of Brandi's red head and pulled her into her crotch. Her legs were locked across her back like the big, shiny bow on an X-mas present.

Bunny started to buck wildly as the frenzy ripped through her body.

* * *

Brandi went to the bathroom to wash up at the sink. I was hoping she'd take a shower so I could have a few minutes alone with Bunny. But no.

"I feel so naked," she said when she came back into the bedroom.

"You look so naked."

"I mean, I feel so naked without a buzz on."

"Well then tie one on, sweetheart."

We drank bourbon in the nude, going shot for shot. Lucky for me she couldn't hold her liquor the way she could hold a hard-on. She was passed out on the floor inside of thirty minutes.

I crawled over and whispered boozily into Bunny's ear. "Where's Peanut? Where'd he go?"

My tongue was thick from the liquor. But the sedatives running through her brain were as good as a truth serum. For once in her life, she was in no condition to lie to me.

"Mmmmm, I dunno," she smiled, eyes shut. She was still luxuriating in the warm pools of orgasm.

"You can tell me. Where's Peanut?"

"Whoze Peanut?"

"Peanut Gaines."

"Pea-nut, Pea-nut," she sang, giggling. "Who's a little Pea-nut..."

"C'mon. Where's he at?"

"Peanut'ssarriot," she slurred.

"The Riot? He's at the Riot?"

"Mm-hmmm," she said. And then she said, "No. Maybe. He was."

"Tell me where he's at right now. Do you know where he's at?"

"Mm-hmmm..." she said, nodding off.

"Tell me where he's got the real crank."

"Nighty-night..."

"No nighty-night." I lightly slapped her cheeks to revive her. "No nighty-night. Don't go to sleep. Bunny?"

"WhyreyoucallingmeBunny?"

"Cuz that's your name."

"I'm not Bunny."

"You're not?"

"N'uh-uh."

"Then who are you?"

"I'm *Sunny.*"

Wow -- them Quaaludes was some good shit. Bunny didn't know who she was anymore. I made a mental note to save some for me.

"Now listen to me, Sunny-Bunny," I told her. "Don't go to sleep."

"Who's goin' sleep?" she said, narrowing her eyebrows. "I wuv you. I wuv you theeeeeeese much!" she giggled, stretching her arms wide.

"Tell me where he's at."

"Holeeeee Haytiiiii."

"Holy Hayti? You mean the town?"

"The Nighty-Night."

Suddenly I understood what Bunny was babbling about. The Nighty-Night was a motel in Holy Hayti, next to the abandoned Bowl-O-Rama. I'd been through there a few times.

I knew of the joint. I knew something else, too. Peanut was a dead man.

* * *

Brandi was still out of it when I shut the motel door behind me.

I climbed into the Plymouth and started going through my pockets, looking for my keys but coming up empty. I checked the ashtray, the glove compartment, under the mats. Nothing.

"Sonofabitch," I cursed, about to get back out of the car.

That's when I saw Brandi stumbling across the parking lot in see-thru plastic sandals, red suitcase full of sex toys in hand. Flapping about her nearly naked body was a green silk Japanese robe. Before I could make a move, her hand was on the passenger door, yanking it open.

"No, babe, no!" I hollered, sprawling across the seat to block her from sitting down.

"Y'all gonna ditch me like Frank did!"

"I ain't ditching you, darlin' -- I'll be back!"

"No, you won't!"

"Honest I will!"

She kept trying to toss in her suitcase but I kept blocking it with my hands. "I don't believe you! Y'all are lying!"

"But I ain't! I'm just going out to get some cigarettes!"

"Then I'm coming, too!"

"*Hell, no!*"

"Why not?"

"Cuz it's too dangerous, that's why."

"Since when is getting cigarettes dangerous?!"

"This ain't a debate, baby."

"Tell me about it," she goes, pulling the car keys from her purse and jingle-jangling them.

"God*dammit*, Brandi. I like you, I really do. You're a good kid. But there's some things you just don't wanna get messed up in."

She thought it over for a second and then she said, "Nice try but y'all ain't getting the keys until I can come, too."

So much for being reasonable. I went for the keys, reaching over to snatch them out of her hands. But she switched them to her right hand and dangled them out of reach.

"*Fuck*," she cursed as I heard them hit the pavement.

She went down to find them and I scrambled across the seat, trying to get there first. I tumbled out the door and fucked my knee up when I hit the ground. But no way in hell was she gonna beat me to those keys.

I saw them gleaming in the light from the strip. I reached for them but she kicked them away and ran for them. I limped after her.

"Quit acting like a brat!" I hollered.

"*Here*," she said, throwing them at me. They hit me in the chest and my fingers caught them. "Take 'em. But I bet this car's *stolen*."

"Aw, whatta you know?"

"I know y'all are in a shitload of trouble. Don't know what it is but I bet it's bad. So if y'all drive off and leave me here, I'll call the cops. I swear to God I will."

I didn't say anything. I just looked at her standing there all smug as she pinched her kimono shut. And then I told her, "Get in."

"Really?" she said, jumping and clapping her hands giddily like she was a schoolgirl and the captain of the football team just asked her to the prom.

We cut outta there and some fifty miles later, out of the blue, she goes, "I just knew y'all weren't going out for cigarettes."

* * *

At one in the a.m. I was drinking alone at the Kozy Korner bar in the little shithole of Pocatalico. The joint was nearly empty, just me and the bearded bartender with the big beer belly.

I sat at the bar wondering how everything got so fucked up -- love and murder and betrayal on top of betrayal. Crank that wasn't even crank. And that got me thinking about money. I needed it bad and that ain't good.

A few minutes later, Brandi came in the door. She walked by me like she didn't even know me. She took a seat at the other end of the bar.

I watched the barman check her out, trying to figure her story and angle his way into her panties. She looked too good to be sitting alone. Probably on the wrong end of a break-up.

"Wanna talk about it?" he asked.

"Y'all are sweet," she goes. "But I'm okay."

He shrugged. "Cheaper than an analyst."

That got a smile out of her. She was doing a good job of warming him up.

Back in the good old days, a grifter had some short cons he could rely on to burn barkeeps. But then the bastards got wise. That's where Brandi came in.

If you can't fuck with their heads, fuck with their dicks -- the money's all the same.

She looked him over slowly, like she was trying to decide something. Finally she was like, "Y'all got an open mind, right?"

"I like to think so."

"Good, cuz this might sound a little crazy."

"*Uh-oh*," he laughed. "Don't worry -- I've heard it all before."

"Y'all believe that we're all alone in the universe? Or maybe there's somebody else out there?"

"Never put much thought into it, really."

"Well, I know there is. And I know they're here on Earth. I've been abducted by them."

"Them?" he asked.

"Aliens," she said.

"Aliens," he repeated.

I cringed. Two minutes into her come-on and she was already blowing it. We might as well get up and leave right now -- find another barman to hustle.

Why didn't she just do like we agreed -- some sob story about a miserable break up and how she felt all ugly and all she wanted was a man's arms around her again? That was a perfectly good come-on. Short and sweet and it got the job done. But even this asshole wasn't rube enough to fall for this E.T. bullshit.

"See?" she goes, like some kind of accusation. "I just knew y'all wouldn't believe me. *No*body does."

"Hold on a second, now. I didn't say that. I just wanna make sure I'm following you."

"Okay, then," she said. "Just be nice to me cuz I'm feeling really vulnerable right now and when I think about everything that's happened I just wanna cry."

"Don't do that -- don't cry. I mean, what do they call that -- a close encounter?"

"Of the third kind," she said.

"Well, I wanna hear all about it."

"It happened not too long ago," she went on. "It's at night. I'm alone in bed. I remember waking up on my back,

251

but I can't move a muscle. It's like a heavy weight is holding me down.

"And that's when I notice the light. Kind of blue. It's coming from outside the window. It lights up the whole room.

"I hear voices, too. Three or four of 'em, speaking in a strange language. I've never heard anything like it. But I know they're not human.

"By now I'm, like, terrified."

He nodded in sympathy. "Who wouldn't be?"

"Exactly. Next thing I know, I'm in a bright, white room. I mean, I have to shut my eyes it's so bright. And I'm floating in the air."

"Floating?"

"Uh huh. I'm just guessing here, but some kind of anti-gravity force field holds me up."

"Sounds about right," he said, playing along and looking to get lucky.

"And I must be drugged, cuz I'm not at all scared. I'm not afraid of falling. My body's totally relaxed. It's almost like I'm underwater. My hair is drifting around my head. I'm completely weightless and feeling very lazy --"

He held up his hand to stop her. "Hold on a minute." He came down to my end of the bar. "Another beer, buddy? Last call."

I shook my head, playing drunker than I actually was, and pulled my last twenty out of my wallet. Brandi better come through, I thought, or else we are fucked in the worst way. We didn't have enough gas to get out of town much less halfway across the country to Holy Hayti.

"Alright then," he goes, taking the bill and dropping it in a slot behind the bar. I couldn't see the safe, but I knew it was there. He popped the register and slid me my change. "G' night."

I nodded but he was already headed back to Brandi.

"Oh," she goes, "did I say I'm totally naked?"

"Uh, no. You left that part out."

"I am. I usually sleep in like a T-shirt and panties. But they must've stripped me cuz now I'm totally nude.

"That's when I become really aware of my, like, pussy. It's totally relaxed, like how all the muscles have to relax before I can pee? It's like that. Only I don't have to pee. Suddenly something starts to touch my pussy."

"Some*thing*?" he said, his voice cracking.

"Uh-huh. Like a probe of some kind. It's smooth and hard like steel. And if feels cold at first, like a surgical tool. But eventually this probe-thingy warms up from my body heat.

"It moves around the outside of my pussy, tracing my lips like it's making a map. And I'm getting turned on, right?"

All he could do was nod. Even from here I could see the blood rushing to his face. He pulled at his shirt collar to release the steam. Lucky for him the bartop was high enough to hide the hard-on that had to be bulging in his pants.

Who could blame him though? It isn't every day a strange and beautiful woman tells you about her pussy. And what description! She had a real knack for it, leaving nothing to the imagination.

My own damn cock lurched ahead. I shifted in my seat, adjusting my hard-on so it wouldn't get pinched. I felt the sticky drops of pre-cum on the inside of my thigh.

"I mean, by this time, my pussy is tingling. It's alive. It's vast. It, like, opens up and swallows my whole body. I can't even begin to describe it."

"You're doing alright," he said.

"There were these things fasted to my nipples, too. Electrodes or something. They were like suction cups. But they're vibrating. I mean, my nipples are super-sensitive as it is."

"Really," he said.

"Oh, yeah. Even now, they are, like, *on*."

"Really?"

"Mmmm," she purred, fixing him in her green eyes. "Y'all must have the air-conditioner on real high."

She cupped her tits, one in each hand, and let her thumbs run back and forth over the excited nipples. She tipped her head back and shook out her hair.

"Suddenly I feel something sliding into my behind. It's extremely thin, no more than a wire. So it goes up my ass like nothing at all."

Oh, yeah -- he was going along for her ride. She had him by the balls now. And to think I ever doubted her! What a fool I was!

"I think," she goes, "the aliens run a low voltage current through it or maybe like a microwave. Cuz my ass is, like, buzzing."

"Your ass is..."

"*Buzzing*," she drawls. "It's so intense. Like my insides are melting.

"Then the wire begins to swell. My ass, like, opens up with it. And suddenly I'm, like, gaping. My ass is stretched like never before.

254

"And, believe me, I'm not into anal. I mean, for other people it's cool. Different strokes and all. But a guy comes anyway near my ass and I tighten up. You wouldn't touch my ass, would you?"

"No, never."

"I mean, everything but, right?" she said, flashing a lazy smile.

"Right."

What the hell was she going on about? Who cares! My girl was merciless! By now he was so horny, he probably didn't even look up to see if I was still hanging around.

I was down on my hands and knees on the sticky floor, under a table in the dark corner.

"But that's not all," she said.

"It's not?" he asked, probably thinking, *What more could there be*? I was thinking the same damn thing myself.

She goes, "They planted a chip inside me."

"A chip?" he said. perplexed.

"You know, like in a computer. But an alien one. To monitor my sexual activity."

He was dumbstruck.

"Y'all believe me?" she asked.

"I believe that you believe," he said carefully.

She groaned like that wasn't the answer she wanted to hear. "Okay," she said at last. "Would you believe me if I showed you?"

"Showed me what?"

"My pussy. So y'all can see for yourself."

"What -- you mean, right now?"

255

"Mm-hmm. Right here, right now."

"Yeah -- I'll, uh, take a look," trying to sound cool and casual about it. "You mean, right right now, right?"

"Uh-huh. We're alone, right?"

"Right, we're alone." I heard him take a look around. "Let me, uh, lock up first, 'kay? Don't go nowhere."

He couldn't lock the deadbolt fast enough. Practically skipping for joy as he made his way around the bar and across the joint. Paranoid pussy on his mind as he turned the deadbolt.

Brandi was on the pinball machine, arching her back and lifting her ass as she tugged her shorts and panties over her hips. She eased them down to her ankles and spread her legs so far her knees were on the table.

"Lord have mercy," he groaned when he turned around and saw her butterfly herself for him. She used both hands, too, crossing her arms and fanning her fingers like the girls in the dirty pictures do.

"Come closer, honey," she goes. "Y'all gotta look real hard to see it. *Closer.*"

"It won't shoot me, will it?"

"Ain't shot anyone yet. Come closer. See it?"

"I think I do. Maybe."

"Closer, sweetie. Don't be scared of a li'l ol' pussy."

He was bent over so close to her cunt you'd think he was gonna dive right in. "Oh, yeah. Uh-huh. I think I see it now. A-yep. There it is. Can I touch it?"

"Touch it all ya want, honeykins."

He lifted his finger. "Well, I'll be godda --"

The blackjack made a soft thunk when it hit the back of his skull. It was made out of a tube sock with twenty bucks in quarters in the toe and the whole thing wrapped tight in electrical tape. But the bastard didn't go down.

He just stood there, teetering a bit -- in shock more than anything else. Brandi craned her neck to see me over his shoulder. Her green eyes narrowed in consternation.

"Hit him again!" she yelled.

But I was way ahead of her, already hauling off to sap him again. This time I brained him in the sweet spot. His legs buckled and I threw my arms around him before he could fall into Brandi's crotch.

"God*damn*," I grunted, trying to pull him backwards but he weighed a ton. It was all I could do to hold him up but he was slipping fast. "Move! Move!" I ordered.

Brandi rolled away and I rode the tub-o-lard like an avalanche as he crashed onto the pinball machine and then slumped to the floor. By the time I got out from under the slob, Brandi was already emptying the register.

"Alien implant in your pussy?" I said, kissing her on the mouth. "I mean, c'mon! But by the end of it you even had *me* going. Bee-yoo-tee-ful!"

I bent down and found the combination safe that he'd been dropping twenties in all night. "Y'all didn't tell me you were a safe cracker," Brandi goes.

And I was like, "That's cuz I ain't. But if this guy's like every other lazy bastard, he's got the combination already rolled..."

I tweaked the dial and heard those tumblers fall into place and the soft give of the lock. I yanked the door and the iron bitch opened for me like a ten-dollar whore.

"Suuu-weet!" I cried as twenties and fifties and a couple hundred dollar bills cascaded out. Brandi knelt beside me, stuffing the loose bills into her purse. I pulled out the bank bag and unzipped it.

"How much is there, baby?" she asked hopefully.

I pulled it open so she could see that it was empty.

"Oh," she goes, deflated.

"Everything can't go your way all the time. But we got enough to get us where we're going."

"Where we going?"

"To settle an old score. And when we're through, we'll be set for life. I think."

* * *

We hit the road with a full tank of gas. I drove the shit out of the Plymouth, relying on the Interstates that ran through townhouse backyards.

Driving by so fast, I could see right through the slats in the tall fences. It was all pine decks and swing sets and emerald chemlawns till I wanted to puke.

Eleven hundred miles in just under twelve hours later, we reached Holy Hayti. It was late afternoon. We went straight to the Nighty-Night. I made Brandi stay in the car. "Keep the engine running," I said.

Ten bucks to the desk clerk got me Peanut's room number.

I held the .38 up as I tried the door. It was unlocked. I eased it open a crack.

My spider sense started tingling as I pushed my way inside. A wedge of golden sunlight shot across the dark room. It was like walking into the end of a horror flick -- the part where the local cop discovers the carnage and mayhem.

The place had been ransacked. Drawers open, clothing scattered, mattress half off the bed. My eyes shot from one detail to the next like connect-the-dots.

The bathroom door was open. I could see a man's leg bent over the side of the tub.

As I came closer, I saw Peanut Gaines slumped inside. He was in only his boxers, his back propped up against the end of the tub. Covered in so much damn blood I couldn't tell where the holes were.

But I could hear him wheezing with every breath, the lungs bubbling as they filled with blood. Yeah, somebody got to somebody, that's for damn sure.

"Who did this to you, old man?"

He ran a dried-out tongue over his lips and tried to speak. A rasp like sandpaper slipped out of his mouth.

"Forget it," I said. "Doesn't matter anymore."

His eyes flared and he wiped the gore from his chest. Through the curls of his chest hair I could see a tattoo of a naked lady. *Bunny* it said in fancy lettering beneath the curvy figure wrapped in a bright green snake.

He kept stabbing his finger at the tattoo but he was delirious, seeing things.

No way Bunny did this. She was still wasted in Jasper-Purdy. Not even Bunny LaFever could be two places at once.

Peanut had fucked with the wrong guy is all. I unwrapped the plastic cup on the sink and filled the poor pathetic bastard a drink of tap water. I tipped it into his mouth.

"Where's the money?" I go, hoping he was thinking straight about that. Hoping there was money -- or something -- worth coming back for. "Where's the drugs?"

"Sixty-nine," he goes, wincing with pain.

Here he was on his deathbed, and the only thing on his mind was a little simultaneous oral. But who the hell was I to rain on a dead man's parade? Let the fucker dream.

"Sixty-*nine*," he said again, reaching up to pull me close to his face. "Car," he croaked.

"What -- it's hidden in a car, or what?"

When he smiled, a string of bloody drool ran over his lip and off his chin.

I nudged his shoulder. He was looking at me and then he was looking through me. His eyes were open but I knew that Elvis had left the building.

* * *

"What happened back there?" she goes as I gunned it to the Laff Riot. "What did y'all see?"

But I was in no mood to talk. A man sees certain things and he's got nothing to say about it. All I could do was play it over in my mind.

I didn't know much about Peanut but I knew a tough guy like that had to be mixed up in a lot of crazy shit. It was only a matter of time before the chickens came home to roost. Whatever went down, the fucker probably deserved it.

* * *

The track at the fairgrounds was on the small side. Not big enough for a full-blown auto race. Number 69 was probably some kind of funny car.

Turns out I was close but no cigar. According to the posters everywhere, it wasn't a race scheduled for that night.

It was a goddamn demolition derby.

* * *

260

At the far side of the track was the derby pit where gearheads were making last-minute repair jobs on their junkers.

I wandered around and in between the heaps, checking out the numbers spraypainted on their sides: 77, 13, 00.

Local guys in coveralls and grease-stained wife-beaters gave me dirty looks over their shoulders. Like I was some kind of spy. Like I gave a shit.

That's when I spotted the elusive 69. It was a Mercury Fire-Eater, sandwiched in between the Chrysler Prowess and Dodge Derringer. The late-model Merc was a real rust-bucket. Primer was the only thing holding her together.

The hood was up, hiding the mechanic. As I walked around to the front, I heard her spitting unimaginative curses as she banged around inside. It was all *fuck shit fuck shit fuck shit fuck!*

I stepped back to give her room and dig the auto erotica. She had an ass that could take on all comers. Short shorts were wedged into her deep crevice. Dreaming about tugging it out of her cheeks with my teeth gave my tongue a hard-on.

At one point she leaned so far inside that her legs spread and her tight ass parted just enough for me to get a good glimpse. How good? So good I could die a happy man because I had finally seen everything this old world has to offer.

She must've felt my eyes on her. Like two laser beams burning holes through her shorts.

"Do you mind?" she goes without looking up -- as if she didn't know what the hell she was doing dressed like that. She was broadcasting the fuck-me vibe like Mexican radio.

She reached around and tried to tug down her shorts but they shot right back up. Her fingers left behind a smear of grease. I would've licked it off if she'd asked. It would've been chocolate syrup to me.

I was like, "So -- can you fix it?"

"Of course I can fix it," she snapped without looking up.

"You got the parts?"

Annoyed, she turned to look at me. My crotch was level with her face. Reflected in her mirrored sunglasses was the hard-on that grew down my leg. That caught her interest.

"What do you think?" she goes, standing straight and cocking a hip.

I inventoried the particulars: tits out to there, slender waist and an ass you'd crawl over broken glass to get at. A real put-together kind of girl.

"I think I just shit my pants. Can I get into yours?"

The hell with it, I thought. Never waste an erection. You never know which one'll be your last. I'd hate to die thinking I missed a good screw somewhere along the line.

* * *

Her name was Dawn Butler, but that wasn't important. What mattered was how I was bending her fender under the grandstand. I was doing a bang-up job of it, too.

She was bent over a beam with her red shorts down around her ankles. Her bottom was up in the air. I went at it, full-tilt and to the hilt. That pussy was humming in no time.

With every in-and-out, I put the knock in knockers. Those galloping gazongas were swinging every which way as I pulled out to the knob and then slammed back in to the hilt. She nearly gave herself a black eye.

Drunk off the smell of gasoline, I spread Dawn's dimpled asscheeks and drove her to the brink of the Big-O-Blivion. She was stretched so tight around my priapic purple piston that it looked like my schlong was dipped in pink rubber. But it's not like this white-knuckled ride wasn't all part of a greater plan. Hell, no. I was gonna win her over with my charms. My magic dick would convince her to give me the car. Or else leave her lying there, exhausted, and steal the damn thing.

Steering her by the hips, I pulled her back onto my pipe as I plowed deeper inside. I wanted to bang her into next week. I upped the rhythm of the free-wheeling friction until I was nothing but a cock quivering in her quiff.

Dawn finally came, screaming like a missile. The roar of the crowd and the rev of engines drowned out her cries. I poured on the gas and then downshifted, suddenly exploding like a backfiring car.

I was still cumming a thick vanilla milkshake when, behind me, a gun cocked. You'd hear that sound in a hurricane. As clear and unmistakable as a fart in church. Sounded like my long, lost .38, too.

"Hi ya, dope," the gunman said, jabbing the barrel in my back and really killing the mood. I mean, I'm always a little down after dogging some broad but this was ridiculous.

I glanced back over my shoulder and saw it was my old friend Pigtails. As ugly as ever.

"Remember me?" he said, cracking an evil smile.

"Not really," I lied.

Dawn piped up: "He's Louie Roulette."

Pigtails/Roulette goes, "Sons of Satan remember you real good, Randy. We remember how you stiffed us fifteen large."

"Wait a minute -- now it's coming back."

"Told you nothing was ever over."

I was like, "Yeah, that reminds me. How's the foot? Looks like you got a little bit of a limp there."

* * *

They walked me out of the grandstand, past the Sno-Kone joint and T-shirt shack. I didn't try anything funny. I'd lost my sense of humor back there with my hard-on.

"Where we going?" I asked as we headed into the parking lot. A mangy yellow dog stood lapping at the puddle of an ice cream cone some kid dropped. When you're about to die, you notice the damnedest things.

"Your car," he said.

When we reached the Plymouth, Brandi was getting out of the front seat. Worry creased her face. "What's goin' on, Randy?"

"I dunno." I looked back over my shoulder. "What's goin' on?"

Roulette lost his smile. "Get back in," he told Brandi, flashing her the .38.

"Listen to the bad man," I said.

Roulette goes to Dawn, "You're driving, babe. Girls up front, boys in the back. Just like fuckin' Kindergarten."

* * *

Dawn dropped us off at the Motel Bouffant.

"You did good," Roulette told her. "Take the car. And win Daddy another trophy tonight."

She got back in the Ambush and roared off with a laugh.

Roulette looked at me and shrugged. "I promised her your ride for the demo derby on account of her alternator's shot. You don't mind, do you? Didn't think so."

264

He walked us to Room 109. He told me to go in -- the door was open. And there she was, all dolled up and waiting for me.

"Bunny!" I said.

"Yeah, it's me, bright boy," she snarled with the hands on the hips and her blonde hair falling over half her face. Her red lips were like a gaping wound in my heart and every word was more salt rubbed in: "Who the hell'd you expect?"

* * *

"If there's one thing I hate," I grumbled, "it's a goddamn double-crossing dame."

"Spare me," she goes, rolling her blue eyes impatiently. "I'm a moneymaking bitch. You just got in my way."

She was dressed in a short, red satin robe. Underneath was a black lace bra that her tits were fighting to get out of.

"Think you're something special, Roulette?" I said. "You'll just get in her way, too."

"Shut up, you," he snapped, aiming that .38 at my head. "Whaddaya think, Bunny -- a little off the top?"

"Why don't all y'all just shoot him in the back?" Brandi bitched.

I gave her a look. "They don't need any pointers, thank you."

Bunny turned on Brandi. "You got something to say, Miss America?"

"I don't think y'all could beat us in a fair fight. How 'bout a little demolition derby of our own tonight?"

"What're you driving at?" Roulette asked.

"An orgy. You and Bunny against me and Randy. The last couple fucking, wins."

"Wins what?"

"Our freedom."

"What do we get when *we* win?" he chuckled.

"Whatever makes y'all happy. Kill us both -- whatever."

"I'm game," said Bunny.

"I dunno..." Roulette growled.

"C'mon honey," Bunny cooed in his ear. "Put your testicles to the test. It'll be fun."

"Easy for you to say," he said. "You just lie there."

"You scared?" she goes.

He got all defensive: "Who said I was scared?"

"Baby, I understand," Bunny said. "If you can't go the distance, you can't go the distance."

"Enough!" he barked. He let his dick make the decision for him. "We're in."

He lowered his gun. I went to Brandi. I was grateful for the reprieve but Brandi was a fool to stick her neck out for me and I told her so.

"You're gambling with your life, darlin'."

"Gambling's for rubes. Right now, I've never been so sure of anything in my life. Remember that alien story I told the bartender?"

"The one about the computer chip?"

"It wasn't just a story," she goes, whispering under her breath. "It's for real."

I looked at her, not saying anything. If she was shitting me, her face didn't let on.

She was like, "Once it starts buzzing down there, there's only one way to make it stop."

"You mean --?"

"Y'all better believe it."

"Is it going off right now?"

"Mm-hmmm..."

* * *

Brandi laid down the rules of the orgy, keeping it simple for Roulette: No holes barred. Any and everything goes. But no time outs.

If anybody stopped fucking, sucking, licking or tricking for more than thirty seconds, the couple was O-U-T spells out. Kinda like a dance marathon, but a helluva lot more interesting.

"Gentlemen, start your engines," Brandi announced with a wink and a wiggle as they began to take it off. My eyes darted from one to the other, desperately trying to keep them both in focus.

Bunny let the robe slip off her shoulders. She unfastened her bra but the cups clung to her breasts. She swung them around like that, teasing us for a while before tossing it aside.

Bunny's big boobs had razor sharp tan lines that tattooed themselves on the inside of my skull. The suntan contrasted incredibly with the milky white flesh. It was like a picture frame for the glowing bullseye of her nipples.

Their pink areolas were as big around as silver dollars. The air-conditioning made Bunny's nipples look like the candied cherries on ice cream sundaes. I wanted to dip my hands in and scoop those big bowls into my mouth.

Even now, after everything, I was in danger of falling for that she-devil again. Lucky for me, Brandi was there working her own bump-and-grind. When she swiveled her hips, it was like Soft-Serv swirling into an ice cream cone.

267

She stretched her tiny cotton T-shirt over her rack. Tits are like snowflakes -- you never see the same pair twice. And believe you me, I've spent a lifetime looking.

Sick of idling in neutral, I dropped into gear and peeled out. My revved-up hard-on led the way across the room. It felt gigantic as it bounced in front of me.

The girls were ready for hard cocks, too. Brandi and I collided in an embrace. Good and sloppy tongue-kisses tied our jaws together. Her long nails strafed my back as her leg wrapped around my waist and squeezed.

It was time for some good old-fashioned tit-worship. I lowered my mouth to sample those scrumptious suck-melons. My fingers slipped into her ever-ready snatch. Peeking from its hood, her clit was as hard and slippery as a ball bearing in a puddle of oil. I rolled it under my finger until she moaned and bit my ear.

With one hand I cupped a firm, round asscheek to maneuver her into a stand-up fuck. With the other hand, I guided myself into the smooth, satin folds. I eased in to the balls.

Out of the corner of my eye, I spied Roulette and Bunny on the floor, missionary style. He aimed for the juicy target between her widespread legs, just below her sun tattoo. Hit dead-center and slid home.

"Know your limits, babe," Brandi coached. "Pace yourself. Nice and easy."

"Sounds like you've done this before," I cracked.

"Just don't get cocky and blow it."

"Don't worry about my cock. Just sit back and enjoy the ride."

"I intend to, dammit. I've *earned* this fuck-for-all."

Instinct told me to drive Brandi fast and hard. I put the pedal to the metal and went all out. She begged me to slow down.

"This ain't a race, honey," she panted in my ears. "Think of our lives!"

But she didn't get it. I had to drive this orgy like a demolition derby. And the only strategy in a Detroit Rumble is SHOW NO MERCY. You gotta beat the other guy into submission.

I knew that if I kept driving hard and fast, Roulette's ego would make him try to keep up with me. All I could do was count on his bone breaking down first. And hope my trusty tool wouldn't backfire on me.

The pleasures of friction changed Brandi's mind about obeying speed limits. Stoked by my strokes, she met me thrust for thrust. We accelerated, bodies banging, skin slapping, balls and bazooms bouncing.

Roulette and I went head to head. Like I'd predicted, he matched my pace. Their bodies crashed together with a force that bulldozed Bunny across the floor. Carpet burns scorched her ass.

"Ow!" she bitched.

"Give up?" Brandi yelled.

"You wish!" she shot right back.

Brandi's pussy gripped me tight as a vise as she clenched her secret love muscles. I thought of fat women on the beach to keep from filling her tank too soon.

I reached down and fingered her trigger until she exploded. Her back arched as the ecstasy rippled out from her womb. Her cunt spazzed up and down my shaft.

I frigged her clit and rammed for ten minutes more as orgasm after orgasm shattered her nerves. It felt too good. She couldn't take it anymore and had to push me away.

Roulette was the first to blow his rod. He pulled out with a groan and trimmed Bunny's tits. She lifted them like she was serving up two tremendous tankards at a dairy bar.

"Lemme show y'all a trick," Brandi said. "Stand up."

I got to my feet. Kneeling before me, she lifted her breasts to sandwich my shaft.

Kneading and pumping my package between her pumpkins, that girl knew how to please a tit man. When my cockhead peeked from her cleavage, she wrapped her lips around my knob and sucked on it like an overripe strawberry.

Stuck in titty city, I tried to hold back. But suddenly my toes curled and I was unloading between her lips. She gazed up at me with wide eyes as she swallowed the high-octane mouthful that pulsed from my pecker. She fellated me until I was deflated.

"Ohh," she said sadly as my gobstopper slipped away.

"Don't worry, darlin' -- the South will rise again."

"Amen to that!" she rebel-yelled.

Down but not out, I bumped her on her back and crashed headfirst into that sopping muff. I made like Evil Knievel and drove her crazy with my motormouth stunt show.

Brandi grabbed the back of my head and ground my face into her crotch. Her legs locked across my back as I tore into her cunt, jawboning until the tangy juices ran down my chin. She careened toward orgasm.

* * *

270

At some point I saw a flash of naked flesh as Bunny darted to the bathroom. "Thirty seconds!" I called out, reminding her of the time limit.

"She's been running back and forth to the bathroom all day," Brandi bitched. "What's up with that?"

"Must be popping amyl nitrates or something," I said. "To keep her going."

"Speaking of going," she said, "there it goes again!"

"Your alien implant?"

"Oh, yeah."

Lucky for the both of us, my dick was all gassed-up and ready to go, go, go. I tossed Brandi on her hands and knees. You know the drill: Tab A, Slot B, all that. She sideswiped my prick, over and over again.

I was giddy, crunch drunk, wanting more. Back and forth we rocked in the Masochism Tango. We were locked together in a knot of twisted flesh and rolling breasts.

Brandi took control. I took a breather on my back. Facing away from me, she squatted above my towering tool and fit my cockhead between her snug lips. She began sliding up and down, fucking herself with my dick. That gal had energy to burn.

I crawled out from under Brandi and blitzed her from behind. Smashed her from the side. Slammed her as she rode on top. Rammed her as she sat on my lap. I went ballistic between those hooters again and again. She was getting more deposits than a bank.

Hours passed by. In between erections, I ate her out till my tongue cramped up. My taste buds were as bald as old tires. My lips were like rubber.

This grueling fuck fest felt like forever. I wasn't afraid of cumming too soon -- I was afraid of coming apart. My

271

whole body was shaking and aching. I felt muscles I never knew I had.

By now my cock was burning fumes. I had the dry throbs -- I was cumming air. My shaft was rubbed red as a dog's dick.

I'd been fucking so long I wasn't human anymore. I couldn't go on. I went on.

I swore I was done for until I saw my competition. Slumped over her backside, Roulette doggied Bunny. He barely moved. It was now or never.

Mustering every ounce of energy I had left, I fired back to life. Brandi's tight bottom was up in the air, grinding invitingly like a neon vacancy sign in the middle of nowhere.

I got up and found a bottle of baby oil. I started to pour like crazy. When it comes to buttscrewing, the more lube, the better. You can't have too much. It cascaded over her cheeks like the waterfall at a megamall.

My index finger slipped into her greasy crevice. Her hips swayed at the invasion. She groaned with deviant pleasure. I was in to the knuckle. I worked it around and then popped it back out.

I massaged her cheeks, kneading the buttflesh while slowly spreading them apart. Her hole was truly open for business. It shimmered like a mirage.

I squeezed more oil over my red-hot cock. I pumped my shaft a few times to coat it completely. Finally I positioned my dickhead at the entrance to her exit.

Inch by greasy inch, my hard-on piled inside. Her nasty ass took it all. She was completely filled. She gripped me tight as a fist as I began to fuck it faster.

Talk about rear-end collision! This was some rectal wreckage. I tried to grab hold of those asscheeks. My fingers slipped across the greasy skin.

My head was pounding. Everything was a blur. The sweat poured off me as adrenaline pumped through my veins.

Sex is a cross-country road trip, and anal is like finally making California. After that all you can do is drop off the face of the earth. I couldn't get there fast enough.

While I'm gunning my nads for the big finish, that chickenshit Roulette wrenched himself free from Bunny and tried to limp away. But he was shot and knew it.

"Thirty seconds," I reminded him, panting. "Or else!"

"The clock's ticking!" Brandi chimed in.

"C'mon, Roulette! Bu-fu that blonde bitch!"

He squeezed some oil on his joint and tried to muscle his way into Bunny's astounding ass. But he was too soft. No way in hell could she take his wreckage up her rectum.

He pried her open with his fingers, just enough to fit his knob. But he couldn't shove in any more. The veins on his neck bulged he tried so hard to jump-start his jizzed-out johnson.

Suddenly I heard his engine sputter and die. His dick went completely limp. Just like that it was over. *Kaput.* He crashed to the floor, totaled, and actually started to cry like a baby and yank his greasy pigtails till I swore he would tear them out.

"We did it!" Brandi cried as our bodies fell into a tangled heap -- too conked to celebrate. My eyes went in and out of focus. I was fading fast, already dreaming of a six-pack of Demerol.

I looked over and saw Bunny's body split into two and then seamlessly merge back into one. They separated again but now, instead of melting back together, there were two of them. Two distinct Bunnies, embracing and kissing, hands exploring matching bodies.

They went tit-to-tit and mouth-to-mouth. Their tongues braided together. One reached between the other's legs.

This was too real to be just a hallucination. This was my tortured brain actually bending reality to the breaking-point. The scariest thing in the world is knowing that you're losing your mind.

There's a certain point, before you're too far gone, when you can still feel your grasp on the narrow ledge of sanity. But your bloodied fingers are slipping fast and you can see the blackness beneath your dangling legs.

Brandi's angry cry brought me back from the other side. "Cheaters!" she screamed. "Dirty, rotten cheaters!"

"Aw, go dry up!" both Bunnies growled simultaneously. I boxed my ears. I was hearing double now, too.

"Randy, they're *twins*!" cried Brandi. "They're twin *sisters*!"

* * *

"And since *we're* still going at it," the one on the left said, wrapping her limbs around her double's body.

"Looks like *we're* the winners," righty goes.

They looked good in their naked and shaved glory. Even covered in oil, sweat, spit, juice and carpet filth, they could make a drunk man sober and a sober man drunk.

"That's not fair!" Brandi cried.

Lefty was like, "Who the hell told you life was fair?"

274

"Never give suckers an even break," righty said, reciting the grifter's credo.

"There's no percentage in it," lefty finished.

"They've been switching back and forth all day!" Brandi cried.

Righty said, "We've been switching back and forth since the very beginning."

"You were fucked the night you first laid eyes on us," lefty said to me.

They started to laugh. But it wasn't one of those friendly *ain't-we-all-in-on-the-joke* laughs. It was one of those cruel *you've-been-fucked-over-bigtime* laughs.

I'm big enough to admit it -- they had me fooled. But the mix-up was an honest mistake. They looked so alike it was spooky. Eerily identical, like mirror images.

"So which one of you is Bunny?" I asked.

"I am," said the one. "And she's Sunny."

Sunny! I thought, shaking my head. So she wasn't shitting me back at the O.K. Motel. The signs are always there -- if only you knew how to read them.

I was like, "That's a lot of trouble to go through just to hustle me."

"You?!" asked Bunny, outraged.

"Who the fuck're *you*?!"

"You're nobody."

"You're nothing but a carny grifter."

"It's Peanut we were really after."

Sunny was like, "O.B. and Peanut were so close that killing one meant killing the other."

"So we suckered Peanut into thinking he was offing O.B. and pinning it on you, bright boy."

"So he and Bunny LaFever could take over the Riot --"

"And the money laundering business --"

"And live happily ever after," finished Sunny. "But he was the one we were setting up."

"We were after the Laff Riot's stash --"

"Three million, cash."

"You were just a tool, Randy."

"Nothing personal, eh, *Actual Size*?"

"What about Roulette?" I said, pointing my chin at his body sprawled out like a corpse. "He's on a mission for the Sons of Satan."

"Not anymore, he isn't," Bunny said with a smirk.

"You'd be surprised what some guys would do for a fuck."

"But you know all about that -- don't you, Randy?"

They'd played a crazy double con. One laid over the other like linoleum on a kitchen floor. It was a beautiful set-up, the best I'd ever heard.

After all, there's only one way to hustle a hustler -- and that's with another hustle.

I was like, "Bravo, ladies. You win."

"We *always* win," said Sunny. "But at least you're smart enough to know when you're beat."

"So be a bright boy and walk away from the game."

"But if you go back to the carny, they'll nail you for O.B."

"Peanut fingered you for the hit."

"And if you go to the cops, they'll nail you for Peanut."

"We planted your name all over the motel room."

"Looks like the only place you can run to is the circus."

"Every circus needs a trained monkey."

"You bitch!" Brandi screeched as she pounced on Bunny and yanked her blonde hair. Bunny fought back, grabbing Brandi's tits. Her fingernails pressed into the soft flesh.

They went at it with claws out, arms flailing and long legs kicking. Nails scraped skin. Angry red scratches pin-striped backs and thighs.

Two naked chicks fighting, and me without a camera. Hell, I shouldn't have been surprised, the way my life was going. What's one more letdown on top of everything else?

The two were thrashing it up pretty good. It looked like a toss-up. But Brandi scored the first takedown.

They rolled across the floor, a tangle of wild legs. Bunny wound up on top, squeezing Brandi's head between her aerobicized thighs until her red face matched the color of her hair.

Suddenly Brandi bared her teeth and sank those choppers into Bunny's thigh. The blonde howled in pain, and relaxed her hold. Their heavy tits swayed as they wrassled around the floor.

The sudden gunshot made me jump. The girls stopped fighting. We all looked at Sunny and the smoking .38 in her hand. She'd shot the first bullet into the mattress but the look on her face said she'd only be too happy to sink number two into me or Brandi.

"Enough," she spat, disgusted.

"I'm thirsty," said Bunny. "Have a drink." It wasn't a friendly offer. It was a command, backed up by the piece in Sunny's hand.

Sunny waved us to the bed, where we sat down. She kept the gun on us while Bunny emptied a bottle of whiskey into two big plastic Gas Guzzler cups. She handed one to me and the other to Brandi.

"Bottoms up," she goes.

Brandi sniffed hers suspiciously. "What's in it?"

Sunny said, "That's for us to know --"

"And you to find out."

It was either take a drink or take a bullet. That wasn't a choice. I lifted the cup and opened my throat.

Whatever spiked the whiskey, they used plenty of it. I could feel its effects almost instantly. The numbness started in my fingers and toes but traveled to my brain. Fuzziness clouded my senses as the sedative went to work and did its job.

I could barely feel her lips on mine as Bunny planted a big wet one on me. Sunny tongued my ear, whispering with her hot, breathy voice: "G'night, bright boy."

Bunny broke her kiss. "It's been *real* real." Her words sounded a million miles away. I faded to black wondering if I'd ever see the light of day again.

* * *

My head was pounding when I came to in the dark room. It was just the two of us on that bed -- me and Brandi.

I felt sick and dirty as I got up and went to the bathroom. My cottonmouth was so parched I had to suck down cold water straight out of the tub's faucet till my belly was about to bust.

I lay back on the bed, replaying the whole thing over and over in my mind. Shit don't come outta nowhere -- just don't-know-where. The set-up was obvious, but I'd been too busy watching their curves to see their audacious angle.

Brandi woke up a few hours later. We cleaned up and got dressed without saying much. "What now?" she finally asked, breaking the silence.

"We're gonna do like they said -- walk away and forget it. They conned us fair and square."

"It kills me to think they're gonna get away with it."

"You'll get over it," I said, "same as me."

* * *

"Looks like Dawn brought back the Plymouth," I said as we stepped outside. "Wonder if she won the derby."

The Ambush sat in the lot, abandoned and crushed like a goddamn can of soda pop. *CHERRY BUSTER* was spray-painted in black on the side. In red, *HIT ME* on the twisted trunk. Three of the tires were so flat they'd been pulled off their rims.

"Why'd she bother?" Brandi wondered out loud.

"To rub it in, I guess."

"People just totally suck."

I ran my hand along the frame. It was wet with dew. I peered inside.

It had been stripped for the derby. Windows removed, door panels and dash ripped out, battery sitting where the back seat used to be. Everything to make it crash worthy.

"At least we got out with our lives, right?" she goes. Her green eyes were big and hopeful and made me feel worse than before.

"If you can call this living," I said. My life had been pulled out from under me like a rug.

Some carnivals can burn a lot so bad that no carny can ever play there again. In a way, that's what the LaFever twins had done to me -- burned me so bad that my life as I knew it was over. I couldn't be with it anymore.

I lost my cool then. When you hit bottom, start digging. I started pummeling and kicking the hell out of the Plymouth -- taking everything out on the car.

I tore open the door, and it came away in my hand. Brandi hit the dirt as I threw it aside and began boxing the seat cushions, the only thing left to destroy.

I heard the springs squeak and fabric tear. I kept pushing and pulling, wanting to pull it apart. The car wasn't dead yet.

But I was gonna finish the job. It felt good when the seat ripped free in my hands. I tossed it ten feet.

"They'll arrest you or something!" she cried and went to fetch it.

"It's my goddamn car," I bitched, collapsing against the side, sweating and holding my throbbing head. "I stole it. I can do whatever the fuck I want to it."

I noticed her silence then and looked up. She was down on the ground, reaching her hand into a tear in the seat back.

"What's this?" she asked.

I came over. She opened her fist. Resting on it was an "egg" of duct tape. I plucked it out of her palm and weighed it in my hand.

"I dunno," I said, pulling out my pocketknife. I sank its blade into the tape and slowly cut a slit straight down the egg. I spread the edges and the contents appeared like raw gem stones.

"*Kee-rist*," I chuckled at the rough yellow crystals. I smelled it and touched it, then tasted the grains that came away on my fingertip to make sure it was pure.

"What is it?" she asked.

"It's crystal meth. Hydro. Good shit, too."

"There's more of those taped-up thingies in here."

We'd discovered Ulysses' stash. A treasure buried in the wreckage. I got down beside her and we started digging out chunks of foam to remove egg after egg.

"I bet there's more of them in the other seat, too," I said, getting giddier by the second. We'd struck the motherlode. This was the payoff of a lifetime.

If Brandi was anybody else, I would've already been scheming against her. Trying to angle her outta her cut. But I wasn't.

The only thing I could see before me was a giant, star-spangled sign off some far-away interstate:

RANDY'S RED-HOT ROCKETS

WORLD'S BIGGEST FIREWORKS OUTLET

CUT-RATE CIGARETTES & RV CAMP

Below it was Brandi, peddling firecrackers, cherry bombs, M-80s and bottle rockets to tourists with out-of-state plates. And me without two of my fingers, blown off by a quarter stick of dynamite, and scaring little kids with my oogly stumps and telling their pops you never hear the one that gets you. Yeah, that'd be the life.

I was through with the carny routine, always moving and getting nowhere. It was time to be somewhere. Once and for all.

* * *

Fate, chance, karma, whatever you wanna call it -- sometimes it comes and pisses on your doorstep. Then again, maybe it's just bringing you a chocolate cake to say, *Welcome to the neighborhood*. You never know till you open the door.

"That's it, darlin'," I said, opening my eyes and grinning like an idiot.

I was battered and bruised but I hear true love knocks you for a loop. And here I thought love was just another lie men told -- like, *I was just helping this sheep over the fence -- but was I wrong*.

I told her, "This score's gonna get me straight in the end."

"Y'all better," she goes and when she stood up, I knew that ass was the best damn thing that ever happened to me, bar-fucking-none. "If y'all wanna get *me* in the end."

About the Authors

Randy Everhard was born in Natchitoches, Louisiana, the son of a traveling Bible salesman. At the tender age of sixteen, he ran away with the carnival and never looked back. A graduate of the "School of Hard Knocks," he sees his future very optimistically and would love to play King Lear.

B.D. Kwiatek is the author of *Unleash Your Dolphin-Human Potential*™ and *The Dolphin-Human Potential*™ *World-Mastery Diet*™.

Lightning Source UK Ltd.
Milton Keynes UK
UKOW051937121011

180206UK00001B/43/A